THE
FIRE
QUEEN

ALSO BY EMILY R. KING

The Hundredth Queen

THE
FIRE
QUEEN

The Hundredth Queen Series
Book Two

EMILY R. KING

SKYSCAPE

SKYSCAPE

Published by Skyscape, New York

www.apub.com

Amazon, the Amazon logo, and Skyscape are trademarks of Amazon.com, Inc., or its affiliates.

ISBN-13: 9781611097498
ISBN-10: 1611097495

Cover design by Jason Blackburn

Printed in the United States of America

For Marlene Stringer, a true sister warrior

AUTHOR'S NOTE

The religion of the Tarachand Empire, the Parijana faith, is a fictional variation derived from Sumerian deities. However, the Parijana faith, and the Tarachand and other empires do not directly represent any specific historical time period, creed, or union. Any other religious or governmental similarities are coincidental and do not depict actual people or events.

1

KALINDA

Death has a stench, and it is not decaying flesh but the bitter scent of smoke clawing into my pores. A wide, dark plume blots out the afternoon sun, an ashy stain rising to the heavens like a sacrificial trail. A lonely wind, hot as dragon's breath, pushes black soot toward our caravan.

Please, gods. Not again.

I click my tongue and press my heels into my camel's side. The long-legged animal grunts, exhausted from long days of tracking. I dig my heels in deeper, rousing a spurt of strength from the beast, and the camel's feet crunch over clumps of dead grass as yellow as the harvest moon. Rays from the late-summer sun beat down, parching the land.

We crest a short hill, and I yank on the reins, stopping to absorb the destruction. Across the expanse of golden hills, dark smoke obscures the temple roof, and red flames chew apart the crumbling stone walls and surrounding cobble courtyard.

Another Brotherhood temple razed to rubble.

Deven leans forward, his chest close to my back. "Great Anu," he says behind me. "They outpaced us again."

Mathura and Brac slow to a halt at our side. We left the imperial city of Vanhi with another camel, but Mathura's fell lame days ago. After being held in the palace for over two decades, the stately courtesan has viewed the outside world with childlike wonder, but a solemn frown ages her striking face. Her son Brac, a Burner, removes his headscarf, uncovering his reddish-brown hair, and scratches his scalp. His golden eyes are red rimmed with fatigue. Two moons' worth of road dust covers him, covers us all. My blouse under my sari itches against my back, sweat clinging to a layer of grime.

Yatin and Natesa catch up, their camel struggling under Yatin's hefty bulk. Natesa, my former contender in the rank tournament, gapes at the pyre. Yatin shakes his head in dismay. His years as a soldier did not prepare him for this level of ruthless destruction.

I lift my chin, stretching the hard lump in my throat. "We'll circle the area."

"Keep an eye out for survivors," Deven orders the group.

Our camels charge down the slope, pushing into the smoke-filled wind and leaving trails of trampled pasture behind us. As we conquer the next rise, we pause, overlooking the temple.

"Captain," Yatin says in his deep burr, "would you like me to ride closer?"

"I see no need," Deven replies with grim-set lips.

I follow his gaze to the closed courtyard gate and barred doors. This is precisely how we found the last two Brotherhood temples. The patrons of the Parijana faith—brethren and young male apprentices—were locked inside when the fire was set. The flames raged into a blazing sarcophagus. We found no survivors.

Tears clear the smoke stinging my eyes. Deven shifts forward, sealing his chest against my back, and his arms come around me. I settle into him, too stricken to question his affection. Deven has been increasingly distant since we left Vanhi. Although I ache to return to our former easiness, we are both still reeling from our escape.

Nothing has been the same since Rajah Tarek claimed me as his last bride. I had to earn my position as his hundredth and final rani in a rank tournament, battling in the arena against his courtesans vying for my throne. I did not grow to love Tarek; I fell in love with my palace guard Deven. After Tarek killed my best friend, Jaya, and sentenced Deven to execution, he had to pay. I won the rank tournament, but I was forced to take the rajah's first wife's life or forfeit my own, a choice I still agonize over. During battle I learned the first wife was my mother's sister—my *aunt*—and the only family I had met since I was orphaned as an infant.

I wed Tarek the evening after my arena duel. That same night, after I enacted my revenge by taking Tarek's life, the Turquoise Palace was attacked by rebel bhutas seeking vengeance against the tyrant rajah. I fled from the bhutas' conniving warlord with the friends who accompany me now. Each day I thank the gods I have them, especially Deven. Wedding Tarek pushed the life we dreamed of together in the lower hills of the Alpana Mountains further away, but I will not give up on our hope for peace.

Deven's calloused thumb rubs my wrist, staying away from the back of my hand where the number one, the rank of the kindred, is dyed into my skin. The henna bridal markings on my arms and back faded a fortnight ago, but my wifely rank was doubly inked on with something stronger and will not leave me, no matter how often I scrub my skin raw. The mark of the rajah's first favored wife is a cursed reminder of the night I became Rajah Tarek's wife—and his widow. I wish this blight on my body, this reminder that I swore my life to another man, was gone.

Flying embers hit the cobble courtyard and bounce to sizzling ash. I worry a stray spark will ignite a brush fire and feed off the arid meadows, but the stone courtyard serves as a buffer to the bone-dry valley. The grounds were well maintained, cared for, loved.

My Burner powers simmer through me like streams of fire, begging for retribution. The bhuta warlord Hastin did this. I anticipated Hastin and his rebels would chase us to steal back the Zhaleh, the sacred book of record I took when we ran from the Turquoise Palace, but I was wrong. I should have known Hastin's hatred for Rajah Tarek would lead him to seek out the rajah's heir, Prince Ashwin.

The prince was raised in one of the four Brotherhood temples—which one is a long-held secret. We have trekked across Tarachand from temple to temple, searching for him, but Hastin has been one step ahead of us. This is the third temple we have located too late. Three sanctuaries of the Parijana faith brought down by powerful bhutas, the guides the brethren believe the gods charged to assist mankind.

"What now?" Natesa asks, her tone forlorn.

"What do you mean?" I reply.

"Prince Ashwin is dead."

"We don't know that," I counter. "The prince could be at the final temple."

"Why should we continue to search for him when he hasn't stepped forward to claim his throne?" Brac questions. "Either Prince Ashwin is a coward or he doesn't care what becomes of the empire."

I gnaw on my inner cheek, locking down my exasperation. Brac is exhausted and frustrated. We all are. Our deliverance from war relies on us locating Prince Ashwin, but finding him is taking longer than we anticipated. We are chasing a spirit, someone we have been told exists but have never seen in the flesh.

"Hastin will own his victory when the prince is dead," says Mathura. "We'll find out if the prince survived this attack in the next few days."

"Until we hear otherwise, we'll assume he's alive," I say, and Brac glances away.

Am I wrong? Should we stop searching for the prince?

I look to Deven for his opinion as a captain, as my guard, as the man I love. He gazes at the burning temple, his eyes pained. Since he removed his soldier uniform and put on a plain tunic and trousers, his attention often drifts elsewhere, lost in thought. Before Rajah Tarek died, he charged Deven with treason and stripped his command for helping me aid the rebels in their attack on Vanhi. But Deven's only mistake was siding with me.

"What should we do, Captain?" Brac inquires.

Deven flinches into focus, cringing every time someone uses his title. He scrubs a hand over his dark beard. His facial hair is scruffier than when he wore the crisp lines of his scarlet uniform, and the ends of his hair are longer, curling out from beneath his turban. His pause lasts longer than usual for his decisive nature. He has come all this way in pursuit of our new leader, and his hesitancy puzzles me.

"Son?" Mathura presses.

Deven glances at Brac, his half brother, and then at their mother, Mathura. "We'll continue onward." Deven points at the Alpana Mountains' far-off shadowy peaks. "Tonight we'll camp above the refugee trail in the foothills, and tomorrow we'll start for the northern temple."

"Thank you," I say quietly.

He registers my gratitude with a short nod, his soft beard grazing my cheekbone. "Stay alert," he says. "The rebels could be nearby."

We lead our camels away from the fiery ruins, the stench of death beating at our backs.

Our caravan rides up to intersect the eastward thoroughfare leading to Iresh, the royal city of the sultanate of Janardan. Rajah Tarek's demise and the bhuta warlord's occupation of Vanhi spurred a mass evacuation. Over the past two moons, thousands of feet have worn a trail into the water-starved valley on the way to the sultanate.

Ahead of us, a small group of refugees wear more tracks into the land. A mother with an infant tied to her chest with a headscarf plods beside a handcart. Two young men heft the cart that holds their scant possessions and supplies for their journey. A little girl runs alongside them, tapping the spoke wheels with a knotted stick.

The woman sees our approach and orders her sons to halt. As the young men set down the handcart and wipe their sweaty brows, the woman watches us guardedly. Pieces of her braided hair fly in tatters around her sunburnt face.

"Ma'am," Deven says.

She clutches her infant closer to her bosom. Gripped in one hand, partly tucked in the folds of her sari, she conceals a knife. The new road has brought evacuees in droves and, with them, thieves preying on travelers.

Brac leads his and Mathura's camel across the road, and Yatin and Natesa follow on theirs. I yank the reins of ours, stopping in the center of the roadway.

"Pardon me," I say. "Do you have any news from Vanhi?"

The woman squints up at me with cold distrust. "None since the bhuta warlord invaded. My husband was stationed in the palace at the time. Word is the warlord executed him and the other guards."

My heart beats slower in my chest. By lingering around village water wells, we learned that Hastin boarded up the gates to the Turquoise Palace, locking everyone inside. The people of Vanhi blame Hastin for Tarek's murder. Few know the truth.

I reach into my saddlebag, and the woman lifts her knife.

"I don't want trouble," she warns.

"Neither do we," I promise.

Deven shifts behind me, his discomfort palpable. We are not safe out near the open roadway.

My fingertips brush the turquoise handle of the dagger in my bag, a twin to the blade strapped to my outer thigh. The daggers belonged to my mother, Rajah Tarek's first-ever wife. Mathura brought them from the palace for me, and Deven has trained me to wield them well. I depend on my daggers as I once did my slingshot. I bypass the hidden knife, find the object I seek, and pull out my hand. The woman peers at the headscarf.

"For you," I offer.

"I don't need your help."

"Maybe so, but what will happen to your children if you fall ill with sun sickness?"

Her scowl lessens, yet she still resists.

Down the road, a larger group of travelers ambles our way, wagons and men. No, soldiers. They are dressed in dark-red uniforms, with the Tarachand Empire's black scorpion crest on their chests, the same uniform Deven no longer wears. They travel without banners. This far from an army stronghold, they must be deserters. Civilians are not the only ones fleeing the bhuta warlord.

Deven vibrates with tension, silently demanding we leave before the soldiers arrive.

I dangle the headscarf between the woman and me, her children solemnly observing our exchange. "Please, take it," I say.

She shuffles forward, pinches the farthest corner of the cloth, and plucks it from my grip. Upon seeing the back of my hand, her eyes bulge.

"Kindred," she says, sinking to her knees. Her sons lower to the ground after her, and she waves for her little girl to do the same. "Forgive us. We didn't recognize you."

The noises from the caravan of soldiers quiver in my stomach. I forgot how much I despise being bowed to. Imagining the lot of them kneeling at my feet, my tone shortens. "You've caused no offense. Please don't speak of seeing me."

"We won't, Kindred. May the gods watch over you."

"And you." I snap the reins for the camel to go.

Deven and I finish crossing the road and start up the rocky hillside. Below, the mother holds her children and weeps. She does not cry from misery or fear but from happiness that twitches my spine. I will add their family to my daily prayers.

Deven's hawkeyed gaze remains on the party of soldiers coming around the bend. Once we are out of sight of the road and the travelers, he relaxes. His voice reaches out to me like a gentle caress down the back of my neck. "That was kind of you."

"I only gave her a headscarf," I say.

"You gave her more than that. You're the kindred. Seeing you gave her family hope."

I shift in the saddle with a frown. I may be nobility, but I am not *noble*. The woman and her family would not have been forced to flee their home had I not foolishly placed my trust in Hastin. I bargained with the warlord for my freedom and lost more than my own. I assumed by ending Rajah Tarek I would liberate his ranis and courtesans, but now they are Hastin's prisoners in the Turquoise Palace. As the first wife, I was the ranis' kindred and leader. Their friend. I failed to protect them, just as I failed to save my dearest friend, Jaya.

"They shouldn't still think of me as their kindred," I say, my voice monotone.

"Your duties to your throne remain until Prince Ashwin releases you from them," Deven reminds me. "Your triumph in the rank tournament has been told far and wide. Our people love you—and you love them. You earned their devotion. Don't diminish what your achievement means to them."

I hold my tongue before I ask Deven what my achievement means to *him*. I fought for my title of kindred, but I have fought harder to forget the bloodshed and horrors of my rank tournament. Most days I succeed. Some days I do not. Yet it is not my victory in the arena or the loss of Deven's command rank that has come between us most. My marriage to the rajah has been our greatest divide. The same reason I am a symbol of hope for that struggling family is why Deven is hesitant to touch me. To the people, my fate and future belong to the rajah's throne. I can no more change their minds—or Deven's—than I can unwed Rajah Tarek or bring Jaya back to life.

As I look out at the trail-worn valley, the refugees' weary footsteps carve blame into my conscience. The empire has changed since I became the rajah's one hundredth queen. Tarachand is gloomier, full of desperate people and massacres of the innocent. I find nothing dignified or noble about being the inciter of heartache.

2

KALINDA

Something strokes down my nose, pulling me from sleep. A ruby silk canopy stretches over my bed. Curtains billow near the balcony, a hot breeze ushering in the rustle of palm fronds. I am in my chamber in the Turquoise Palace.

A finger brushes my nose again. I blink fast, and a face comes into focus.

Rajah Tarek's white teeth flash predatorily in my darkened room. "I've missed you, love."

I try to jerk away, but my hands and legs are pinned.

"Shh," he croons. "We're going to have the wedding night the gods intended for us." He lies beside me, turns his body into mine, and buries his face in my hair.

I wrench at my bindings, struggling to kick free, but my ankles are tied to the bedposts and my arms are stretched over my head. I reach inward for my powers to burn away the straps—and find a well of emptiness. No soul-fire flickers within me.

"What did you do?" I ask, my voice hitching on terror.

Tarek answers while kissing a trail across my cheek. "I poisoned you as you did me."

His hands roam down my body. A wild, hot scream rises up my throat. Tarek slams a palm over my mouth.

"Don't fight me, love. You are my wife"—he kisses my cramping neck—"and I am your husband. The gods have bound our souls in matrimony. You're mine, forever and always."

I struggle against my bindings, tears flooding my sight. Tarek presses his hand harder over my mouth to muffle my screams.

"Kali."

My head jerks up, my breath thrashing against my rib cage. I am not in my bedchamber. The Turquoise Palace is far away. And Rajah Tarek . . . Tarek is dead.

Brac is sitting beside me, his honey eyes shimmering with worry. Mathura, Natesa, and Deven finish a supper of dried fruit and toasted nuts across the campfire. Yatin stands guard on the outcropping over-looking the valley, a shadow against a starlit night.

"Are you all right?" Brac asks.

I wrap my arms around myself to suppress a shiver. "I drifted off."

"Did you dream of *him* again?"

"Yes."

Brac curses under his breath and glances across the campfire at his brother. "You should tell him."

"No," I answer with finality. Deven can hardly stand to speak of my marriage to Tarek, let alone hear that the rajah dominates my dreams. Neither Natesa nor Mathura have asked what privately took place between Tarek and me on our wedding night, and Yatin only sends me glances of sympathy from time to time. Brac was on guard when I first woke from a night terror in a cold sweat and confided in him. He already knew that I had been poisoned—he had burned the toxins from my body when he and Deven found me—but he did not know *how*. After my explanation, I swore I would not tell anyone else that I used poison-laced lotion to kill Tarek, or that I was prepared to die with him.

I stare into the crackling fire, fatigue wearing a path down my spine. I wish I could sketch to alleviate my mind, but those days of quiet pleasure are on hold until after we find Prince Ashwin and determine what to do with the Zhaleh resting in my satchel. We have not discussed where best to secure the bhutas' sacred book, but that is a concern for after I am free from my throne.

Brac gazes into the campfire and speaks, his tone thoughtful. "It's said that when a Burner looks into the heart of a fire, they can see the reflection of their soul. I used to spend hours watching for mine, waiting for my blood to sing to the flames and reveal my inner self."

"Have you ever seen anything?"

"No, but I imagine my soul's reflection would be a wolf." An apt choice. Brac is stealthy and sly, and his golden eyes shine like a canine's. He bumps his shoulder into mine. "What do you see?"

I look into the campfire, uncertain what it will show me. My inner self has done some awful things. "I don't see anything either."

"Let's try this." Brac reaches for the campfire and plucks out a spindly flame as he would a loose thread. The filament of heat suspends between his palms, hovering above his skin. He rotates his hands, and the long flame winds through his fingers like a serpent weaving through tall grass. He is trying to cheer me up, and I cannot help but be amazed. The sight of him playing with fire is mesmerizing.

"Nature-fire is the last element the gods created. When the sky-god Anu bestowed godly gifts on the First Bhutas, the Burner was feared above them all. People saw her as a peril."

"Her? The first Burner was a woman?"

"Her name was Uri," Brac says. I stare, transfixed, as the flame twists between his fingers. "Uri knew she had to master nature-fire or she would always be feared, so she trekked up the highest mountain and spent several moons learning to manipulate a single flame." Brac holds out the strand of fire. "Take it."

"I don't think so." Brac has been training me to expand my abilities with soul-fire, but I am not ready for nature-fire.

"Kali, you can scorch and parch soul-fire as well as I can, but until you master nature-fire, you're a danger. See this campfire? You cannot extinguish it without an outside source. You need a pail of sand or water. You can start the fire, but you cannot *control* it." Brac comes nearer with the hot flame. "Anu created mortals in the image of the gods. Sky in our lungs, land beneath our feet, fire in our soul, and water in our blood. The First Bhutas were each given dominion over one of these powers. So you see, you have nothing to fear. You are fire, and fire is you."

"But soul-fire is contained within the body." I maintain a firm eye on the flame dancing over his hand, mistrustful of its cheerful movements. "Nature-fire is wild."

"All the more reason to revere it. Galers respect the storm. Aquifiers idolize the sea. Tremblers worship the mountain. And we . . . we respect this. Soul-fire and nature-fire come from the gods. The only divide is how your mortal half perceives them. Your mortal side fears death and pain."

"I wonder why," I say dryly. Across the fire, Deven glances away from us, pretending he is not watching my lesson.

"Ignore your mortal half," says Brac. "Listen to the half of you that connects to the gods. *That* is your strength." He brings the swirling flame closer. "Hold out your palm." I do not comply, so he lifts my hand. "Ready?"

Not at all. But Brac will not leave me alone until I try, so I nod.

He tips his hand and drops the flame into my open palm. The instant the fiery tendril hits my skin, I draw back in pain. The wispy flare falls to the ground and catches the dry grass afire. Brac extinguishes the small brush fire with the wave of his hand and then aims an accusatory scowl at me.

"You're being absurd. You're a *Burner*. You shouldn't be afraid of fire."

"Shouldn't I?" I show him the scalding boils on my palm. They are minor, but they hurt.

Brac grasps my forearms and pushes in his powers, awakening radiance beneath my skin. Tiny rivers of soul-fire brighten up the veins in my arm. I gawk at the powers now visible within me. "You *are* fire, and fire is you," he explains. "You cannot fear fire or it will turn on you. Burners are the ones to fear. Nature-fire will obey *our* command."

Deven steps over to us, avoiding looking at the pathways of light running up my arms. "Brac, that's enough for now."

Brac slings an irritated frown at his older brother and releases me. The shining trails along my skin fade like a star subject to a new day. "I don't interfere with your and Kali's weapon training. Don't interfere with ours."

"*I* haven't burned her," Deven retorts.

"Oh, hush," Mathura orders her sons and then carries a small pot of salve over to me, limping on her bad knee. Deven stays at my side, his temples bouncing from his clenched jaw. Mathura slathers the cool medicine on my blisters and speaks soothingly. "Don't be discouraged, Kalinda. Fear of fire is perfectly rational."

Deven's frown deepens. His interference with my training bothers Brac and me for different reasons. Deven wants my powers to remain hidden from our people for my protection. Rajah Tarek spread lies to teach his subjects to hate all bhutas, and now that the bhuta warlord has run them out of their homes, they may link me to Hastin's insurgence. Bhutas look like full-mortals even though they are half-gods, and so my people do not know what I am. But I suspect Deven takes personal issue with my powers. He dislikes any reminder that I am a Burner.

My blister stops stinging, and a sudden wind hits us, rustling our clothes.

"I don't like the mood of that wind," says Natesa, batting away a loose strand of her hair. She has not bathed in days, yet she is still one of the prettiest women in Tarachand.

Another flurry whips at us with dusty swipes. Gooseflesh springs up my arms. These are not natural gales. Something—some*one*—comes.

"Kali, where is the Zhaleh?" Deven asks.

My pulse skips in alarm. "Inside my satchel."

Deven slings my bag over his shoulder. Yatin returns to camp, and they both unsheathe their khandas. I draw my dagger, my injured hand free to employ my powers. Mathura and Natesa stand back to back, weapons ready. The camels exchange high-pitched moans and bunch together to stave off the errant winds.

Brac steps out of the circle of firelight to search for what approaches. He leaves camp, his figure waning to a silhouette, and shouts, "There!"

I expect to see rebels, but a great bird soars over the valley. I peer at the monstrous fowl, its moonlit wings frosted ghostly silver. The bird is as large as a passenger carriage. I have not seen anything this gigantic airborne; its wingspan is wider than a wagon is long. We watch the immense bird, hypnotized by its graceful approach in the high winds. The flying monster banks right, zooming in our direction.

Brac dashes for camp. The bird races after him, harnessing the force of the gale, and dives. Brac drops to the ground, and the monster skims over him—flying straight at me.

Deven knocks me down. We roll twice and land with him on top, a barrier between me and the sky. The great bird swoops over us. Everyone else has stretched out on the ground. We stay down as the enormous creature soars back with the moon facing its front. The bird is actually an extraordinary flying contraption. A boy rides within it, lying with his belly perpendicular to the land. He steers the flyer down and lowers his legs. His feet connect with the land, and he sprints to a stop with the contraption.

Another flyer cuts across the sky. The birdlike device dives for an open patch of hillside, and a girl lands with the same skilled poise as her partner.

Deven and I rise together. Yatin straightens from his protective crouch over Natesa, and Mathura steps forward from behind a boulder. The boy and girl climb out of the flyers. Their plain clothes do not reveal who they are or where they come from. All I am certain of is that they are bhutas, Galers. Their flying contraptions ride their conjured winds. The only Galer I have met is Anjali, the warlord's sneaky daughter. I gather soul-fire into my hand, fingers glowing.

Brac plants himself between our visitors and camp. He throws a blast of fire to push them back. The flame lights up their surprised faces and sizzles out. They raise their hands in peace.

"We aren't rebels," the boy says. His dark hair flops casually across his forehead, fringing his overly round eyes. He takes a tentative step forward. "We were sent to find you."

"Goal accomplished. Now go." Brac tosses another heatwave at them.

"Stop that," says the girl. She is short and reed thin, with a confident full mouth and wide, flat nose. Her looks are plain, but beauty and intelligence reside in her sleek cheekbones and thin brows. She lowers her arms and throws a squall at Brac, swiping him off his feet. He lands with an *umph*.

I hurl my dagger. The tip embeds in the ground shy of the girl's toes. "That's far enough," I call out.

"Kindred." She drops to her knees, and the boy follows.

"What do you want?" Deven's voice is sharp and flat, like his outstretched blade.

The girl—I wager age sixteen, and her male comrade a year younger—shows us a sealed letter. "We bring a message from Brother Shaan."

Brac gets up and snatches the message from her hand. He stalks back to us, his attention locked on the pair, and hands me the sealed letter. I open it and read.

Trust the messengers. They will guide you.

I hand the letter to Deven. He reads the concise instructions and frowns.

"That *is* Brother Shaan's handwriting," he says. Like me, he is not ready to trust these strangers. "And that sounds like him, cryptic and all knowing."

I consider our young guests and the possibility that they would know who we are *and* carry a note from Brother Shaan. I lower my glowing hand. "Let's hear what they have to say."

Brac does not disengage his glower as the Galers cross into the firelight. Natesa and Mathura lower their steel but keep the blades close. Yatin flanks our visitors, his huge size provoking wary glances from the girl.

"May we sit?" The boy gives a flimsy smile. "We've been flying for hours, and our wings are tired." He flaps his arms for good measure. None of our expressions budge. The boy coughs awkwardly into his hand.

"I'm Opal, and this is my brother, Rohan," says the girl.

"Please rest," I offer. Opal sits beside her brother, and I join them. Everyone else remains on their feet, distrustful and wary. "Your flying contraptions are remarkable."

"Wing flyers," Opal corrects. "They were made in Paljor."

Their nondescript attire bears no insignia linking them to the northern tribal nation of the Alpana Mountains, or any nation for that matter. "Are you from Paljor?" I ask.

"Paljor is our mother's homeland," answers Opal.

"Where is Brother Shaan?" Deven asks.

"Safe," she replies. "We flew him to the northern temple where Prince Ashwin was hiding and then took them both to Janardan a few days ago. Per their request, we've been searching for you since."

A light sparks inside me, bright and warm. *Prince Ashwin is alive.* Mathura sets down her weapon and sits near us to listen, resting her bad knee.

"Why did the prince leave the empire?" Natesa asks, crossing her arms over her chest. "His people need him here."

"It isn't safe," Opal avows. "When Hastin discovered Brother Shaan escaped Vanhi, he rounded up the brethren for questioning."

"The wind told us of their fate." Rohan's grimace reminds me that Galers hear secrets on the wind that no other bhutas or mortals can. "Anjali tortured them to find out the prince's whereabouts. The brethren wouldn't tell, so Hastin ordered his daughter to winnow them."

"Buzzards," Brac says. At my confused glance, he explains. "A Galer can use their powers to siphon the air from their victim's lungs. They call it winnowing."

"Only amoral Galers use that technique," Opal says in aversion. "None of the brethren knew where the prince was hiding, only Brother Shaan."

My mouth turns dry. Mathura takes up her handheld hookah pipe to cope with the accounts of torture. I am close to asking for a puff of the mind-easing smoke myself.

"And the imperial guard?" Deven asks tightly. He has been reluctant to speak about the palace guards, but the rumor the woman told us of their being executed must be wearing on him.

"Hastin stoned the guards and beheaded the higher-ranking officers," Rohan replies.

Deven pales. He and Yatin would have faced the same fate had they not fled with me. My worry for the ranis and courtesans Hastin is holding captive surges.

"What are the prince's orders?" I ask.

Rohan trains his gaze on me. "He requests that you join him in Iresh as a guest at the sultan's Beryl Palace."

Iresh is the imperial city of the sultanate of Janardan, ruled by Sultan Kuval, whom Rajah Tarek was rumored to despise. During Tarek's early days of attacks on bhutas, the sultan welcomed refugees into Iresh. Tarek had planned to go after the bhutas who slipped through his grasp after he eradicated those within his borders.

Deven stabs the tip of his sword into the ground and leans against the hilt. "Why does the prince need Kali?"

"Prince Ashwin went to the sultan to seek military aid," Opal says, "but the prince is an untried ruler. The kindred's reputation is known far and wide, and the refugee camps are filling. The prince needs her to gain the favor of his people. They need a ruler they know and trust."

"I'm no more experienced a leader than Prince Ashwin," I say, drawing back.

"You won your rank tournament and earned their devotion," Opal replies, her gaze insistent. "The prince believes your endorsement will reassure the refugees and have the added benefit of convincing the sultan to provide troops to unseat Hastin from Vanhi."

I begrudge Opal's reasoning but understand why Tarachandians view the prince as a stranger. He has been in hiding all his life. I suppose I can comfort the people until he earns their loyalty.

And then I will walk away from my throne for good.

"I need to speak to my friends alone," I say, rising.

Opal and Rohan start to leave, but Rohan pauses. "Do you have anything to eat?" he asks. Mathura hands him a bag of dried dates. Rohan licks his lips at the larger supply sack she took the fruit from. "Are those cashews?"

"The fruit is fine," Opal says, dragging her brother away.

Brac squints at them in the dark as they sit beside their wing flyers and munch on their food. "You know they can hear everything we say," he remarks.

"I know," I reply, sighing, "but this gives us some semblance of privacy."

I glance from face to face, seeking my friends' cooperation. I have convinced them to follow me this far, but asking them to leave the empire, their home, is a lot to require.

"So now we know where the prince is," I start carefully.

"I cannot believe he ran." Natesa's voice crackles with condemnation. "He left us. He left his people."

"He went to seek aid, little lotus," says Yatin. Natesa's frown fades, charmed by his nickname for her.

"That's true," I say, still proceeding cautiously. I will thank Yatin for his support later. "The prince needs our help."

Brac tips his head to the side in deliberation. "I was the first to call Prince Ashwin a coward, but he's right to seek aid." Natesa mutters something snide under her breath. She has adapted to the brothers—Deven, who does not let her boss him around, and Brac, who parched her with his powers the first time they met—but she is less tolerant of Brac. "We should go," he finishes.

"Absolutely not." Deven draws an unequivocal line in the air. "The sultan could be using the prince to lure Kali into his borders."

Brac confronts his brother's scowl straight on. "The imperial army is disbanding. Our soldiers are running to escape a war they're ill equipped to fight. We need an army that can stand up to Hastin. The sultan has bhutas in his royal guard. Bhutas can better fight bhutas."

"No mortal army will stand against Hastin," Yatin agrees in his low voice. "The fall of Vanhi has proven that."

"Once we set foot in Janardan, we'll be under the sultan's rule," argues Deven.

Natesa scoffs. "We're no safer in our borders."

The same may be true for the Zhaleh. I am hesitant to mention the sacred book—I do not know how much Opal and Rohan know—but

Brother Shaan must believe it will be safe in Janardan. I hold my tongue and wait for Mathura to offer her opinion.

She puffs on her pipe and answers, pushing out smoke. "I've always wanted to see the sultanate."

Deven glowers at each of us in turn. I step to his side, tug on his arm, and lure him out of the circle of firelight. He stares down at his dusty boots, distant and tight-lipped.

"This is our best chance at defeating Hastin," I say.

"I understand . . . I just . . ." Deven raises his beseeching gaze to me. "Let's be done with this, Kali. Leave the prince to fare on his own. This is his war and his empire. He'll find a way to defeat Hastin without us."

"What if he doesn't? What happens then?" The weight of my throne is tethered to my ankles, weighing me down. Prince Ashwin must claim his throne in order to sever me from mine. "Once the prince steps into power, we'll be free."

"What if he's unfit to rule? He *is* Rajah Tarek's son."

"Not every son is destined to become his father."

Deven drops his pleading gaze and glowers at his boots. His distrust of the prince is unlike him. He believed serving the rajah was his fate, but that changed when we planned to run away . . . the act that led to his accusation of treason.

Gods, does Deven blame me for Tarek stripping away his military command? I cannot handle yet another toppled fate on my conscience.

Deven's gentle voice breaks our silence. "I'm worried for your safety."

I step closer and run my fingers up his neck. I feather the silky locks beneath his turban, trying to remember the last time we kissed. "We're so close to freedom." My entreaty sounds like a desperate prayer, but my optimism swells within him through his softening mouth and loosening shoulders.

"All right," he says finally.

I squeeze Deven nearer in thanks, and his arms come around me. I inhale his calming sandalwood scent, masked slightly by the campfire smoke, and soak in his sweet warmth. As I burrow into his cozy arms, the frown line between his brows eases and his dark eyes soften. For an idyllic moment, the strain between us lifts away.

The brother and sister Galers rejoin us by the fire. "We, ah, couldn't help but overhear you've made a decision," Rohan says.

Deven lets me go and threads his fingers through mine. We step back into the firelight.

"We're going to meet the prince," I say.

"How about we go right now?" Opal suggests.

"Why?" Natesa challenges. "Will you be paid upon our delivery?"

"We aren't being paid," Rohan says. "The rebels are on their way."

Deven drops my hand and stalks to the cliff's edge. A storm gathers in the distance.

Brac glares at the Galers. "You were *followed*?"

"We thought we lost them," says Rohan, ducking his head in chagrin.

My skin tingles with the first ominous stirrings of wind blowing through camp. No one need give the command; we all rush to pack up at once.

"Rohan and I can each carry up to four additional people on our flyers," Opal says.

Stronger drafts battle us, building one powerful strand at a time. Across the valley, a wind tunnel careens our way, throwing a curtain of dirt and heaving silver lightning bolts. Thunderclaps roll across the grassland valley. The camels squawk in alarm and kneel, hunkering down for the storm.

I walk toward the weather, nearer to the cliff side. Flashes of lightning emphasize the silhouette of a young woman suspended inside a giant wind tunnel. *Anjali, the warlord's Galer daughter.*

"Opal," Deven barks, "take Kali and go."

I whirl on him. "I'm staying. Anjali has come for *me*." I betrayed her father when I took the Zhaleh and ran. I must be the one to face her.

"Kali," he says, uttering my name with commendable calm, "you have to think like a rani. Protecting yourself is preserving the empire."

Must the empire come first, before me, before him, before us? Duty would say yes, the empire should be my priority.

"What about you?" I grip his forearm, the force of the whirlwind shoving us back a pace.

"We'll hold them off and meet you in Janardan." Deven drops my pack over my shoulder, the Zhaleh within. "Brother Shaan said we could trust these Galers, but be careful."

Panic takes hold of me. I fist his tunic and drag him close. "Promise you'll meet me in Janardan?"

"I swear it." Deven cups my chin, his touch tainted by hand-shaking alarm. Part of me is relieved that he is not composed either. But if Deven is afraid, then we have much to fear. He rubs his thumb across my cheek and steps into the punishing wind.

The camels are frightened by the violence of the sky and scatter. Deven braces behind a boulder with Mathura, and Natesa does the same with Yatin. Brac crouches low to the ground, closer to the storm.

I run for Opal's wing flyer into the wind's dusty grip. Opal creates a peaceful air bubble around her like the eye of a hurricane. I throw myself into her safe haven and draw in mouthfuls of clean air.

"Get in and hold on to the navigation bar," she says.

I grip the bamboo bar, and another wider beam braces my hips. I lie suspended over the ground on a platform. Opal climbs on beside me. A gale catches the canvas wings and tries to rip them off like leaves from a tree, but she holds the wing flyer steady and lifts us into the sky.

A greater squall hurls us back—Anjali is nearly here. Opal fights to level us, one wing precariously close to crashing into the ground. Below, Rohan throws a draft and straightens our lowered wing. Another well-timed gust lifts us higher into the night. I close my eyes, which are now streaming with tears. This would be exhilarating if it was not so terrifying.

Hail pelts us. Beneath Anjali's wind tunnel, a young woman rides a horse with her arms raised to the storm. Indira, an Aquifier, is conducting the thunderheads. Two bhutas against two bhutas is a fair match, but my friends have a better chance of winning if Opal and I stay.

"Turn back!" I shout to her. "They need our help."

"I have my orders!"

Her almighty winds usher us east, away from Tarachand. Away from our friends and family. Away from Deven.

3

DEVEN

Opal's wing flyer banks east, out of range from the deafening winds.

Thank the gods. Kali got away.

The driving rains drench me. Anjali hovers before us, the wind tunnel of hailstones whipping around her. While Rohan runs for the second wing flyer, Brac sends a heatwave at her from behind his boulder. The rainy gales extinguish his fire to smoke. Anjali's relentless wind pushes aside my brother's safe cover. He sprints to Mother and me and ducks beside us. Anjali pummels our boulder with gust after gust. I crouch over Mother, our heads bowed, while the hail thrashes against our backs. I have been trained for battle, but my sword is useless here. I have no way of defending my family against these higher powers.

Something darkens my side vision—Rohan is airborne in his wing flyer. Anjali harnesses her ripping winds and thrusts them full force at him. He twirls, trapped inside the vortex.

"Help him," I command Brac.

He throws several fire blasts in a row at Anjali, each weaker than the last. Nothing slows her. Brac's hands are barely glowing.

"Deven, you aren't going to like this," he says and then grasps my face. A sudden hold comes over me, and the light inside me jerks. He pulls at my soul-fire, drawing it out like a loose thread. He lets me go, and the strength in my bones goes too. I drop to my side in the mud.

"What did you do?" Mother demands.

"I borrowed his soul-fire." Brac's hands glow bright again. The gods created all mankind with fire in their soul—and my brother has stolen mine.

He leans around the boulder and tosses a ribbon of flame into the air. I watch his fire—power he parched from *me*—careen toward Anjali. She redirects the stream of heat away with a gust and directs it at Rohan. The wing flyer catches on fire and free-falls. The smoking wing tip spirals near the overhang, reeling toward the valley below. Rohan leaps from his flyer at the ledge and rolls behind a rock. The wing flyer disappears and crashes below with a bang.

Anjali chases Rohan with another flurry. He lies on the ground and shields his head with his arms. I spring up to go to his aid, but rocks and dust bombard him and barrel onward to us, forcing me to hunch down again. Without warning, the howling winds and rain die to a startling halt.

Yatin peers over the top of his and Natesa's boulder. "She's leaving."

I push myself up onto shaky legs. Anjali has veered her wind tunnel east. My heart pitches.

"She's following Kali." I stumble to the edge of the cliff. Rohan runs to my side. I pick up a rock the size of a melon. "Can you give this a boost?"

"Throw it," he replies.

Anjali pulls farther away. I take aim and hurl the stone. Rohan flings his winds behind the rock, and it arcs across the sky. I lose sight of our weapon in the dark, and then Anjali's twisting winds fail, and she plunges to the valley. A plume of dust mushrooms when she lands. Sudden quiet rushes in around us.

Rohan tilts his ear to the sky. "She's breathing."

"You can hear that?" Natesa asks doubtfully.

"I can hear her and another," Rohan replies. "She had an accomplice driving the storm, an Aquifier. Their heartbeats sound like crickets in the night. The Aquifier is riding to her on a horse."

"Can you repair the wing flyer?" I ask, pressing a hand to my chest. My heart feels withered and worn from Brac's parching.

"The rain put out the fire before the damage spread," answers Rohan. "I can fix the wing in half an hour with my patch kit."

"You have ten minutes." My tone leaves no quarter for discussion. "We have to leave before Anjali wakes."

Rohan stands taller. "Yes, Captain."

Skies above, I wish everyone would quit using that title.

My brother steps forward. "I'll help Rohan."

An inner cold heavies my core, like impenetrable hoarfrost. "Don't ever parch my soul-fire again," I grit out.

Brac's mouth turns downward. "Deven . . ." He reaches for me, but I tug away. Brac's offered hand falls at his side. "I'm sorry," he says and then goes with Rohan.

My mother strokes my forearm. "Your brother didn't mean—"

"Not now," I say.

When Brac and I had disagreements as children, even if he was in the wrong, I would make amends with him to end our mother's distress. Mother said I was born a peacemaker. Her belief in my capacity for goodness inspired me to join the Brotherhood for a time and later influenced my training as a soldier. I still prefer levelheaded diplomacy over posturing and strong-arming. But Brac did not borrow my toy sword without asking. He took a piece of my soul and sent it burning across the sky.

Mother brushes the front of my wet tunic, her touch laced with understanding, and leaves to salvage our supplies strewn across the hillside.

Facing the night sky where Kali disappeared, the stars shine down on me, full of wisdom. *I didn't kiss her good-bye.* The last time we kissed was when I found her on the rajah's balcony, lying in the desert rain, Tarek dead inside the open doors behind her. That was two moons ago. *Has it been so long?*

I hobble to the cliff to view Brac and Rohan's progress repairing the wing flyer; they are nearly finished. I scrub mud off my face, irritated at myself. Anjali came upon us so *fast.* I chose the advantage of the hillside so we could see our enemies' approach, but after Rohan and Opal arrived, I lost my vigilance. My error could have gotten us killed.

Rohan and Brac soar up on the wing flyer and land near camp.

"We're ready to go," says Rohan.

I eye the flying contraption and its repaired wing. I am not fond of boats, and I doubt navigating waves of wind will be any less unpleasant.

Brac assists Mother onto the flyer, and Natesa and Yatin squish on next under the opposite wing. Rohan stretches out in the center of the platform. The room left is hardly wide enough for me.

"Opal said you could carry four additional people," I say, boarding the contraption. "How overloaded are we with five?" I almost say six, since Yatin's size could easily count for two men.

"I can manage," Rohan says and then lifts us with a gust. My stomach dips to my knees. We tip left, and the toes of my boots brush the ground. Rohan straightens us out, but I do not trust his capacity to carry us all the way to Iresh.

I do not look down, trying to avoid further aggravating my uneasy gut. "What if you find out midflight that you cannot manage?"

Rohan grins. "You don't do well when you aren't in command, do you, Captain Naik?"

"I try not to let that happen."

On a laugh, Rohan pushes us higher, wings wobbling like a spin-top toy. I grip the bar in a stranglehold. *Who thought flying was a good idea? People don't have wings for a reason.*

We reach a calmer altitude, and Rohan summons a gale that flings us forward. Air rushes at us, expanding my lungs. My turban flies off my head. The wind slicks back my hair over my ears. Brac hoots in pleasure. My mother smiles, her long dark hair streaming behind her. Natesa and Yatin beam at each other.

I swallow to keep my supper down. *I wish I hadn't eaten the last of the toasted nuts.* With my gaze planted on the dim horizon, I promise never to grumble about boats again.

4

KALINDA

Hours later, after flying over the seemingly endless eastern rice fields and marshlands, the road twists south, but Opal stays her course southeast over an endless expanse of trees. We fly above the jungle while I watch the treetops rippling beneath us like emerald waves.

"I need to rest," Opal says an hour or so later. "Be ready to descend."

The wind lessens, and we dip. I grip the navigation bar as the greenery comes nearer. The emergent trees, tualang and kapok, rise above the rest of the canopy. We dip past one, still coasting downward.

"Um, Opal? Where are we going to land?"

"Ever see a myna perch in a tree?"

I groan. *Oh no.*

Opal decreases the wind again, and we drop. I turn my face away from the incoming leaves. Branches snap and slap my face and legs. Opal's wind dwindles off, and foliage surrounds the wing flyer, slowing us to a jolting halt.

Our legs dangle behind us, our bodies held up by the passengers' plank. The wing flyer suspends high above the ground in a giant banyan tree. We are not mynas relaxing in the sun, more like floating lanterns tangled in a maze of branches.

Opal swings down off the flyer onto a sturdy bough and waves for me to go next. I lower myself beside her, sending the tree limb swaying, and grip another offshoot for balance. The abundant leafage veils the sun. Strange, discordant birdcalls echo across the treetops, and buzzing insects flit about, large as butterflies but with menacing pinchers and iridescent wings. Mists obscure the far-off trees and skulk across the hidden jungle floor.

"Sorry for the height," Opal says. "Any lower and the wing flyer couldn't take off again."

"Where are we?"

"The Morass."

Wariness settles inside me. From what I recall of my topography studies, the Morass straddles the border between the Tarachand Empire and the sultanate of Janardan. Old as the primeval gods, the nearly impassable tropical forest is home to deadly serpents, man-eating beasts, and poisonous plants.

Opal passes me a persimmon from her satchel. "The roadway the refugees travel goes south around the Morass. This is the most direct path. We should arrive in Iresh by nightfall."

I cup the ripe fruit loosely and turn my palm over to check my burns. My blisters have popped and scabbed from holding on to the wing flyer for hours.

Opal devours four pieces of heart-shaped fruit in the same time I eat one. She covered more ground in her wing flyer than I thought possible, but she needs to store up strength for the final portion of our journey.

"How do you know Brother Shaan?" I ask.

Opal flicks a beetle from the tree branch, and it vanishes in the fog below. "Soldiers visited our hut in the middle of the night and broke down the door. Mother told Rohan and me to run to the Brotherhood temple. Brother Shaan hid us from them. A few months later he sneaked us into Janardan."

"And your mother?"

The Galer pauses, her voice quieting. "She didn't make it."

"I'm sorry."

Opal contemplates the persimmon in her hand. "Sometimes I hear her voice on the wind, whispering that she loves me. She's gone, but I know it's her, speaking to me from her next life."

What I would give to hear Jaya's voice again.

"Then it must be her," I reply softly.

Opal tosses off her nostalgia. "Are you really a Burner?" she asks, more inquisitive than accusatory, but I am reluctant to answer. "Even before I saw your hand glowing last night, I knew you were. Brother Shaan swore Rohan and me to secrecy, but I had already guessed that's how you defeated Kindred Lakia in your rank tournament. You parched her." I startle at her perceptiveness before I can catch myself. Opal grins. "I told Rohan that's how you won. Wait until he hears I'm right."

I lean against an intersection of boughs, unwilling to discuss my rank tournament. I work too hard to forget it. I try to relax and recuperate from our long flight, but my muscles refuse to unwind. Did my group escape the rebels? Duty to the empire or not, we should have stayed together.

"Have you heard anything from the others?" I ask Opal.

"Not yet, but the wind always leads my brother and me to each other."

I hug my knees to my chest, wishing I had her certainty. "Do you like hearing the secrets of the wind?"

Opal answers after finishing a yawn. "I don't hear all secrets, but I know yours. You carry the Zhaleh."

My spine stretches in alarm. The Zhaleh contains the bhutas' lineage records leading back to when Anu gifted the First Bhutas with godly powers. The book also holds the incantation to release the Voider, a darkness sent to this world by the demon Kur to combat bhutas' godly light. The warlord seeks to unleash this caged power for revenge

32

against those who persecuted his people under Rajah Tarek's reign. Hastin desires the promised favor the Voider is said to owe the soul who releases it. One almighty wish.

"May I see it?" asks Opal.

"Why?" I lower my fingers to my dagger sheathed against my thigh. The book cannot be taken by someone who would use it for violence or personal gain. I tire of the responsibility of guarding it. But with whom *does* the Zhaleh belong?

"Every bhuta's name from the time of the First Bhutas to when Rajah Tarek stole the book is recorded within." Opal adds in a small voice, "My mother's name is inside."

I have been too intimidated by the Zhaleh to thumb through its pages, not even to see my father's name. I shiver at the thought of disturbing the book's slumbering powers and fist the hilt of my dagger beneath my skirt. "I don't think that's a good idea."

"All right," Opal says. I frown at her hasty compliance. She yawns again, her expression anything but sinister. "I won't fight you for it, Kindred. I'm just curious."

She tips her head back against the tree trunk and closes her eyes. I leave my grip on my dagger, should her cooperation be a ruse, but the only movement near us comes from a mosquito landing on my arm. Before the insect can feed off me, I heat my skin with my powers, and the mosquito shrivels to ash.

A bone-chilling yowl rises from the jungle floor. The short hairs on my arms prickle. While Opal rests, I stand watch over the rolling mists and count the minutes until we leave the Morass.

Opal frees the wing flyer from the trees with a hearty breeze, and we rise from the murky canopy into afternoon daylight. I inhale deeply, breathing easier above the closed-in jungle.

Refreshed by a nap and food, Opal calls brisk, fair winds, and we fly eastward. Drowsiness tampers with my attentiveness when the sun begins to sink at our backs and the copse of trees below is parted by a mighty green-hued river.

"The River Ninsar will lead us the rest of the way," Opal shouts above the rushing air.

Minutes later, twinkling city lanterns manifest on the purple horizon like waking fireflies. She summons a strong gale, and we speed toward the shining beacon of Iresh, racing the final rays of daylight.

We plunge down and graze the river's surface, our reflection darkening the jade waters. Opal dips her toe in and splashes our legs. I smile, rejuvenated by its coolness.

I've done it. I've left the Tarachand Empire.

I may as well have stepped into another world. No spiky mountains haunt my peripheral vision, and the dull orange and brown of the desert have been replaced by a flourishing oasis that could revive the whole of any wasteland. Civilization nestles in the heart of the Morass, the reddish-yellow lights the jungle's lifeblood.

Our wing flyer stays low, gliding over the river alongside a battalion of flitting bugs. Huddled between a tremendous cliff and the River Ninsar, Iresh molds into the lush foliage.

We soar over riverboats that bob along the merchant-lined waterfront. Opal draws a wind beneath us, and we climb steeply. My stomach drops and then floats back up when we level off. I gaze down at circular bamboo huts with domed roofs. Vines buckle the narrow roadways and scale walls, the jungle veins connecting everything and everyone.

Opal flies us higher, trailing a wide, zigzagging stairway etched into the side of a craggy cliff looming over the riverside city. We crest the top, and a tremendous gold-leaf domed palace with low, flat columned outer buildings spans the breadth of the plateau. Living, breathing vines cover the Beryl Palace's mossy walls. A waterfall engraves a raging path from the center of the palace grounds down the cliff and lays root in the river. Even here the Morass encroaches on man, but the Beryl Palace maintains firm hold against the jungle, a pillar of fortitude for the city at its feet.

The wing flyer glides to an open strip of grassland in a garden within the palace grounds. Opal reins in her winds. We land effortlessly, and she hops off the flyer. I slip down and stretch, my arms and back aching with fatigue.

Soldiers file out from the covered patios stretching alongside the grass. They line a stone path leading to a palace entry and stare straight ahead. Opal stays by the wing flyer. I hover near her, my hand tight on the turquoise hilt of my sheathed dagger. I eye the guards, absorbing every detail of their loose, buttonless tunics and skirted legs, along with the machetes at their hips and the khandas strapped to their backs. The guards in the Turquoise Palace wore stiff, high-buttoned collared jackets and long trousers. This is the first time I have seen men sporting skirts. The bagginess of their apparel must be cooler in this muggy heat.

An elegant young woman in a lime-green sari sweeps down the pathway. "You made good time. Where's Rohan?"

"We were separated in a rebel attack," Opal replies. "He and the remainder of the kindred's party will join us later."

"You must be Kindred Kalinda," the young woman says. "I'm Princess Citra, Sultan Kuval's eldest daughter." She speaks the same language everyone on the continent does, but her *s* sounds like a *z*.

The princess examines me up and down with a summary frown. I am not known for my beauty. I am too thin, too tall. I wear no eye kohl or rouge staining my lips and cheeks. No makeup colors Princess Citra's face either, yet her eyes shine like the River Ninsar, dark pools reflecting the green of the jungle. Her blackish hair hangs straight down her back, the top strands braided and twisted up in a crown. Her silky yellow-brown skin hints of floral perfume, but she is no delicate bloom.

A machete hangs at her waist, and judging from her trim figure, firm stance, and sandaled feet fastened to the land, she is skilled with her blade.

Princess Citra meets my survey of her with a self-assured smirk. "Prince Ashwin requests your company straightaway." Something possessive, even predatory, takes hold of her when she mentions the prince.

I slide a questioning glance at Opal—*is the princess always this intense?*—and she motions for me to follow her.

The princess leads us down the path and through a high-arched doorway into the Beryl Palace. Torches light the vacant halls. Ceramic pots with bushy plants bring the verdure of the jungle indoors. Emerald banners hang from ceiling to floor. Each corridor has a gold-framed portrait of the land-goddess Ki wearing a huge black snake draped over her shoulders—a dragon cobra—the sultanate of Janardan's imperial symbol.

My soul-fire flickers as we navigate the corridors, shrinking and growing every so often. I would think it odd if I was not so tired. I must stoke my inner fire with food and rest. I will not be found defenseless on foreign soil.

I maintain cautious awareness of the Janardanian soldiers. Some wear a yellow cloth band tied around their upper arm, embroidered with one godly symbol: sky, land, or water. No fire symbol, so far. They must be the sultan's bhuta guards.

"Why don't you wear a yellow armband?" I whisper to Opal, depending on her sensitive ears to hear me.

After a glance at Princess Citra's back, she answers. "Bhuta refugees have two choices: sign the peace treaty and agree not to use their powers or swear fealty to Sultan Kuval and join his army. Rohan opted for the latter. The sultan doesn't retain women in his army, so I signed the treaty. I've been given special permission to use my powers so long as I serve as a personal servant to the prince."

"And who are they?" I ask of the white-clad guards with shaved heads alongside the princess. They are plain faced and fit, with toned torsos and arms.

"Eunuchs. They protect the sultan's queens, courtesans, and children."

How strange this place is from home. Not only did Tarek not employ eunuchs to guard his women, his courtesans were forced to entertain his men of court. I grimace at the memory of Tarek's ill-treatment of Natesa and Mathura.

Princess Citra stops before a curved doorway. Stationed on either side of the entry are guards dressed in baggy dark-green uniforms. My longing intensifies to a piercing ache. The Janardanian guards' postures and strict demeanors remind me of Deven.

"Your chamber is down the hall," the princess says and then ushers Opal and me through the door.

Brother Shaan rises from a chair near an empty hearth. A smile rips across my face. He devoted his life to the Parijana faith—and to protecting me, the daughter of Rajah Tarek's first-ever rani.

I hurry to Brother Shaan, and he wraps me in his arms. "My child," he says, "you're safe."

"Anjali attacked us." I draw away. The wrinkles on his weathered face are permanently creased into a state of concern. "I left ahead of Deven and the others."

He grasps my cold hands in his warm ones. "You did what was right."

Princess Citra taps her nails against her leg, her voice short. "Prince Ashwin asked to see Kindred Kalinda as soon as she arrived."

"His Majesty is in his study," says Brother Shaan. "I'll look after the kindred from here. Good night, Princess."

She bottles her breath, then exhales sharply and marches out.

"Where's the book?" Brother Shaan asks. I lift the flap of my pack, and he peeks in at the Zhaleh. "And the oil vessel?"

"Here as well." I nearly forgot the oil vessel was in my satchel. I try not to think about carrying around a vial that contains a thousand drops of bhuta blood acquired from years of Rajah Tarek's merciless bloodlettings and stonings. Tarek needed to consume the blood before speaking the incantation in the Zhaleh that releases the Voider, but he did not live long enough to start the ritual.

Brother Shaan lowers the flap of my bag. "They're safer with you. Continue to protect them. We're beyond Hastin's reach here, but others will seek them for their advantage." I would rather give Brother Shaan the Zhaleh, but I can withstand a couple more days watching over it. "And, Kalinda, Burners are not welcome in Iresh. The sultan isn't prejudiced; he's an opportunist. Burners are historically harder to control. If Sultan Kuval discovers what you are, he'll take action against you. For now, your heritage must stay private."

I have lots of practice hiding my powers to put others at ease, so I see no harm in continuing.

A low voice sounds behind us. "Brother Shaan—oh. I didn't realize we have visitors."

I swivel to see a man in the far doorway. *Great Anu, it cannot be.*

His shiny dark hair is trimmed and combed back, his smooth face beardless. His soft skin is oily, like a freshly molted snake, and his apparel is sewn from the finest silk, purple as a field of irises. The regal man stands tall, perched above the world like a proud bird of prey.

Rajah Tarek is alive.

The rajah's face lights up, as though he has been waiting for me here all this time. I whip out my dagger and push Brother Shaan behind me.

"Stay back," I warn.

Rajah Tarek's smile shrinks, and he closes his book. "I—I apologize for startling you, Kalinda."

His voice is wrong.

The realization triggers an avalanche of other details that my startled mind only now registers. His chin is softer and eyes rounder. He is a tad taller and thinner than Tarek, gangly and less muscular. His clean-shaven face is young, placing him a year or two under me. And he carries a book that he was reading when he walked in. I never once saw Tarek interested in reading.

Brother Shaan steps out in front of me. "Your Majesty, please forgive the kindred. You've given her quite a shock." He pushes my arm down, lowering my dagger. "You came in before I could prepare her. Kindred, this is Prince Ashwin."

I stare at the man—no, *boy*—before me. The longer I gape at him, the more obvious my mistake. He is a twin of his father, but the subtle dissimilarities are apparent enough for my face to heat with humiliation.

"Your Majesty." I manage a short bow, my guarded gaze firm on him.

The prince steps fully into the chamber, and, on instinct, I raise my dagger. He sidesteps, skirting me near the exterior of the room. "I'll shake your hand later."

I tremble at the thought of touching him. The prince notices my disdain, and injury fills his eyes. Did I not tell Deven to give Prince Ashwin a chance? I rush to recover my abysmal first impression. "We traveled across Tarachand from temple to temple, searching for you."

"We?" he asks, glancing behind me. Opal sits in the chair Brother Shaan vacated, picking dried carob seeds from a dish on the table.

"I had to leave my companions behind with Rohan. They'll join us soon."

"Are they all right?" he asks.

Prince Ashwin's concern causes me pause. "I . . . I don't know, Your Majesty."

Remorse flickers across his face. I am entranced by his openness; I cannot recall seeing Tarek regretful about anything. Prince Ashwin turns away from me, and his voice softens. "I appreciate your coming, Kalinda. I was uncertain if you would."

I frown at his back, desiring to see his haunting face and read his expression. "Of course, Your Majesty. I am here to help you with your transition onto the throne."

The prince swivels back around. Even after listing their dissimilarities, I am still unprepared for how closely he resembles his father. *Don't be a fledgling. He isn't Tarek.*

"I cannot express how grateful I am that you're here," says Prince Ashwin. "I was worried you would decline to come for the tournament."

I go still, my stomach lurching with unease. "What tournament?"

The prince flashes a startled look at Brother Shaan. "You said you would tell her."

"Tell me what?" I demand, my voice rising.

Brother Shaan gestures at Opal, a half wave. "You may go now." She hops to her feet and scoots for the door.

"Tell me what?" I call after her as she leaves. I fix Brother Shaan with an impatient glower. "What is this about? What tournament?"

Prince Ashwin toys nervously with a gold cuff around his wrist. "The sovereigns of the neighboring countries are alarmed by Hastin's insurgence. They want to see him displaced and his rebel army stopped. They agree we require aid, but not on how much and who will supply it."

"We need allies," says Brother Shaan, "but the other rulers are reluctant to risk their manpower and resources without being invested in Ashwin's new empire. Sultan Kuval offered to host a trial tournament to determine who would be responsible for aiding us. All four sovereigns will submit one female competitor to vie as a representative from their nation. Ashwin consented on the condition that he could select the competitor from Tarachand. Your reputation is hailed all over the continent, and as the current kindred, your continued reign would assure our people's cooperation."

"What's the reward for winning?" I ask, dreading the answer.

"My kindred's throne," Prince Ashwin replies with a bright smile that does not warm me. "The champion will have the honor of marrying me."

"I don't want to marry you." Prince Ashwin frowns in hurt. Has he already envisioned me as his wife? I will have to put a stop to that right away. "I don't want the throne."

Brother Shaan licks his lips with cautious hope. "You must see the diplomatic advantage the other sovereignties would gain should one of their competitors win. The Tarachand Empire is the largest territory on the continent and has the richest resources. Prince Ashwin has promised to open trade negotiations once he is seated on the throne and offered a treaty of arms in support of lessening tensions. The sultan has agreed to provide bhuta military aid, regardless of the tournament's outcome. It's in all our best interests to bind states in defense against the rebel insurgents."

His diplomatic reasoning does not explain the need for a tournament. "Why doesn't the prince wed a wife from each sovereign?"

"I recommended that," Prince Ashwin insists. "I suggested the champion be my first wife, and the other contenders would be my second, third, and fourth wives, according to the succession of their performance in the tournament. But Sultan Kuval felt the strongest alliance should remain solely between us and the champion's nation. Too many competing agendas would frustrate the purpose for uniting nations, which is to defend against our common threat—the warlord."

Brother Shaan finishes the explanation. "All Sultan Kuval requests is that Princess Citra has a chance to contend for the throne. Female representatives from Lestari and Paljor will arrive soon to compete."

"I swore I would never step foot in the arena again." Of the three of us, only I have fought and killed in a tournament. My memories of the bloody duels dredge up horrors I have struggled to bury. I will not relive them.

"This will be unlike your rank tournament," assures Brother Shaan. "Each contender will be tested in a series of challenges intended to find the most worthy queen. The final test will remain a traditional match between the last two competitors, a duel to first blood."

Back home, "first blood" means competitors battle until someone's throat is slit. But a series of trials *would* be less life threatening. "What will these trials be?"

"We don't know particulars," answers Brother Shaan. "Sultan Kuval will devise them."

"Then you cannot guarantee this will be different than my rank tournament!" I hear how rancorous I sound, and with great effort, I level my voice. "What happens if I refuse?"

"We haven't considered that outcome," Prince Ashwin admits. "You're the only rani who escaped Vanhi. We have no one else."

"Then I suggest you get used to the idea of wedding a foreigner." I storm for the door.

"Kalinda," Prince Ashwin calls, catching up. "Please—"

"I won't fight for you."

He smiles, a dashing tilt of his lips. "I was going to ask if you would like me to escort you to your chamber."

I deflate a tad. He must know I cannot find my way alone. "Fine."

He joins me, leaving a gap between us. I widen our distance even more. I am not skittish, but Prince Ashwin has brought my nightmares of Tarek back to life.

We leave his chamber in silence, the Janardanian guards following us. I peek at the prince from the corner of my eye. He catches me, and I swiftly glance away.

"You aren't the first to fear me for my appearance," he says.

"The resemblance is incredible." I assumed the prince would have more of his mother in him. Prince Ashwin is Lakia and Tarek's son, and I am Lakia's niece.

The prince and I are cousins. Family.

I mellow my voice. "It isn't you they fear. It's him."

"I'm born of Tarek's blood. Isn't that the same?"

"I—I don't know." I walk faster. We do not choose the circumstances we are born into or the gods' will for us, but which shapes us the most? Do our parents' choices bind us to an inescapable fate or do our own?

Prince Ashwin pauses at an open door. "Brother Shaan told me of your tastes and hobbies. I took the liberty of requesting a few comforts for your stay. Opal will be your personal guard. I hope you find everything to your liking."

I step inside the chamber, and my knees weaken with want. I have not slept in a bed since I left Vanhi. Adjacent to the large bed is a table with three chairs, and near the hearth is a raised lounge. More potted plants and trees stand in corners, as though the jungle could not spare a single room from its intrusion.

"Kalinda." The wistful way Prince Ashwin speaks my name compels me to face him. The strength of his optimistic gaze spears me to my spot. "I would like for you to join me in defending our homeland. I need you to stand on my right-hand side."

"I've stood on the right-hand side of the rajah's throne. No matter what you were told about me, that isn't where I belong."

His shoulders draw up, his elbows tucking into his sides, holding himself tight. "I'm not blind to the legacy I've inherited. Rajah Tarek was a tyrant, but he also made you a champion."

"*I* made myself a champion. I won't make the same mistake twice." I slam the door in his startled face, letting the satisfaction of the brusque echo vibrate through me.

A servant bustles in from an antechamber. I wave her away. "I don't need a servant. Tell them to reassign you."

She retreats the way she came, and I prowl the bedchamber, searching for possible exits, an escape route, should I need one. None of the closed windows have latches. I check the balcony, dissatisfied with my findings. The exit is too high to jump from, and armed guards patrol in the garden below, either to protect me or to lock me in. Most likely both. And Opal will be stationed outside my door.

I am stuck.

I take off my satchel and drop it on the bed. A note addressed to me rests on the table. Beside the note are a sketchbook and a tray of fine quills, ink bottles, and charcoals. I run my fingers over the rainbow array of inks. I have always wanted to learn how to paint, but I pull away. Prince Ashwin cannot bribe me.

But perhaps the prince's gift could have another use . . .

I tug the leather cover off the sketchbook and fit it around the Zhaleh. *That will do.* After slipping the Zhaleh back into my bag, I stretch out on the bed and try to relax into the downy pillow and silk sheets, but noises carry in from the balcony, lonesome birdcalls and warbling cicadas. My bedsheets smell oddly of musty moss.

A dull throbbing swells inside me. I wish for the crackle of a campfire, the grit of dust on my hands, and the comforting scent of warm sandalwood and leather. *Where are you, Deven?*

A yawn pops out of me. Shutting my eyes, I picture home to force my muscles to unwind, but Rajah Tarek's spirit looms over me in the dark.

5

DEVEN

I slog across the marshlands, surveying the inky edge of the Morass in the distance. In the other direction, Yatin and Brac forge for cattails and Natesa and Mother pick long-stemmed reeds. Rohan is resting from our long flight. The wind told him Anjali and Indira are retreating back to Vanhi, so we have the wetlands to ourselves.

At last, we are on the ground again, but I cannot see where I am stepping in the dark. I misjudge a mound of grass and slosh through a puddle. Cold, muddy water pours into my boots.

Son of a scorpion.

I finish surveying the area—with *wet boots*—and then squish back to Rohan, propped up against the wing flyer. His young face is disconcertingly pale. I heard no complaint or grousing from him today, but it was clear from his shaking arms that his Galer powers were overexerted by too many riders.

Natesa and Mother huddle upon a higher mound of land, piling willow reeds. Brac holds his glowing hand to the heap of grass, and it ignites. Firelight brightens the area, revealing the dampness on our clothes and the bugs zipping through the balmy air.

Yatin heaves rocks over for Natesa and Mother to sit on and then takes first watch near a glassy pond. He removes his uniform jacket and rests on top of it. Out of habit, I go to do the same and remember half a second too late that I took mine off in the desert after we left Vanhi. Eventually I will get used to not wearing my uniform, even though I am viewed as half the man I was with it. Yatin still thinks of me as his captain, but to the troop that passed us on the road yesterday, I am a traitor. I would be a fool to think my execution sentence is behind me. The trained soldier within me knows I deserve whatever punishment comes my way. But the man stripped of my uniform wants my title, my honor, back. An impossible wish. Traitors are neither forgiven nor forgotten.

I find another rock for my seat, then pull off my boots and set them near the fire to dry. Mother passes out cattails for supper. They are all we have to eat. Our food stores were destroyed in the attack.

Natesa curls her lip at the grassy stalk. "I'm not eating that." She throws the cattail at the feet of the fire and rises.

I shift out of her path before we touch. The one time I tried to help Natesa onto her camel, she drew a blade on me and nearly took off my finger. She only lets Yatin near her. She was wary of men when we first met, and her time as Rajah Tarek's courtesan made her even more cautious. I would not admit this aloud—Natesa would probably slice me open if she knew—but I sympathize with her, as I do my mother. Rajah Tarek was not good to his courtesans.

Natesa joins Yatin, his silhouette big beside hers. My chest pangs in envy. *Skies, I wish I knew Kali was all right.*

Rohan picks up Natesa's discarded stalk and nibbles it away, his eyes flat with fatigue. He finishes the cattail, curls up on his side near the fire, and goes to sleep.

Across the campfire, Brac is missing his trademark grin. I know he regrets parching me, but I cannot forget that he threaded out my life source and used it as a weapon.

Mother flickers her gaze between us, preparing to heap her motherly guilt upon my peacekeeping ways. I am sure I will give in. I am no good at holding a grudge. My instructor at the Brotherhood temple once told me I was quick to forgive—a compliment, I think. But Brac needs to realize the full ramifications of parching me and to never do it again. I tug on my wet boots and trudge away, facing the fields.

Alone in the quiet, my evening prayers meander from expressing gratitude for surviving another day to requesting protection for the next. But prayers cannot curtail my restlessness. By now, Kali must have met Prince Ashwin. The events that have befallen the empire since Rajah Tarek's death are not her fault. She did as the gods directed her. Even so, her ending the rajah's life may dissuade the prince from retaining her in his court.

But should Prince Ashwin take a liking to her . . .

Mother and Brac speak in hushed voices behind me, probably *about* me. Brac does not understand how he is viewed. His abilities are terrifying. When he uses his Burner powers, I am reminded that he is a half-god. A literal spiritual offspring of Anu.

And so is Kali.

The harder I hold on to her, the brighter she shines and the further apart we grow. Kali is a shooting star. I do not know how much longer I can keep her close without burning up in her wake.

———————

Early light reveals a mist over the marshlands. Rohan is up and alert, his strength and color returned overnight. He gnaws down the rest of the cattails for breakfast while we take turns marching across the soggy plain to use the latrine.

Brac comes up to my side. "Mother and I spoke last night. We agree it would be better for her and me to find another way to Iresh. You go ahead with the others. We'll take the road east of here."

Several paces away, Mother hugs Natesa and Yatin. She must be telling them good-bye.

"Why Mother?" I ask, masking my hurt. *They decided this without me.* "Yatin could stay behind with you." He is the obvious choice to free up the weight of the wing flyer.

"Natesa wouldn't allow it," Brac says lowly so they cannot hear. Separating Natesa from Yatin would be like trying to untangle a monkey from a tree branch. A monkey that *bites.* "This was Mother's idea. She wants to see more of the empire."

"What about her bad knee?"

"I'll trade work for a horse and supplies in the next village, and she can ride to Iresh." Brac glances at Rohan drinking from our water flask. "We'll arrive a few days behind you."

"Sounds like you've already made up your mind." I pull on my pack and tighten the straps with brisk tugs. Brac reaches out to console me, and I lean away.

"I *am* sorry for parching you, Deven," he says, lowering his hand. "I was trying to protect you and Mother. I don't want you to fear me."

I am not afraid of Brac. I am afraid of what he can *do.* Since we were boys, I have distanced myself from his powers. I hate that I am weak. Weaker than him.

Brac starts to go, and, despite my anger, I refuse to part on bad terms. "Wait," I say. "No matter what, we'll always be brothers."

Brac hauls me into a hug. A moment later, Mother wraps her arms around us both. "I knew my boys couldn't stay mad at one another."

"This is solely for your benefit," says Brac.

"That's right, Mother," I add. "As soon as you turn your back, I'm going to throttle him."

Mother shakes her head at our teasing and rests her palm against my cheek. "Be good to yourself. Your fate may not seem to be leading you where you want to go, but following it will bring you more peace than you could dream." I squint down at her, sensing a lecture. She pats my cheek affectionately. "I'm proud of you, son."

Heavy regret lands across my chest. At one point I may have deserved her praise, but not anymore. I take off my pack and pass it to her. "My supplies should last until the next village. Look after each other. Brac likes to wander off when pretty women are near."

My brother barks a laugh, lifting my mood. Then the first stirrings of Rohan's gales disperse the mist hanging over the marshland and wash away my smile. I have spent long stretches of time away from my family before, but the empire is days away from falling to the warlord's control. I do not like leaving them behind.

Yatin and Natesa are already on the wing flyer. I climb in beside Rohan, and the flyer rises. Brac wraps his arm around Mother's shoulders. They shrink below us until they are the size of ants. Rohan's winds switch direction, and the wing flyer banks deftly, agile with less weight, like a moth instead of a fat bumblebee. We turn southeastward over the wetland, and my family sinks out of sight.

On the horizon, I spot a regiment of soldiers bearing the Janardanian flag traveling the roadway alongside the Morass.

"Why are those troops this far west?" I call to Rohan.

"Routine patrol," he yells over the wind.

The ranks of the slow-moving battalion—about a thousand men— and numerous wagons suggest they are hauling heavy artillery. They are well within their borders yet are marching northwestward, nearer to Tarachand. They could also be traveling around the Morass.

Before I can determine their destination, we turn east into a red dawn.

6

KALINDA

Opal waits while I strap my daggers to my thighs. She arrived moments ago, wearing the loose dark-green uniform of a Janardanian palace guard, and summoned me to meet with the sultan.

"Any word from Rohan?" I ask.

"Not yet, but he and the others are probably a day or so behind."

They could be here by tonight. If I can win over the people's affection for the prince today, we could leave tomorrow.

"Before we go, put this on." Opal offers me a veil. I recoil like it is a lit match. Married women wear veils. I am *not* married. "Brother Shaan said you mustn't be seen in public without the lower half of your face covered." She attempts to put the veil on me, but I tug it from her hand and crush the flimsy cloth in my fist.

"My husband is dead."

I toss the veil, and it flutters to the floor beside my unmade bed. The sheets are crumpled, like my nerves. My nightmares of Tarek were worse last night, heightened by this strange place and the deception that brought me here.

The rest of our party waits in the corridor. Prince Ashwin offers me a shy smile.

"You look lovely, Kalinda," he says.

Having every inch of me clean is a luxury I have missed. I woke to the noises of servants filling a bath for me and leaving. I bathed in the mint-scented water for nearly an hour and then spent longer than usual combing my hair. I wear no eye kohl or lip stain, as I never bothered to learn how to apply them. Any attempt would be heavy-handed and make me look garish.

Brother Shaan bows. "Kindred, please behave in the meeting today. The sultan doesn't often allow women into the war room."

"I'll do my best," I say stiffly.

Opal leads the way. The palace is opulent, with plant life at every corner, and swathed in tapestries of the land-goddess Ki. We leave the corridor to a covered walkway. A tall bamboo fence lines one side, so high I can only see the treetops peeking overhead.

"What's in there?" I ask.

"That's the tiger paddock," Opal replies. "They're the sultan's pets."

Tigers are pets? I *have* come a long way from home.

We are lead to an entry, past two tall potted plants on either side of a door. I step into the chamber with Brother Shaan and Prince Ashwin, and my inner flame snuffs out.

I back out of the doorway and grip Opal's arm. "I lost my powers. What's going on?"

"Protection." She waves at the potted plants. "White baneberry and snakeroot."

The plants she speaks of are noxious to bhutas, given to mortals from the land-goddess Ki as a defense against us. They block bhuta powers, leaving us exposed. White baneberry and snakeroot have been used as safeguards from bhutas for centuries. I assumed the greenery was for decoration, but the palace is covered with *poison*. I must have experienced its effects last night while I walked the corridors.

"The sultan doesn't allow bhuta powers in the war room," Opal whispers, glancing at Prince Ashwin, waiting for me inside. "Sultan

Kuval doesn't know what you are. The prince might, but I don't know for certain. You should go. The sultan has limited patience."

Looking inside, I see a stout white-mustached man sitting on a pedestal across the sunken room. More pots of white baneberry and snakeroot line all four walls. A knee-high, rectangular table occupies the middle of the oblong chamber, with richly colored cloth floor mats laid about. Military officers are seated and ready to begin the meeting.

Prince Ashwin eyes me with concern, attune to my discomfort. I am tempted to go back to my chamber, but I have come all this way to support him. Moreover, I have faced a room full of ranis, all experienced sister warriors. These men cannot be scarier than them.

I step to the prince's side in the war room, and my powers shrink to a useless ember.

A middle-aged military officer with a gaunt face greets us. "Kindred Kalinda, I'm Vizier Gyan, the sultan's head military adviser. We've heard much about you." His gray-streaked hair is tied back, and he carries two machetes, one on each hip. His poor attempt at a welcoming smile broadens his austere appearance. He, with the other Janardanian men, wears a loose-fitting skirt instead of trousers, folded so there is a slight crease separating his legs. The vizier sizes me up in turn but with scrutiny that surpasses polite interest.

Prince Ashwin leads me to the steely-eyed man on the throne. "Sultan Kuval, this is Kindred Kalinda."

The sultan lowers his double chin as if to inspect me better. "They call you the indomitable Kalinda, the reincarnation of Enlil's hundredth rani." His tone borders on ironic.

I wince at the comparison to the fire-god's triumphant intended queen. Tarachandians started a myth that I was Enlil's final wife in another life, and Rajah Tarek fed their fantasy, expanding my reputation beyond the believable. I temper the urge to correct the sultan.

"Thank you for having me, Your Majesty."

"I heard you refused the prince's invitation to join the trial tournament." His gruffness carries a note of satisfaction.

"I'm undecided."

"We anxiously await your answer," Sultan Kuval replies, returning to his ornery tone. "Please be seated."

Prince Ashwin and I kneel at the table, and Brother Shaan sits across from us.

Vizier Gyan addresses the council. "Before we begin with other matters, we have questions for Kindred Kalinda about the recent events in Vanhi. Kindred, you were in the Turquoise Palace when it was occupied by rebels, were you not?"

His question, and the subsequent dozen or so probing stares, catches me off guard. I clasp my unsteady hands in my lap, seeking some semblance of composure. "I was."

"How did Rajah Tarek die?"

A phantom finger strokes down my cheek, and a deep voice whispers *my love* in my ear.

I jerk my chin sideways. The sultan's watchful presence hovers at the brink of my vision. "I—I don't know. I fled when the rebels attacked."

Vizier Gyan takes hasty notes in front of him with a quill pen. "How did you escape?"

"The captain of the guard led me through a secret passageway below the palace."

Their silence fires a flush over my skin. They do not know that I bargained with Hastin and slayed Tarek. Prince Ashwin shifts in his seat beside me. How much does *he* know?

"On the night of the attack, did you see the bhuta warlord?" Vizier Gyan asks.

I falter on a reply. All I can think of is the truth: Hastin tried to kill me in the underground cavern, but I used my powers and fled.

Brother Shaan speaks up. "We must contest this line of questioning. We didn't bring the kindred here so you could interrogate her."

"Our apologies," replies Vizier Gyan. His flat offer of remorse is meant to appease Brother Shaan's protest on my behalf. The vizier does not extend his apology to me. "The kindred is the only member of Rajah Tarek's imperial court who escaped the insurgency. We must establish how and why she was spared."

They suspect I might be a traitor.

But I am.

I scatter the thought before guilt lands on my expression. "I'll answer." I level the vizier with a cool stare. "I didn't see Hastin in the palace on the night of the attack."

Vizier Gyan leans forward, resting his forearms on the table. "Did you see Rajah Tarek's body?"

Brother Shaan lifts his hand to gain the council's attention. "The kindred lost her husband on her wedding night. Upon fleeing the warlord, she searched for Prince Ashwin and came here to join him. Her devotion to the empire is undeniable."

No one contests him, though the council's blatant disapproval of my fleeing Vanhi remains evident in their frowns.

"One last question." Vizier Gyan returns his meddling stare to me. "Where is the Zhaleh?"

Finally, a question I have rehearsed an answer for.

"I don't know," I say, reciting the reply I practiced with Deven in case the rebels caught me. "Tarek had it for years. The book must still be in Vanhi."

"Very well," the sultan clips out. "Vizier Gyan, proceed with the other matters."

The vizier aims his disgruntled glowering face at me, instead of at the sultan, for cutting his interrogation short and then tugs down his long sleeves in preparation of the shift in topics. An emblem is sewn onto the lapel of his uniform jacket, the land symbol. Is he a Trembler?

Prince Ashwin's even voice sounds beside me. "What news do you have, Vizier?"

"I have the latest report on the encampments," he replies, shuffling the parchment papers before him. "Conditions are holding, but we are receiving more refugees every day. We're working to improve their access to clean water and expand the dining tents."

"When can Prince Ashwin and I visit the camps?" I ask.

"Your presence will slow our improvement," replies the vizier. "It's best you stay away for now."

I startle at his brusqueness. "You mean we cannot see our people?"

"Your people are safe," interjects Sultan Kuval. He folds his hands across his ample belly, his movement too controlled for his testiness. "I'm feeding them, housing them, and protecting them. I will continue to leave my borders open and care for them for the duration of the tournament. You may visit them then."

After the tournament? I came to Janardan to shift the people's devotion from me to the prince. How can I do that if I am not allowed to see them? I open my mouth to object, but Brother Shaan shakes his head at me. I clamp my mouth shut and wait for the prince to protest on my behalf. He fiddles with the gold cuff around his wrist and says nothing.

The rest of the meeting is more of the same, Vizier Gyan telling Prince Ashwin what to do and the prince acquiescing. My anger raises by the moment, but I hold my tongue until we are dismissed; then I grab the prince by the arm and drag him out of the war room. Brother Shaan follows close behind, Opal a few steps after him.

"What's the matter with you?" I hiss in the prince's ear. "You need to stand up for our people."

"I cannot offend the Janardanians," he answers, his expression perplexed. "We need their aid."

"The sultan wishes only to help himself," I say louder, not caring who hears me. My powers reignite as soon as I am away from the potted poisons. I pull back from Prince Ashwin before my temper inadvertently singes him. "He's taking advantage of you."

"We have to make concessions," he replies, his surety weakening.

I slow my pace and stare at him. The prince's imperial rule swallows him up, like he is wearing a uniform that is too large. I cannot understand how I mistook him for Tarek.

"Good gods." I step away, understanding why Brother Shaan lied to bring me here.

The fate of the Tarachand Empire has been left to a naive, sheltered boy.

"Kindred," Brother Shaan says softly, "may I have a word?" I nod, defeat falling through me. Without a strong rajah, the empire is lost. "Opal, please escort His Majesty back to his chambers and rejoin us."

"Did I say something wrong?" Prince Ashwin asks, glancing from Brother Shaan to me with an unblinking gaze.

"No, Your Majesty," Brother Shaan replies. "I need a word alone with the kindred. I'll return shortly."

The prince lowers his shoulders, disappointed that we have left him out. Brother Shaan loops his arm through mine, and we stroll off into the gardens. Brother Shaan waits to speak until Opal returns.

"You see now why we need you," he says.

Frustration shortens my strides. "The sultan has Prince Ashwin by the gullet, and the prince is all too happy to hand him power."

"Be patient. Ashwin is more capable than he appears."

Opal trails a couple steps behind us. A slight breeze kicks up as she twirls her finger at her side.

"We may speak without danger of being heard," says Brother Shaan.

Opal must be using the wind to divert the sound around us, giving us the privacy to talk without another Galer overhearing.

"Before coming here," Brother Shaan says, "Prince Ashwin wrote a letter to each sovereign requesting military aid. He anticipated the sultan would be self-serving and try to profit off of our circumstances, and Kuval did exactly that. Within hours of our arrival, the sultan tried to persuade Ashwin to take Princess Citra as his rani. The prince would have been forced to accept, but the letters he sent to Paljor and Lestari prevented Kuval from strong-arming him. The trial tournament may not be ideal. Ashwin is giving up diplomatic power in exchange for aid. In the end, the empire will be vastly different than it is today, but the prince feels the distribution of power is best in the long run. He is doing all he can to establish allied relationships that have been neglected for years."

I sink down on a bench beneath a neem tree that overlooks the green-brown river and the domed roofs of the city. Staring out at this foreign land, a part of me understands Ashwin's uncertainty. The first days outside of the temple, I longed for home. I still crave the cold nights of Samiya and for Jaya in her cot beside mine. The world of men is endlessly challenging, and the prince has entered it as a ruler of a warring empire.

"Your prince needs you, Kalinda," Brother Shaan says quietly. "Imperial blood runs through your veins, and you know what it is to earn your throne."

Do I? I fought my throne every step of the way.

"Ashwin is doing a kindness, leaving this choice up to you," Brother Shaan states, implying I should be grateful. "By law, he can compel you to compete."

I lift my chin at the word "compel," a more tactful way of saying the prince can force me against my will. "What law?"

"I assumed Deven told you."

"He didn't," I snap, impatient for clarification. What does Deven have to do with this?

Brother Shaan gentles his tone. "The Binding of the Ranis is a law as old as the first rajah. The law states that should the rajah pass away, his wealth—including his wives and courtesans—passes on to his heir. Should the heir choose, he may accept his father's ranis as his own wives and step into his reign."

A loaded beat of silence hammers down on me. I was aware that Prince Ashwin would have to release me from my throne, but as a formality. I had no idea I had to overcome a *law*. Is this why Deven has been distant? Why he was indifferent about finding Ashwin? Why he asked me not to come here?

Disbelief and defiance shake my core. My voice emerges from the aftershock, quivering with outrage. *"I—I belong to the prince?"*

"You belong to your throne, and your throne belongs to the prince."

"I see no distinction," I snap. Brother Shaan's optimism for my uncertain fate is beyond tedious.

"Under the law, Prince Ashwin has first rights to you. As the current political unrest is too dangerous for the prince to travel to a Sisterhood temple and claim a kindred of his own, this is his only option."

"I'm a convenience." I grip my teeth together to contain my fury.

"You're the people's kindred," Brother Shaan replies, all patience and calmness. "If you don't compete, what will it mean for them? This is more than a battle for marriage to the throne; it's for the future of the empire. Prince Ashwin is doing all he can to save his homeland and his people."

"I came here to help the people through assisting *the prince*," I remind him. His implication that I am not doing enough to aid Prince Ashwin chafes.

"Yes," Brother Shaan answers, "and the prince needs you to compete."

I will do what I can for our people, but the last time I contended for my throne, I altered the empire, and not for the better. After my interrogation, the prince must realize I am not trusted by Sultan Kuval or his court. I will do more harm than good here.

But if Prince Ashwin does not see reason . . .

"Will he . . . will he force me?"

"I don't know," Brother Shaan answers. "The prince will do what he deems is right for the empire."

Right for his empire or for himself? I fist my skirt, digging my fingertips into my thighs. This entrapment, this false benevolence, is all too familiar. It reminds me of Tarek.

Brother Shaan gazes up, seeking solace in Anu's ever-present sky. "The other tournament competitors will arrive tomorrow. You have until then to decide."

I *have* decided, but Prince Ashwin may still compel me against my will. Soon I will find out how alike the boy prince is to his father.

7

DEVEN

We soar into Iresh on a tailwind and land in the grounds of the Beryl Palace. I have never wanted to stand on my own two feet more than I do now.

The gardens are magnificent and clean, luxuries afforded to the affluent. No sooner do we jump down from the wing flyer than footsteps drum around us. Janardanian guards flock into the courtyard, and one points a machete at my nose.

This isn't the warm welcome I expected.

I lift my hands away from my sword. One green-clad guard confiscates it, and another pats me down for hidden weapons. More guards disarm Yatin and Rohan, but when they reach Natesa, she shoves them away.

"Don't touch me," she hisses.

She is promptly wrangled and her haladie taken. Unarmed, she tosses them a look that would send a pig squealing.

A narrow-faced older man wearing a Janardanian military uniform strides into the garden. "Who are you?" he asks, coldly scrutinizing us.

"Vizier Gyan," Rohan answers, "I'm an imperial guard here at the palace. These people are Kindred Kalinda's party, come from Tarachand."

"Refugees," the vizier surmises.

"We're the kindred's personal guard, sir," I explain.

Vizier Gyan arches a slim brow at Yatin's filthy uniform and my lack of one. "And you are?"

"Captain Deven Naik, sir." I use my former title, as Kali probably gave it to them to identify us upon arrival.

"Welcome to Janardan, Captain," says the vizier. "Are you or your companions bhutas? We are required by law to ask."

A snap of apprehension hits me. Did Kali reveal she is a Burner? "We are not."

Vizier Gyan squints at me a long moment, skeptical of my answer, and then swivels away and speaks to his men in a low voice.

Natesa studies the mossy palace walls in consternation. "If this is our reception, what did Kalinda walk into?"

Yatin gently squeezes her elbow for comfort.

The vizier returns his attention to us. "Rohan, you may go."

Rohan, unable to argue with a higher-ranking officer, twists on his heels and enters the palace. Four guards with yellow armbands flank the rest of us.

Vizier Gyan smiles without warmth. "Captain Naik, your party will come with us."

"Where are we going?" I ask, heedful of the armed escort.

"We have protocols regarding refugees." A muscle in the vizier's cheek jumps slightly from his insincere smile. "As a military man, you must understand our need for order."

What I understand is that this man controls whether or not I see Kali. "Lead the way." I will comply with him, for now.

Vizier Gyan and his soldiers direct us down a steep stairway to the dense jungle below. Everything is so *green*. Vines and wild fruit trees grow alongside the stairs, and moss lives in the cracks of the stones. Life thrives on every surface. The jungle is suffocating compared to the barrenness of the desert.

White patches of tents appear below. The encampment is barricaded with a fence patrolled by soldiers. A smaller compound is organized opposite the other and is closed in by high dirt walls. Watchtowers with mirrors for spotlights are posted at either end. Each camp has one gate near a guardhouse so soldiers can observe all those who enter and exit. A small locked hut is stationed between them, a weapons bunker.

I could not have designed more secure compounds myself, but the measures do not protect the refugees from outside forces. They lock the refugees in.

Vizier Gyan stops between the entranceways to the camps. "Captain Naik, I'll escort you and your man to the military encampment." He means the high-walled compound guarded by soldiers wearing yellow armbands, an identifier of some sort. "My guards will lead the young woman to the civilian camp."

Yatin sidesteps closer to Natesa's side. His great bulk is intimidating, but we are grossly outnumbered. Our last line of defense is our words.

"Sir, the kindred is expecting us," I say. "Before we go in, please notify her of our arrival, or if she's unavailable, Prince Ashwin."

"That's not a possibility," Vizier Gyan replies. "You see, neither Kindred Kalinda nor the prince told us you were coming."

I do not believe him. Kali would not forget to arrange for our arrival. More likely than not, Prince Ashwin has taken a liking to her and is keeping her from us. Or keeping *me* from *her*.

"This is our procedure for all refugees," says the vizier, his words crisp. "Civilians and military personnel are to reside in separate camps."

"These aren't camps," Natesa says, glaring. "They're prisons."

Vizier Gyan sniffs his nose at her. "These arrangements are temporary, miss." He signals to his men. "Take them inside."

Natesa jerks away from a guard. Yatin plants his feet apart, preparing for a fight. My fingers go for my sword—but they confiscated it. Our chance of running and hiding in the jungle tree line across the way is too risky. I will not endanger Yatin or Natesa.

"Yatin," I say. He hears my command in my colorless voice. *Stand down.*

"Do as they say, little lotus," Yatin tells Natesa.

She places her palm on his wide chest. Though her touch is gentle, her eyes are hard. "Don't let them mistreat you."

"I won't," he promises.

Guards escort Natesa to the gate for the civilian encampment. Additional guards nudge Yatin and me toward the high walls of the compound. One of them throws out his hand, and a sudden wind unlatches the gate. *The guard is a Galer.* I spot a sky symbol on his yellow armband. The armbands must distinguish the elite bhuta guards from the regular soldiers.

Vizier Gyan leads us to an open quad amid rows of canvas tents. Loitering men quiet when they see us. All of them are from home, some having served under my command. They wear prison garb, plain brown tunics and flowing trousers. A younger man, four years shy of my twenty, stalks up to me.

"Manas," I breathe. He was a fellow palace guard who served under my command. The last time I saw him, he was battling the rebels beneath the Turquoise Palace. "I thought you were—"

Manas punches me in the jaw. I fall back a step, and he strikes me again, his knuckles slamming into my cheekbone. Yatin grabs Manas by the back of the shirt and lifts him away. Manas hangs from Yatin's hand like an infuriated kitten in its mother's maw.

"Traitor!" Manas bellows. "You betrayed Rajah Tarek!"

Vizier Gyan steps between us. "What's the trouble here?"

Yatin sets Manas on his feet, and Manas yanks his shirt from Yatin's hold. "Ask Captain Naik," he growls.

I glower back at him, my jaw and cheek burning.

"You're a disgrace to the imperial army," Manas says, spitting at my feet.

More caustic glares from the other men box me in. These soldiers were my comrades. Manas and I were friends. I thought he died in the rebel insurgence and I would never see him again. I ball my vibrating fists. If the vizier were not involved, I would strike Manas for betraying our friendship. He turned me in to the rajah.

"Detain Captain Naik until I confer with Prince Ashwin," Vizier Gyan calls to his guards.

Yatin puffs out his gigantic frame to protect me, but I signal for him to bow out. He crosses his arms over his chest and lobs a disgruntled look at Manas.

Guards usher me across the yard to a windowless shack, shove me inside, and slam the door. The dark cell stinks of stale body odor and rotten moss. A ray of sunlight sneaks through the crack at the bottom of the door.

Traitor. My men think I should be dead. I strike the wall with my fist. In the wave of pain that carries up my arm, my shock and anger at seeing Manas dissolve to bleak acceptance. Try as I might, I cannot entirely fault him or the men for their resentment. I *did* betray our empire by breaking my oath to serve the rajah. My penalty was not absolved, only postponed. I could pound against the door, demand to speak with the prince, and plead with him for forgiveness, but he is within his right to discipline me. Gods know, disobedience has a cost. The sky is everywhere, and Anu's justice sees all.

Laden with regret, I bow my head. *I'll face my dishonor with humility. Just please, Anu . . . forgive me.*

Minutes pass as cold fear trickles into my heart. My mind falls silent, but my heart prays on.

8

Kalinda

I spend the afternoon with Opal, though she is not much for company.
She naps while I stare blankly at a book. The colorful inks and sketch-
ing parchment call out to me, beckoning me to open them. My mind
floats with imaginings of all the vivid pictures I could draw, but I go no
further. I will not be bribed, even by so lovely a gift.

Sitting by the hearth, I ignore the book in my lap and scratch at
the rank marks on the backs of my hands. I wish they would go away.
But even if they do, the prince still has first rights to me. What if he
compels me to compete in the tournament? What if he *doesn't*? Will he
exercise his first rights to me regardless?

Opal sits up and tilts a listening ear to the sky. "Brother Shaan
needs me." She jumps up without further explanation and leaves.

My sigh hitches on disappointment. She said Rohan and my party
were a day or so behind us, so they must not be here yet.

I return my attention to the book, but in the stillness of the chamber my awareness prickles. Someone is watching me. I rise with my
hand firmly on my dagger and search for the source. Seeing nothing,
I step closer to the bed. Gooseflesh flares up my body. No one is here,
yet a steady pulse like a heartbeat drums in my ears.

My hand slips into my satchel hung on the bedpost. The pulsing intensifies. I pull out the Zhaleh, and the throbbing behind my eyes stops.

Did I imagine that? Or did the book lure me to it?

I pull off the cover of the sketchbook Prince Ashwin gave me. The real front of the Zhaleh is worn and creased like an old man's face. I run my hand over the tanned deer hide, and my pulse hitches. I should leave it alone. The Zhaleh holds darkness. And yet . . .

As I open the true cover, I brace for an assault on my senses. I assume the mere act of unsealing the book will unleash evil, but nothing happens. Exhaling shallowly, I start in.

The first page is divided into four columns. At the top are symbols, one each for water, sky, land, and fire. Names are written beneath the symbols. The top four names are the First Bhutas, including Uri under the fire symbol. Below them, line after line, page after page, are the proceeding bhuta generations. After twenty pages or so, the column of Burners becomes shorter than the others. Starting at the bottom, I skim the list backward. My finger stops.

Kishan Zacharias.

I brush my thumb over my father's surname. *KZ.* We have the same initials.

"Kalinda Zacharias," I say, testing how it sounds. The last part rings foreign, like an off-tune sitar string. I whisper my full name to myself once, twice, a third time. "Kalinda Zacharias." The last time the sound slides out of my mouth and sits right in my ear.

A shadow appears on the wall, cast from behind me. Someone *is* here. I whirl around and grasp the intruder by the throat. My fingers glow, pulsing with fire.

"It's me." Prince Ashwin gulps hard, his gullet bobbing against my palm.

I drop my hold on him and retract my powers before he sees. With my pulse charging, I hide the Zhaleh behind me. "I didn't hear you come in."

"I entered quietly." The prince rubs his throat where my handprint fades. "I thought you might like to come with me to the encampments."

I shield the Zhaleh with my body while I stow it away in my satchel. "You told the sultan we wouldn't go there."

The prince grips the strap of a bag slung over his shoulder. "I gave it some thought, and I agree with what you said. We should see our people. Will you come with me?"

I have no qualms about defying Sultan Kuval, but I will not go anywhere with the prince until we discuss the Binding of the Ranis. "Brother Shaan told me of the law. You have first rights to me."

"He mentioned your conversation to me." Prince Ashwin's tone is maddeningly neutral. How can he be offhand about my future?

"You tricked me into coming here," I say, venting my anger.

Hurt crosses his face. "I was told you knew about the law. Remember it was my will to tell you about the tournament prior to your arrival. I'm truly sorry you were misled."

The prince's apology dumps icy water over my temper. I do not recall Tarek apologizing for anything. Ever. Either Prince Ashwin is a terrific liar or he was also misled. Gods, I hate that I feel sorry for him. *I* am the one wronged.

"As I said," Prince Ashwin goes on, "you can leave at any time."

"You won't compel me to compete?"

"No, but I will do my best to persuade you to stay."

His eyes shine with sincerity, driving me to look away. I simply cannot trust him. Prince Ashwin may not be Tarek, but he holds the same power over my fate.

"All right. I'll go with you." I came here to support the prince, after all.

"Good. I've arranged for a distraction, so we need to hurry." Instead of going to the corridor, he strides out onto the balcony.

I follow him into the late-day sun. "There's no way down."

"Certainly there is. I used to sneak out of the temple all the time." His smile is a tad daring and plenty dashing. He swings his leg over the banister and offers me his hand. Ever so cautiously, I rest my fingers in his. He brushes his thumb over my wifely rank. Sympathy emanates from him with a trace of understanding. We are both tied to the throne.

Shouts rise up from the garden below. The prince helps me over the banister and grips a vine growing up the palace wall. He climbs down hand over hand.

Brother Shaan's voice carries to us. "I tripped on that rock! Who put that there? Are you trying to injure an old man?"

I pause at his ranting. Brother Shaan is the most even-tempered man I know.

"Kalinda, come on," Prince Ashwin whispers. "He won't buy us much time."

Oh. Brother Shaan *is the distraction.*

I scale down the vine. At the bottom, we duck behind a flower bush and check the path. While Brother Shaan berates the guards, we dart across the empty pathway into the tree cover.

A shrill voice erupts from across the garden. "What's all the commotion?"

Princess Citra marches up to Brother Shaan and the palace guards. As her back is to us, we sprint to the overhang where the stream lunges off the cliff in a waterfall. Prince Ashwin reels up a rope that hangs over the edge.

"I was assured this is safe," he says, tugging me against him. "Hold on."

Before I can object, he leaps over the cliff with me. I strangle a scream, clutching him with all my might. We swing down in an arc. Wind whooshes through my hair, and then we break through the streaming water. Cold wetness shocks me, drenching me down to my skin, and Prince Ashwin lets go of the rope. We drop to the floor of a cave behind the waterfall and roll to a stop, lying beside each other and dripping wet.

"You could have warned me," I snap.

"I wasn't sure if I had the nerve for it myself." The prince grins. "You didn't scream."

"I'm not the hysterical type." I shove away from him. The gushing waterfall mists our faces and muffles our voices. "How did you know about the rope?"

"Princess Citra's little sister Tevy told me about it. Tevy said young people use the rope to swing into the cave through the waterfall."

"Why?"

"For excitement." He wiggles his eyebrows, rousing a droll smile out of me, and then walks deeper into the cave. Away from the surging water, the light wanes to grayish blue. From his pack, he removes dry sparring garments for me and an extra set of clothes for himself.

I accept the clothing, cautious of his thoughtfulness. He peels off his wet tunic, and his smooth, bare chest robs me of all coherent thoughts. I twist around, my face heating.

"Get changed," he says.

I glance over my shoulder at him. Ugly scars run across the length of his back. I have a similar scar from my rank tournament down my arm from a khanda wound, but Prince Ashwin was the most protected child in the empire. How did he get his?

I hear him start to undo his belt and twist back around.

"Are you finished?" he asks.

"Almost." I unpin my wet sari, leaving on the petticoat and blouse. Shivering in the dampness, I drape and pin on the dry scarlet sari. I lift the finished edge of the cloth up through my legs and tuck it into the back of my waistline, leaving my covered legs free to move.

I slip my sheathed daggers to my hips and straighten. In the familiar training uniform, I face Prince Ashwin. "Done."

He turns back around. He has changed into coarser clothes, shedding his royal finery. If he were any other boy, I would look twice at him. Tarek was handsome, but his ruthlessness repulsed me. Prince Ashwin is equally attractive without the cruelty.

The prince smiles widely at me. "Brother Shaan told me that color flatters you."

"He did not."

"No, but you do wear scarlet well." A blush blossoms on his cheeks, and a tingling sweeps across my face. Prince Ashwin packs my wet clothes and then offers me a corked bottle. "Rub this on your skin. It's lemon-eucalyptus oil to repel the mosquitoes."

We take turns rubbing the smelly oil on ourselves, and then he shoulders his pack.

"There's a stairway at the back of the cave that leads to a lower door," he says.

"Your Majesty—"

"Ashwin. We swung over a cliff together. That merits the use of my first name."

"All right, *Ashwin*, what will happen if we're caught?"

"I don't know, so let's not find out."

I am far from reassured, but he knows how to get out of here, so I follow him deeper into the dim cave. The farther we travel from the waterfall, the darker our surroundings. Ashwin stops in the scant light and draws a torch from the pack.

"Will you please?" he asks, holding it out for me.

I draw back. *Brother Shaan must have told him I'm a Burner.*

"Are you going to leave us in the dark?" Ashwin presses.

I search his expression for any warning of loathing but find only ardent expectancy. Ashwin has known all along what I am, yet he still invited me here and asked me to compete for the throne.

Holding my finger to the torch, I push out my powers, and the wood ignites. Torchlight illuminates the wonder on Ashwin's face.

"Incredible," he breathes.

I start down the steep stairway. Could Ashwin respect my powers?

"I'm sorry I didn't mention I knew about your bhuta heritage before now," he says, his footsteps at my back. The ease of his apologies continues to astound me. "Brother Shaan swore me to secrecy. He's concerned Kuval would accuse you of working with the rebels and blame you for Rajah Tarek's death."

I stumble downward a step in surprise. His arms come around me and steady my balance. I pull away in haste. *He knows about the blood on my hands.*

"Brother Shaan explained everything," he rushes on. "None of it was your fault, Kalinda. You were forced to defend yourself against Kindred Lakia, and you couldn't have saved Rajah Tarek."

Ashwin's defense of me against his parents is the last reply I expected. Brother Shaan must have left out that I conspired with Hastin. Ashwin does not know that *I* killed Tarek.

"Did you . . . did you love him?" Ashwin asks, misinterpreting my silence as sorrow for my late husband.

"No," I reply fast. *Gods' virtue, I sound so coldhearted.* "I mean to say I hardly knew him."

"I barely knew him too." Ashwin passes me on the stairs. I trail him, eager for him to go on. I never observed Tarek act as a parent. "Far back as I can recall, I was raised by the brethren. *They* were my family. Kindred Lakia and Rajah Tarek visited me once a year, if that."

I never met my mother or father. Having parents would be a blessing, but Ashwin speaks of his like they were a scourge.

"Tarek was a selfish leader." Ashwin's voice hardens with contempt for his father, paired with an undertone of resigned acceptance about his legacy. "My duty is to fix Tarek's mistakes, but I cannot redeem the empire alone. I need someone at my side, someone who will stand for what's right, someone who has already found favor with the gods."

I arrange my features into apathy. Spinning at the back of my mind is the law that promises Ashwin my future. How far will he go to fix his father's mistakes? Will he rescind his promise and force me to compete? I agree the empire must heal from Tarek's rule, but I cannot assist Ashwin in the way he wishes. I did my godly duty. I won my rank tournament and ended Tarek. The most I am willing to do is help Ashwin find another competitor from the encampment to represent Tarachand in the trial tournament. He will have to find another champion.

Silence closes in around us as we continue into the dark. The stairs flatten out to a high tunnel. Many paces later, the torchlight reveals odd clay markings across a gray wall face. We pause to inspect the strange symbols.

"Runes," Ashwin says.

"They're beautiful." Whoever left them must have lived a long time ago. I run my finger over the rough stone. "I wonder what they mean."

"They teach the origin of the Morass." Ashwin sweeps the light over the ancient drawings. "Would you like me to read you the tale?"

"Can you?" Runes are an ancient language, rarely taught or spoken in Tarachand.

Ashwin answers by beginning to read. "Long ago, when the world was new, Abzu, the freshwater-god, was the first deity, the begetter of all. Soon after Abzu came Tiamat, the saltwater-goddess. Abzu and Tiamat met at the horizon, and when their waters intertwined, Tiamat birthed Anu and Ki."

Abzu and Tiamat are not deities I worship. The sisters taught me to pray to the sky-god Anu; his consort, Ki, the land-goddess; and their children, the fire-god Enlil and the water-goddess Enki. Though I have heard of Abzu and Tiamat, our temple studies did not focus on the primeval gods.

Ashwin lowers the torchlight and continues. "Anu sought to possess his father's glory and become king of the gods, so he killed Abzu and usurped his lordship. Enraged by her son's betrayal, Tiamat birthed the First-Ever Dragon and filled the creature's body with fiery venom. Together, they made war against her son. Armed with the arrows of his winds, Anu, the god of storms, fought Tiamat and the dragon. Anu cut through the channels of Tiamat's blood and made the north wind bear her body away into secret places, creating rivers that ran into the salty seas. From her ribs, Anu crafted the vault of sky and land, and from her spine, she sprouted the Morass."

I rub my chilled arms. "What happened to the First-Ever Dragon?"

Ashwin scans the wall but finds no more runes. "Doesn't say, but I once read that another name for the demon Kur is the First-Ever Dragon."

Demons and dragons are one and the same?

A foreboding wind flickers our torch. "We should move on," I say. We carry onward down the tunnel, more cautious than before. "Who taught you to read runes?"

"My instructor, Brother Dhiren. I wasn't allowed to go outside or train with the other apprentices, so Brother Dhiren filled my days with lessons."

I try to picture Ashwin as a child, buried in books instead of playing outside, and my heart squeezes. When I was younger and suffering from fevers, I was often alone. Then I met Jaya. She was a torch in the dark, brightening my world.

"Where is Brother Dhiren now?" I ask.

"He passed away." Pain Ashwin lacked when he spoke of his parents jams his voice, a sadness that stems from losing someone he loved. He speeds up his pace. "It should be sundown by now, and we still have a ways to go."

I walk faster, mulling over our conversation. Nothing Ashwin has told me about himself has caused me to doubt him. In fact, his disapproval of his parents and affection for Brother Dhiren are endearing. I do not dislike Ashwin, but I am not ready to trust him yet either.

9

DEVEN

The sunlight under the door weakens to pale silver. Footsteps approach, and the door swings open. I squint at the dusky sky; weak as it is, my eyes still sting in the twilight.

"You may come out now, Captain," says Vizier Gyan.

I push away from leaning against the wall. Days of traveling without much food weaken my knees, and I weave a step as I exit the hut. Vizier Gyan waits with guards. One of them holds out a whip, the other a sword. I force my face to granite.

Vizier Gyan links his hands behind him. "I've spoken with the soldiers. They informed me of your prior accusations. Do you admit to conspiring with the bhuta warlord Hastin and betraying Rajah Tarek?"

Be humble. I draw in a shallow breath. "Yes, sir."

Vizier Gyan's staid expression does not change. "I reported my findings to Prince Ashwin. He has no room in his army for traitors. Fortunately for you, he is more lenient than his father. He said if you confessed he would spare your life and deliver a less severe sentence."

"Does the kindred know I'm here? What did she say?"

The vizier pauses at my unanticipated inquiry. "She's in accord with the prince. Neither will excuse treachery."

Kali sided with Prince Ashwin? Something must have happened between them. He could be exercising his first rights to her and forcing her to comply with his wishes.

"I want to see the kindred," I say.

"You have no rights here, Captain."

"I understand, but when they arrive, if you would please let me speak—"

"Neither the prince nor the kindred will attend your punishment. They have more immediate affairs that require their attention."

Kali isn't coming. I stiffen my jaw, locking down my frustration. Prince Ashwin is keeping her away from me. Why has *he* not come? He should be here to order my sentencing, not hiding behind the vizier. "What affairs?" I chop out.

"Sultan Kuval is hosting a trial tournament," explains Vizier Gyan. "Each of the four sovereigns will select a contender to compete for a chance to wed Prince Ashwin. He wishes for Kindred Kalinda to represent Tarachand against the opposition."

Another godsforsaken tournament.

"Did she agree?" I ask.

"As far as I'm aware, she's competing."

My stomach collapses in dismay. I do not want to believe him, but, regretfully, this makes sense. Kali loves our people, and blames herself for their recent suffering. She will compete in another tournament to protect them from a foreign queen and more hardship.

The vizier swivels around, and his guards drag me behind him to the quad. My fellow soldiers line the open area, facing a post staked in the center. Manas's glare burns into me as I pass. His acrimony is nothing new—he turned me in for treason back in Vanhi—but his lack of concern for me demolishes any remaining memories I have of our friendship.

I am led to face the post. The guards tie me to it, strapping my hands above my head. Another guard uses his machete to rip the back of my shirt open and finishes by tugging it off. Clammy air rushes over my skin.

Vizier Gyan calls to the men—*my* men. "Prince Ashwin won't tolerate traitors. Nor will Sultan Kuval provide refuge to dishonorable guards. Captain Deven Naik has confessed to treason; hence the prince has granted him mercy. He will not lose his life but will receive thirty lashes."

I rest my forehead against the pole, my insides cramping. Thirty lashes will rip me apart. I have seen men fall to pieces after ten.

The vizier approaches in my side vision with the whip. I widen my stance and bend my knees to avoid fainting. Bracing my forehead against the pole, I hold myself for the first strike. Vizier Gyan counts down.

"On my mark. Three, two, one . . ."

Pain slashes across my back. My shoulders bunch in recourse, sharpness ricocheting down my legs. *I brought this upon myself.*

Before I can recover, the snap of the whip comes again.

"Two."

Another hit, deeper and more painful than the last.

"Three."

My vision grays at the fringes. I have to anchor my mind to something or I will float away. Where is Kali?

"Four."

I cry out, an unbidden groan, and then grip my teeth together. I will not dishonor myself with another sound.

"Five."

Gods, grant me strength. I wish I could rescind my guilty plea. I wish I could scrub clean every mistake I have made.

Eight more hits, and my knees slacken. Agony pushes past my resolve to endure. My weight sinks against the pole. I cannot lift my head. More strikes, and the vizier's counting fades to a distant call for justice.

More pain. More darkness.

My knees thunk to the ground. *Forgive me, Anu. Forgive me.* I do not cry out, but my heart weeps for absolution. I am a soldier. I swore my life in service to the Tarachand throne.

The damned whip strikes again.

I am a traitor. I fell in love with the rajah's queen. I betrayed my calling, and the gods will have their wrath.

I remain on my knees, refusing to coil into a ball. I honored my duty to protect Kali. I gave my life to *her*. She is my rani. She is my ruler.

Another vicious hit. Blood seeps across my back and down my chest.

Kali *is* the Tarachand throne. And I . . . I will always be a disgraced guard. If she knows I am being punished, if she did side with the prince, I cannot fault her. Our dream was a fool's wish. From the start, she belonged to the empire, first as a temple ward and now as the kindred. She must think of the good of Tarachand above all else.

Above herself. Above me.

I curl into my knees, my strength shredding away. The vizier counts on dutifully. Each lash scores into my soul . . . until, finally, I am broken.

10

KALINDA

Ashwin and I step out of the tunnel into sticky air and the persistent night calls of creatures hunkering in the dark. Predatory plant life walls us in, gray-emerald shadows partially blocking the starry sky.

"Brother Shaan said there's a path," Ashwin remarks. He walks to the thick trees with the torchlight. My fingers hover over my dagger as we search for a trail into the Morass. He notices my hand near my weapon. "Expecting a monster to jump out?"

"Can you guarantee me one won't?"

He expels a breathy chuckle. "Here it is."

A narrow path has been scored into the jungle floor, hardly wide enough for a rabbit's trail. I draw my knife and step into the darkened trees. I pause and listen intently. Branches rustle around me, and animal noises quit or carry away, but the awareness of something watching me prickles at my scalp. I have heard clouded leopards, porcupines, and macaques call this jungle their home, none of which I would like to disturb.

Ashwin joins me, our shadows cast by the torchlight. "I'm glad I didn't make you that guarantee," he says.

"Watch your step."

I lead the way with my dagger and slash at spiny ferns. Up and down, the trail weaves through underbrush alive with zipping insects. We duck under great boughs, lunge over heaving tree roots carpeted with orchids, and come to a murky waterway. The mirrorlike surface burns the fiery reflection of our torch. My feet splash along the bank.

"Stay away from the water," Ashwin warns. "The Morass is home to crocodiles."

Another predator I would rather not run into. I follow him back into the trees without argument. Soon the trail widens, releasing us from the vine-strangled tree trunks and bristly weeds. Tiny lights sparkle in the distance. As we near the end of the path, a large grouping of white tents comes into view. Ashwin extinguishes the torch in the dirt, and we stop behind a teak tree.

Janardanian guards armed with machetes patrol outside a waist-high blockade around the camp. Within the fence, torches burn every ten paces or so, lighting the tight rows of tents. Mosquitoes congregate near the torches like clotting clouds.

Our people are everywhere. Some mill about, while others sit on the dirt ground outside their tents. Many are so thin I can see their angled cheekbones and the knots in their spines. All are in need of several good meals. They have little furniture, and what they do have is run down. The stench of refuse from overfull latrines wafts off the tented city.

My pulse echoes hollow in my ears. This is worse than the poverty in Tarachand. Tarek was not a generous ruler, but at least he did not pen them in like livestock.

"How many are here?" I ask.

"Last count was five thousand." Ashwin's guttural whisper teems with condemnation. "Sultan Kuval said he was caring for our people. But this . . . this is inexcusable."

I swallow the bitter tang of regret. Ashwin understands now why he cannot trust the well-being of his people to anyone else.

He pushes away from the tree, his movements jerky from anger. "Brother Shaan said the second encampment is north of here."

We stick to the underbrush to avoid the guards and skirt the camp. The encampment goes on and on, endless tents and people. Ashwin pauses to frown at two lookout towers stationed at the south side. The people are locked inside the camp with no defense. What threat do they pose? We move on to the end of the camp. Across from the main entrance, a dirt wall encircles a second smaller compound.

"This must be our military internment camp," Ashwin says, more weary now than outraged. "Our soldiers reside here."

"Are all of the refugees sorted into one of the camps?"

"That's the Janardanians' protocol. The sultan demands it."

A warning crawls inside me. Deven and the others may have arrived by now, or if not, they will soon. What if they were brought here instead of to me? I whisper to Ashwin, "Did you see Opal before we left? She said Brother Shaan needed her."

"I was with Brother Shaan. I didn't see her."

My gaze zips to the high walls of the military compound, my alarm expanding. Opal lied. Maybe she did not want me present when my party arrived. I draw my dagger and slip out of the underbrush.

"Kalinda!" Ashwin reaches for me, but I tug from his grasp.

I sprint across the clearing to the military encampment. A soldier on watch spots me and rings a gong. I peek through the slots in the gate to the compound but see only tents and guards within.

"Deven!" I call. "Deven!"

Janardanian guards block the gate. "Move away," one orders.

I try to look past him. "You may have detained my guards."

Across the way, people in the civilian encampment notice the disturbance and peer at me over the chest-high bamboo fence.

"Deven!"

My shouts prompt a hum of low voices . . . "The kindred."

The guards shuffle agitatedly. They recognize me now too. My revered name flies across the camp behind me and lures more onlookers. In moments, people press against the bamboo fence.

"Kalinda!" Natesa shoves her way to the front of the crowd.

Hearing her, I swivel around and start for the other camp. Janardanian guards block my way, stopping me in the clearing. I could throw them back with a heatwave, but everyone would see my powers.

"Put down your weapon," says a large guard.

I drop my dagger. He kicks it from my reach and tries to seize me. I wrench away from him. "I laid down my weapon, but I am not defenseless. I can work that curious crowd into a mob in seconds. Release my friend, or five thousand people will be upon you."

The large guard who disarmed me, a bhuta commander by his yellow armband, presses his lips into a hard slash. Cords of muscles twang at his neck. I hold my stance, unmoving in my demand. At last, he signals to the guards at the far gate, and they release Natesa.

She pushes through the armed men. "Kalinda," she says, grabbing me to her. "We told them you were expecting us, but they wouldn't let us see you."

"Where are the others?"

"All of us were too heavy for Rohan to carry, so Mathura and Brac stayed behind in Tarachand. They're coming by foot." Natesa points at the compound. "They put Yatin and Deven in there."

I face the bhuta commander. "Release my guards."

"I cannot do that, Kindred. Tarachandian guards must remain under watch."

I put on my haughtiest voice. "They're my personal guards. I'll watch over them."

Janardanian soldiers wave the people in the civilian camp away from the fence. Some obey, but most stand their ground. I threatened a riot, but I do not want any of them hurt.

"I take my orders from the vizier," says the commander. "No one is allowed in or out without authorization."

"*I'm* your authorization." Ashwin strides up to the guards' line of defense. "Commander, bring us the rest of the kindred's party."

"My apologies, Your Majesty," says the commander, bowing. "My orders come from Vizier Gyan. No one may enter either camp without his permission."

"Those are *my* soldiers," Ashwin says louder, with more backbone than I thought he possessed.

Natesa gapes at Ashwin in disbelief. "That's the prince," I whisper to her.

She shakes her head slightly to dispel her shock at his resemblance to his father. Our onlookers comprehend that their prince stands before them, and their muttering starts anew.

"I understand, Your Majesty," replies the commander, "but those men deserted their posts. They're cowards and traitors."

Ashwin steps up to him, radiating authority. "According to your reasoning, I too am a traitor. Do you believe I'm a coward, Commander?"

"Prince Ashwin," Princess Citra calls from above. She and Opal soar down on a wing flyer and land nearby.

"Who's *that*?" Natesa asks me.

"Princess Citra," I say lowly. "She's all beauty and, as far as I can tell, no heart."

The princess struts up to our group and snaps orders at her soldiers. "This spectacle will end now. Return the refugees to their tents."

The guards corral the bystanders away from the fence and back inside their temporary quarters.

"She stays with me," I say, stepping in front of Natesa.

"Refugees aren't permitted inside the palace," Princes Citra replies with icy contempt.

"Kalinda requires a servant she trusts, Your Highness." Ashwin follows up his statement with a deferential nod. "Surely you must understand."

Princess Citra offers him a mild smile. "I appreciate your consideration for the kindred's comfort, but my father's decrees are final."

"I wouldn't ask you to disobey your father." Ashwin accentuates his charming good looks with a conspiratorial smile. "This would be between us. I would consider it a personal favor."

Princess Citra sidles closer to him and skims a trimmed nail down his arm. "I suppose the kindred may retain *one* servant."

"What of my guards?" I ask.

The princess's attention slides to me. "They'll remain here."

"I'm not leaving without them." I raise my hands to employ my powers, but some of the refugees still watch from inside the camp. My people cannot know I am a Burner, or I will lose my influence to help them. As much as it pains me to leave Yatin and Deven, I do not see this quarrel ending in our favor.

I retrieve my dagger from the dirt and sheathe the blade. "We're done here."

Princess Citra loops her arm through Ashwin's. "Ride with me back to the palace?" she asks, dripping sweetness. After a swift glance at me, he agrees. She tips up her nose in victory, and they stroll to the wing flyer where Opal waits.

"Kindred, I'll have your servant escorted to the palace," the commander says.

Natesa bristles at being called my servant, but I am in no mood to pacify her. I go to the wing flyer and climb on opposite Ashwin and Princess Citra. Opal's summoned draft elevates us into the night sky. Looking down, I quickly memorize the layout of the military camp.

My throne is a noose around my neck. I must be careful that what I do next does not trip the trapdoor.

~~~~~~~~~~~~

Ashwin escorts me back to my chambers. As soon as the door shuts, I step up to him. "You aren't the naive boy you put forward, are you? I saw you with those guards. You have mettle when you want it."

He waves aside my recounting of his bravado. "I'm whatever my people need."

"Your people *need* a leader. Release Captain Naik. He's the reason I escaped Vanhi."

"I have no authority here." Ashwin holds up his empty hands. "This isn't my land. I cannot release him or anyone else until after the tournament."

"You haven't even tried," I growl.

Ashwin edges nearer to me. "I'm not blind. You care for this Captain Naik." He reads my answer in my defiant gaze, and his voice softens. "Should you win the tournament, I'll free you from your wifely rank."

"You lie." I dare not trust the prince's tempting offer.

He comes right up to me, our eye level equal. "I was bold tonight because you were there. I'm a better ruler with you beside me. But if you compete in the tournament and win, I vow you'll no longer be a rani unless that's your wish."

"You'll let me go?"

He sweeps my hair behind my shoulder, his gaze roving my face. "I'm willing to let you go, but I will fight for you, Kalinda."

I turn away, undone by his forwardness. "I need to think."

Ashwin blows out a heavy breath. "Are all women this frustrating?"

"Only those of us with minds."

He squelches his irritation and replies with politeness. "I need your answer by morning. I hope . . . I hope you will accept my offer."

I hear him draw away, his feet dragging, and I shove the heels of my hands into my eye sockets. He offered me freedom, but with a stomach-churning contingency—I must battle for my throne. Why must I continually prove my worthiness? I swore when I left the arena that I would not return. Should I break my vow for the ranis being held prisoner in the Turquoise Palace? For the thousands of people trapped in the encampments? For Deven?

I drop my hands, my arms limp beside me. Ashwin is certain I will compete. Is this the arrogance of a prince, or has he inherited Tarek's domineering will? I cringe from the thought. Ashwin's intentions aside, can my aversion to violence and my abhorrence for diplomatic necessities justify my doing nothing? The fate of the Tarachand Empire teeters on the edge of a blade. Someone must stand up to Hastin. But even after witnessing Ashwin defend me against the guards, he is not the one. Only a bhuta can defeat the warlord's Trembler powers.

Perhaps this is my godly purpose. Perhaps the gods are not finished with me yet.

Only one person can clear my confusion. I hurry to the balcony and throw open the door. Opal stands there, blocking my path.

"You shouldn't go," she says. "You'll get caught."

She must have been listening to my conversation with Ashwin. "Why didn't you tell me my people had arrived?"

"Brother Shaan asked me not to." Opal drops her gaze, her dark eyelashes resting against her reddened cheeks. "He wanted you to go with the prince tonight. He thought if you saw the state of our people, you would agree to compete."

Brother Shaan is trying to coerce me into joining the trial tournament. Was Ashwin privy to this manipulation? The beginning of a headache shortens my reply. "I won't leave my guards imprisoned. If you have any compassion for what happens to them, you'll get out of my way."

Opal opens and then closes her mouth, locked in hesitancy. Then, without a word, she steps aside and allows me to pass.

Kneeling at the banister, I find the vine from earlier. I shimmy down and land in the shadowy gardens, the sweet scent of hibiscus around me.

"Kindred," Opal calls down quietly, chewing her lower lip. "Captain Naik is being held in a hut on the south end of the military compound. Guards are patrolling the other side of the gardens right now. Take the stairs to the jungle, and hurry. Night watchmen do their rounds every fifteen minutes. If you go now, you should miss their next pass."

I nod at her, the only apology I can dig out of my anger, and dart through the hushed garden. Sneaking around the palace, I locate the stairs that lead to the base of the hill and down into the Morass. Cicadas chorus loudly, concealing my footfalls through the brushwood. The jungle night air is so thick with bugs I breathe through my nose to avoid swallowing them.

Outside the military encampment, near the wall where Deven's cell should be, I hunker down in the ferns and memorize the path of the patrolling guards.

Ready . . . and go.

I dash into the clearing, leap onto a fallen tree for height, and jump off the log to the partition. Gripping the lip of the wall, I pull myself up and slide over to the other side. I land in a crouch and survey the still tents.

Dagger in hand, I sneak up to the boxy, windowless hut. No guard stands watch. I lift the crossbar over the door, open it, and slip into the darkness. An iron grasp clamps around my neck. My dagger is wrenched from my hand and held near my eye.

"You bruise my ego, using my own weapon against me," I garble out.

Deven lowers the blade on a prayer. "Thank the gods."

"You flatter me."

He twirls me around and crushes me in a hug. "I haven't stopped praying for your safety since I saw you fly away in Tarachand."

"No one told me you'd arrived. Are you all right?"

He nods against my forehead. "You smell like home."

I smile, and he presses his lips to mine. I link my arms around his shoulders and tuck my curves against him. In the dark, he is all warm arms, hard muscles, and satin lips. My hands roam to his back and find wetness. Deven hisses and pulls away. I light up my hand with my powers.

Blood.

"You're injured." My fingers glow hot in fury, and Deven backs away in fear. My powers are blinding in the darkened cell, scarier than they should be. I promptly let the light inside me fade, leaving just enough so I can still see him. "What happened?"

"My men turned me in," he says, slumping against the wall. "Prince Ashwin ordered me whipped."

"*Ashwin* did this? But I was with him all evening."

"He commanded my sentencing."

My temper brightens my hands again. Ashwin's openness and thoughtfulness were a diversion, a manipulation to convince me to compete in the tournament. I wipe Deven's blood off on my clothes. "You aren't staying here. You're coming to the palace with me. I'll find you a healer."

"I cannot leave. My men aren't safe here. I cannot abandon them."

My expression slackens. Deven wants to stay to look after the same men who turned him in?

"I betrayed the rajah, Kali." His voice is so small it nearly shatters me. "I won't betray them too."

I cross to him and lift his chin. I do not miss his flinch when I touch him. "You opposed Tarek to protect me. Now let me protect you."

Deven unpeels my dimly shining hand from his face and frowns at the faint number one on the back. "I heard about the trial tournament. You need to compete."

My voice snags on a surprised breath. "I haven't decided yet."

"What's to decide?" Deven strokes his thumb over my rank number, his lips pinching. "You wed Rajah Tarek. Your life belongs to the empire."

He is wrong; my life belongs to me. I take a moment to regroup, and then answer. "I married Tarek to end his life. He told me you were *dead*. Stop punishing me for wedding him."

"I'm not punishing you," Deven says, infuriatingly calm. "But I cannot undo the past or change the law."

"We don't have to change the law. Ashwin promised me freedom if I win."

Deven shakes his head forlornly. "The prince would be a fool to let you go. Even if you prevail in the trial tournament, he'll need you by his side to win the war and rebuild the empire." Resignation tempers his tone, wrenching my gut. "Kali, the prince will always need you."

His assertion frays at me, scoring away at the part of me that believes we have a choice in our fates.

An alarm sounds outside the door, followed by agitated shouts. Feet thump nearby, rattling the thin walls. *They know I'm here.*

The door bangs open, and the first light of dawn falls inside. Guards charge in around us. Deven lowers to the ground and places his hands on top of his bowed head.

Prince Ashwin steps into the hut and observes Deven with open curiosity. Brother Shaan stands at the doorway.

"How did you find me?" I ask.

"One of the Galer guards heard you sneak into camp," Brother Shaan says, his voice quieter than usual. "Vizier Gyan threatened to apprehend you, but we promised we would bring you back to the palace without incident."

"Deven is coming with me," I say.

"Kali—" Deven attempts to look up, but a guard hits him over the head with the hilt of his machete. He stoops in pain.

I yank out my daggers and aim them at the guards. "Leave us." After a nod from Brother Shaan, they back out of the hut. The torn flesh of Deven's back bleeds anew. I glare at Ashwin. "You did this to him."

"I . . . *what?*" Ashwin asks.

"You ordered Captain Naik lashed."

"Where did you hear this?" asks the prince.

"Vizier Gyan said you gave the order, Your Majesty," Deven grits out, his gaze down.

Ashwin raises his square chin. He does not deny Deven's claim, but his burning resentment causes me to pause.

"Kalinda, we must go, or they'll imprison you too," says Brother Shaan, one eye on the exit. "I'll see that Captain Naik is cared for."

"Deven has done nothing worse than I have," I reply. "Release him or I'll tell everyone the truth."

Ashwin's baffled gaze volleys from me to Brother Shaan. The prince is the only one in the hut who does not know I killed Rajah Tarek.

"Your reputation mustn't be tarnished," Brother Shaan pleads. "The people need a champion. They need hope."

"They need their rani," adds Deven. He hangs his head so low his hair falls into his face. "May the gods protect you, Kindred."

I reel at his use of my imperial rank. "Don't do this, Deven. Come with me."

He offers no reply, so I sheathe my daggers and bend down to search his face for a weakening of resolve. His chin quivers, but he does not meet my gaze.

"I'm sorry," I whisper, tears stinging my eyes. "I didn't want any of this." I never wanted Tarek to claim me or to fight in his rank tournament or to be the people's champion.

But I became what Tarek wanted. I am a slave to his throne.

"I won't stop fighting for us," I promise. "Even if it means competing in the tournament. Even if it means owning my throne. I will not quit until I have the power to return for you—and then we will walk out of here together."

I lay my hand over Deven's, yearning for him to vow to fight with me—fight *for* me. His thumb brushes across my finger. *Gods, let that be a sign. Let him understand that what I do next is for us both.* I wait for a stronger signal from him, but none comes.

As I rise, I avoid looking at Ashwin for fear that I will throw a heatwave at him and roast him like a goose. "An Aquifier will heal Captain Naik," I order Brother Shaan. "Tell the healer not to leave a single scar."

"Yes, Kindred."

I search out Deven's support one last time, but his head stays lowered.

Wiping my face dry, I sweep past Ashwin out of the hut. Dawn rests upon the eastern horizon, tucking away the night. Tarachandian soldiers, groggy from sleep, amble out of their tents to view the source of the ruckus. They spot Ashwin and me surrounded by guards and murmur to one another. I wish I knew which one turned Deven in. I would scorch him to ash. Can they not see we must stand together? We have been divided by those who claim to aid us, and these camps are only the beginning.

"I am Kindred Kalinda," I call out to the men, and they hush to listen. "My throne is *mine*, and no foreigner will take it from me. I will compete in the trial tournament—and I will win. The next time you see me, it will be to release you to your families."

Shouts of praise ring out. The guards hastily usher Ashwin and me from the compound, but the hollers of the imprisoned soldiers follow us. "Kindred . . . Kindred . . ."

I loathe that title, but it is all I have left to cling to. My throne, my power, can release these people and provide me a path back to Deven.

But outside the gate, where I can no longer see his call, doubts crowd in around me. Can I win? Can I retain my throne in this strange land? The peaceful life I dreamed of is so far away. I grasp on to my beautiful wish for Deven and me and shove it down safe. I must hold on to it or my determination will tear in two.

Across the way, our people line the fence of the civilian encampment to glimpse Prince Ashwin and me. They cry my name, and a memory chills me. They chanted for me the day I won my rank tournament.

Ashwin grasps my arm to demonstrate our unity. I allow his touch to linger, but as we begin the climb to the palace, I tug away.

"Kalinda," he starts, "I didn't—"

"Don't." I will not hear his defense of Deven's punishment. The damage is done.

We reach the pinnacle of the hillside, and our people still intone my name, their emboldened cheers heard on high. I pray their shouts wake Sultan Kuval, for when he hears their voices sounding as one, he will know we are not beaten.

11

KALINDA

As Natesa finishes brushing kohl around my eyes, her knuckle grazes my nose, triggering an itch. I reach up to scratch it, and she smacks my hand away.

"You smudged the corner!" she fumes and then fixes the blemish with impatient brushstrokes.

After I slept until the early afternoon, Natesa dragged me out of bed to ready me for the declaration ceremony. I have been avoiding the mirror glass since earlier, when I stole a glimpse of my pallid reflection. Every broken shard of my heart was visible in my bloodshot eyes.

Natesa stands back to admire her work. She has been short with me since we were told servants are not allowed to attend the tournament proceedings. She does not like being left out almost as much as she dislikes people ordering her about.

"That'll do," she proclaims.

I brace myself for disappointment and look at my reflection. My makeup is flawless. My hair is brushed to a shine that could outdo a brass gong in the sun, and the plum sari is elegantly majestic. Natesa has fashioned me into a rani.

Our days of eyeing each other maliciously are over. We have come a long way since she conceded to me during our rank-tournament battle. She no longer calls me names, and I do not bait her. We are not friends, but we are friendly.

She rests a fist on her hip. "Well?"

"Thank you," I say, my tears swelling.

She pats my back awkwardly. "Don't spoil your face."

"Sorry. I'm tired." And raw, inside and out. I was daring last night, brash in my purpose, but the light of day has revealed the truth.

Deven has pushed me away.

I am a mosaic of busted pieces desperately held together. I long to burrow under my bedcovers and shut out the world, but I have to face the trial tournament and act every part the collected rani the mirror glass pretends I am.

"Would you like to tell me what happened?" Natesa asks, her voice quiet.

Her offer is kind, but I doubt I could answer without shedding more tears and spoiling her hard work. "Maybe another time."

Natesa turns away before I can see her full reaction, but her jawline tightens.

The door opens, and Opal slips inside. She stays near the exit, her gaze full of pity. She must have heard what took place in the prison hut. Opal holds up a sheer gold veil. "This is from Brother Shaan. He said you only have to wear it tonight."

So I am to play the part of the grieving widow before the sultan's court and other foreign dignitaries, am I? Brother Shaan knows wearing a symbol of devotion to Tarek disgusts me. But he is concerned about keeping what I did in Vanhi a secret. Someone could see through my lack of grief over losing Tarek and ask questions.

I go to Opal and let her hook the veil behind my ears. The gossamer cloth brushes my nose, hanging from below my eyes to my chin. "About yesterday," she begins. "I'm sorry—"

"I'm not mad at you anymore. I understand you were only following Brother Shaan's orders."

She relaxes a tad, relieved and grateful for my forgiveness. "I won't hide anything from you again, Kindred," she promises. I smile at her through my transparent veil. "Prince Ashwin is waiting for you in his chambers."

My smile falls. "I can walk to the garden myself."

"His Majesty wants to tell you what he learned about Captain Naik's punishment," Opal says with an unsaid plea. She has been sent to retrieve me and could be in trouble if I disobey. I am not afraid of defying the prince, but not if my rebelliousness will wrong Opal.

"Oh, all right." I stride out the door ahead of her. I may as well face Ashwin before the declaration ceremony. Who knows what I could do to him in public should he upset me further? But with each step down the corridor, my anger strengthens. Nothing Ashwin has to say will relieve him of his culpability.

Rohan stands guard outside the prince's chamber. He opens the door, and I careen past him inside.

Ashwin is waiting, dressed in his finest apparel, an elegant gold-embroidered scarlet tunic over fitted dark-gray trousers. He gapes at me. "Kalinda, you look . . . you look radiant."

My cheeks warm despite myself. Rajah Tarek saw me as a possession to own and control. Everything I did reflected upon his greatness. Ashwin's compliment is sheer, unselfish approval.

Across the palace grounds, a gong rings three times, jolting Ashwin out of his daze. "That's our summons," he says.

"Opal said you wanted to speak with me first."

He rakes a hand through his combed-back hair. "Yes, of course." He shoves his fidgety hands into his pockets. "I wish to explain about last night. I'm very alarmed by Captain Naik's punishment. I give you my word I had nothing to do with it. Vizier Gyan claims to have received a written order from me. I swear to you I sent no such message. Brother

Shaan did not make me aware of your party's arrival, and, as you recall, I was with you at the time of the . . . incident."

We both know he could have conspired with Brother Shaan before we left for the encampments, but I set that aside for now. "Then who hurt Deven?"

"I don't know. I asked to see the message that supposedly came from me, but Vizier Gyan had thrown it away." Ashwin's apology means little without resolution. He must realize he is failing to convince me, and he hurries onward. "Kalinda, I think someone used Captain Naik to hurt you, probably to dissuade you from competing. As I would do nothing to discourage you from the tournament, it would be counter-intuitive for me to have done this."

My shoulders sink a little. In that case, whoever hurt Deven must be involved in the trial tournament and could stand to benefit from securing my throne. Princess Citra or Sultan Kuval could have forged the prince's order. But how did they know that hurting Deven would hurt me? Worry flips my stomach over and over like a tarnished coin. Whoever used Deven to get to me could do it again.

"I had a word with Brother Shaan about holding back information," Ashwin says. "He has assured me it will not happen twice. I've also asked Opal and Rohan to listen to the happenings in the military camp to prevent another debacle. They're also investigating who the culprit could be." Ashwin maintains an even tone, but his expression darkens. "My authority will not be undermined again."

Indecision lurks over me. I tire of questioning his intentions, but his anger reminds me too closely of Tarek's.

"Do you believe me?" Ashwin asks.

I choose my reply with careful regard. "I believe it doesn't make sense for you to have done this." The first motive I can think of would be jealousy, but Ashwin did not know of my affection for Deven until after the lashing.

The prince loosens some but still holds his pocketed hands tense. "A healer is attending to Captain Naik, per your request. I wish there was another way I could make this up to you."

"As soon as the tournament ends, you can grant me my freedom."

"I'll do so gladly." Ashwin offers me his arm and a smile. "Until then, I'll enjoy your company."

I link my elbow through his, worry turning my lips downward. Ashwin said his mantle of authority weighs lighter on him when I am by his side. He claims he is acting in the best interest of our people, but when he smiles at me, he is not thinking of his empire.

He smiles at me as though I am his entire world.

⁂

Ashwin escorts me to the palace gardens, down a walkway with shorn shrubberies and across an arched bridge over a slow-moving stream. The placid water flows to the nearby cliff and transforms into a roaring waterfall. I am the stream in both its forms: calm on the exterior, raging inside.

We pass a statue of the land-goddess Ki with a dragon cobra slung over her shoulders. I have always admired her plentiful curves and fiery gaze. Ki is equal parts the tenacity of the mountains, asperity of the desert, steadiness of the grasslands, and carnal bounty of the forest. This likeness of her reminds me of the painted murals in the temples back home, except for one part.

"Why do Janardanians depict Ki with a snake?" I ask Ashwin as he walks beside me.

"If I recall my studies correctly, snakes are distant relatives to dragons. In the Janardanians' portrayal of the land-goddess, the dragon cobra represents the demon Kur. Some people believe Kur and Ki were lovers. Others have gone as far as to say their union bore a child."

I rear back to look at him. "Ki would never take a demon for a lover."

Ashwin shrugs. "Ki supposedly had a wandering eye, and Kur was said to dote on her."

"You're a romantic," I say on a laugh. "You think the myth is true?"

"It's possible. Everyone has redeemable qualities."

"Even demons?"

His smile waivers, but his answer remains resolute. "Especially demons."

Guests and palace attendees gather in the lattice-roofed terrace that has a view over the twilight sky and city. Flowering vines twist up the exterior columns and latticework overhead to the gray dome ceiling. Teardrop lantern chandeliers light the late-afternoon shadows.

Veiled women of various ages, with inarguable beauty, kneel on one side of the terrace. They must be the sultan's wives, his sultanas. Additional lovely women in slightly less gaudy finery sit behind them, the sultan's courtesans. Kuval's court is smaller than Tarek's, and his women are soft and plump from their privileged life. I do not see a single sister warrior among them. They have never set foot in an arena. Tarek reinstated rank tournaments, even though they were abolished centuries ago. He alone hungered for the arena violence, and his wives bore the scars from the ruthless duels he forced upon them for his entertainment. I would be in different circumstances had I been claimed by a man like Kuval. His sultanas and courtesans are pretty possessions to pet once in a while, not sister warriors to pit against one another in the arena.

On the opposite half of the terrace, representatives from Paljor and Lestari congregate in groups. I cannot tell which of them will be my opponents, but they all wear formfitting clothes made of thick material and carry strange, flashy weapons.

Sultan Kuval oversees the gathering from his throne on the dais. The back of his seat is fashioned from elephant tusks. I recall hearing that elephants are sacred in the sultanate. Janardanians believe elephants are the first animals the land-goddess introduced to the Morass.

Ashwin follows my gaze and speaks into my ear. "Years ago, Rajah Tarek poached an elephant herd from the jungle. When Sultan Kuval demanded them back, Tarek sent him the ivory husks of the oldest and largest elephant he stole." Ashwin gazes pointedly at the large tusks of the sultan's throne. "I've been told those are they."

Sultan Kuval beckons to Ashwin. The prince goes to occupy the empty throne to the sultan's left. Brother Shaan kneels across the aisle from the sultan's court. I would rather sit alone, but to prevent others from noticing that we are at odds, I join him. I do not meet the brother's seeking gaze. I am still fuming at him for not telling me when my party arrived. His omission cost Deven the skin on his back.

The sultan rises, and a hush falls over the terrace. "Welcome, honored guests," he says. "We're joined by representatives from Lestari and Paljor, as well as Prince Ashwin of the Tarachand Empire. The prince has asked for aid, and we have heard his call. The rebels are not his responsibility alone. Together we will unify the continent with this trial tournament. At this time, each competitor will come forward and declare their intent to vie for the Tarachand throne. First we welcome Indah, Virtue Guard from the Southern Isles of Lestari."

He swings out an arm to direct our attention to the stream. A young woman floats over the water on bare feet, a cloud of vapor around her. A short skirt is wrapped around her legs, and a twisted band covers her chest. She is tall, taller than me, and built to weather a tide, with strong sculpted legs and arms. Her bare waist is thin, her shoulders broad, and her golden-brown skin dewy. Ashwin's mouth falls open. Lestari has sent a woman who exudes natural strength and sexuality, and who is also an Aquifier.

Indah reaches land, and the ethereal mist dissipates. She pads on bare feet to the dais, carrying a trident and a large shell. Her eyes are the same golden hue as the interior of the shell and reflect the bronze sheen of her painted lips.

Indah bows and holds out the shell to Ashwin. "Your Majesty, please accept this gift from my island as a token of my devotion." He takes the shell, his hands exploring its rough ivory surface. "Hold it to your ear, and you can hear the sea."

Ashwin lifts the shell to his ear, and his eyes widen. Indah bows to him with a smile, and then descends the dais and joins the Lestarians in the audience. She moves with the grace of a wave and the might of the moon. Ashwin sets the shell in his lap, pleased and stunned by her magnificence.

Sultan Kuval announces the second competitor. "Next we welcome Tinley from the alpine cliffs of Paljor, daughter of Chief Naresh and Guardian of the North Wind."

A gale rushes through the terrace, tousling hair and skimming cheeks. A sound like a whip cracking snaps overhead, and everyone looks up. Something large flies above us, a bird with red-orange feathers and the sharp beak and talons of an evolved predator. A mahati falcon, king of the sky and natural enemy to serpents, mocks the wind with the speed of its flight.

On the back of the mahati rides a sleek young woman. Her opaque eyes and silver hair are striking against her warm sepia skin. She lands the falcon with a whoosh that disperses all sound to wind song. Only a Galer could dominate the skies with such flawless form.

Tinley dismounts and strokes the bird's feathery breast. She pulls a scorpion from a pouch around her waist and tosses it into the falcon's open beak. A long sarong covers her upper thighs, a high slit revealing long, lean legs, and her chest is banded with a single strip of dark cloth. A crossbow is strapped to her back. Her milky eyes take in the crowd, sharp as the long nails jutting from her fingers like talons. She stalks into the terrace and down the aisle before the dais.

Tinley bows and removes a feather from her pack. "Prince Ashwin, as a token of my devotion, please accept this feather plucked from my falcon, Bya, sky-friend to all mankind and guide to the heavens." Her musical voice rings like copper wind chimes.

Ashwin takes the feather and runs his fingers over the flexible blades. Tinley assumes her place among the crowd beside her people. A small current of sweet air flows around her, a sip of pureness that is intoxicating.

Dread imbeds itself in my belly. I am not competing against mere warriors. These women are bhutas and masters of their inner element. Another lesser concern nags at me. *I did not bring a gift for the prince.* I have no more time to think of this as the ground begins to tremble.

Sultan Kuval raises his voice. "It is now my pleasure to introduce my firstborn and eldest daughter, Princess Citra, Sentinel of the Morass."

Trumpets peal, startling the crowd. The ground shakes harder, rising up through my thighs. A group of elephants stomp across the gardens, decorated with headpieces of golden tassels and rich green and purple cloth. Princess Citra rides bareback on the first of the animals. She and her majestic mount stop shy of the pillars, and she emits a ground-shaking yip. Her elephant lifts its two front legs and holds the balanced stance. Princess Citra hangs on, one arm raised above her head. Another yip from her, and the elephant drops, vibrating the pillars.

The only other person surprised by Princess Citra's powers is Ashwin, who gawks along with me. The princess has not worn a yellow armband like the other bhutas in Iresh, so it did not occur to me that she is a Trembler.

Princess Citra slides off the elephant, moving gracefully in her heavy breastplate and helmet. She lifts her arms and clucks her tongue. The elephants bow before her, and the crowd hushes in reverent awe. Princess Citra clucks her tongue twice. The herd rises and plods away, their thin tails swishing.

The princess slinks up the dais to Ashwin and removes her helmet, her hair falling over her shoulders like strings of black sapphires. "I offer a token of my devotion to Prince Ashwin." Planting either hand on his armrests, she leans over him. "A kiss," she says and presses her lips to his.

Ashwin's eyes fly open. The audience titters. Sultan Kuval scowls at his daughter's audacious display. Princess Citra withdraws, and Ashwin droops in his throne, red faced. The princess licks her lips and grins. Has she any decency?

The princess struts down the steps and kneels with the sultan's women of court. A girl no more than twelve sidles up to her, and Princess Citra loops her arm around the youngster. They have similar features—they are sisters. The girl must be Tevy, the one Ashwin told me about.

Sultan Kuval clears his throat, calling the audience to attention. "And finally, we welcome Kindred Kalinda, rank-tournament champion of the Tarachand Empire."

I rise without fanfare. I have no majestic beast to ride on. No fancy armor. No grand weapon besides my mother's daggers, hidden beneath my skirt.

Sultan Kuval's lips twist smugly. He does not know that I am a bhuta, yet he pitted me against three. He has set me up to fail. How far does his scheming go?

Silence digs into my back. I stare up at Ashwin, my heart hammering. I do not know what to do. I cannot be seen as weak before my competitors, but I cannot reveal my powers without word spreading to the camps that I am a Burner.

"Kindred Kalinda, what's your offering?" Sultan Kuval presses.

"I . . ."

Reading my panic, Ashwin rises from his throne. "Kalinda needn't offer me a token of devotion. Her coming here is the only gift I require." He crosses to me and kisses my cheek. I jolt a little. This close, he is a mirror of Tarek. Ashwin frowns, understanding that he has unsettled me. But instead of moving away, he kisses my other cheek. "I'm not my father," he whispers.

I scrounge up a smile and turn to the audience. Princess Citra's face screws up in jealousy. Tinley inspects her sharp nails, unimpressed by my introduction, and Indah remains collected, unconcerned by my closeness to Ashwin. He and I return to our seats, and Sultan Kuval addresses the assembly.

"I have given great thought to this trial tournament, as to what qualifications make an outstanding rani. My pondering led me to our history. In ancient days, Anu challenged his children, Enlil and Enki, to prove their godliness in a number of trials. Our competitors will face a series of similar tests. But before they begin, each one must complete an exhibition of ability. Skill demonstrations are customary before any tournament. They provide each contender the opportunity to boast her weaponry expertise and intimidate her opponents."

For my last skill demonstration, I broke glass orbs with my slingshot. But I suspect the sultan will require something more strenuous of my bhuta opponents and, subsequently, me.

"Tomorrow at sunset," says the sultan, "competitors will meet at the mouth of the Morass. There they will receive further instructions." With that ominous declaration, he adds, "Let us feast!"

12

DEVEN

I lie on my stomach, all strength bled out of me. To blink is to harness the power of a thousand men. To swallow is to employ the gods. The Aquifier pours more healing waters over my back. The warm liquid releases a cascade of fresh smells, from sun-warmed muslin to coconut to white sandalwood. My skin tautens painfully and then tingles with welcome coolness.

A member of the brethren has not come to offer a healing blessing on my behalf, as is customary in Tarachand, but I did not expect it. During my time training with the brethren, I learned Janardanians do not worship the Parijana faith as we do but a varied sect that places the land-goddess above her husband, the sky-god. Janardanians believe returning to the ground to feed the land, Ki's domain, is an honor. They accept that they will die when the land-goddess chooses, and they do not interfere with her will through prayer.

The Aquifier trickles more of his fresh-scented water over my back. Foggy dreaminess drifts over me with the lifting pain, my mind flowing from one abstract thought to the next. An image of a fox arises from the darkness.

"I'm finished for now." The Aquifier's voice sharpens my focus. With great effort, I turn my head to see him gathering his empty jug and bandages. "I'll leave your back unwrapped. The air is good for your wounds."

I thank him, and he leaves, shutting me in the dark.

Closing my eyes, I relish the release from pain. I intend to sleep, but Kali's grave stare blooms in my stream of thought. The rest of her materializes next, her willowy frame, thick dark hair, and delicate face. I reach for her, and the second my fingertips touch her cheek, her expression changes to hurt. She backs away and runs into the shadows.

I set out after her, calling her name, and my surroundings transform into snowy woods. I run through the dark forest, and a snap sounds behind me. I round a tree and stumble to a halt. A fox lies dead at my feet, scarlet staining the snow around it, a snare wound around its leg.

The door to my cell creaks open, bringing me back to the present, and a hulking figure comes in. I drum up an ounce of strength to clench my fist in defense.

"Hello, Captain," Yatin says. I uncurl my hand, and my friend pulls up the healer's stool. "I cannot stay long. The guards check the prisoners' tents twice an hour. The Galer guards may start listening to us, if they aren't already." Yatin lays his wide palm on the top of my head. "I am sorry I didn't stop them."

"My punishment was just. You did nothing wrong."

"Neither did you," he asserts.

"That's a matter of perspective."

Yatin leans forward and clasps his hands. Shadows play with my sight, revealing sections of his solemn face. Yatin is the youngest of six children. His older siblings are all sisters, and his mother a widow. Like me, when he joined the imperial army, he was more accustomed to women than men. I was brought up at the Turquoise Palace, surrounded by nursemaids, courtesans, and ranis, an experience my mother insists made me the peacemaker I am. Yatin is even more of a peacemaker.

I admire his long-suffering temperament and belief that every soul is fundamentally good. He speaks carefully, with deliberate thoughtfulness. "The vizier announced the trial tournament to the men . . . I don't understand. Why is the kindred competing?" His words carry another question. *Don't you love each other?*

I lick my parched lips. They feel dry, like tree bark. "Do you remember when we were camped in the lower Alpana Mountains, traveling with Rajah Tarek to the Samiya Temple?"

"That was before Rajah Tarek claimed Kalinda," Yatin recalls.

"I was on watch one night. It was snowing and especially still, the snowflakes muffling the noises of the forest. In the distance, beyond the quiet, I heard scratching noises. The rest of the men were asleep, so I took a lantern into the woods and came upon a trapped fox. A hunter had set a snare, and the fox had the misfortune of finding it. When the fox saw me, it growled and tried to wrench free. In its struggle, the snare wrapped tighter around its hind leg, and blood soon flecked the snow."

I wet my dry lips again. My body is dragging me over a cliff of exhaustion, but I hang on to consciousness. I need Yatin to understand. "The fox was unharmed other than the snare strangling its leg. I knew if the animal worked itself free, it would survive, but it would not calm down and outsmart the snare so long as I was near. So I walked back to camp, and soon its growls and yips ceased.

"The next morning, I rose before dawn and returned to the trap. As I got closer, I heard no sound of struggles. With some dread, I thought the fox had died trying to twist free. But when I reached the trap, the fox was gone, and the snare had been chewed apart. Tracks led into the woods. The fox had wriggled and gnawed its way to freedom. When I returned to camp, Rajah Tarek asked me where I'd been, and I told him about the fox. He said I should have harvested its pelt. He saw the trapped fox as something to take advantage of." I shake off the memory of Rajah Tarek and go on. "Last night with Kali, I remembered that fox.

She asked me to go with her, and I was tempted. But that snare . . . It would have still been around her leg."

Yatin processes my meaning. "You think Kalinda can break free from her throne?"

"I think she has a better chance if I leave her be. The closer I am to Kali, the harder she resists the snare that has her." For two moons I have tried to find a way to release her from her throne, but her fate belongs to the gods. "I cannot save her, nor should I try."

"Even if it means walking away." He is silent a long moment. I begin to drift off, but his low voice tugs me back. "Will the prince exercise his first rights to Kalinda?"

"He will try." I despise Prince Ashwin for dangling Kali's freedom before her for his gain. He is like Rajah Tarek was with the snared fox, extorting control over another's pain and misfortune. "But she will find a way to break free."

"What if she doesn't?" Yatin asks.

Exhaustion pulls me toward sleep, but I rasp out one more answer. "Then I have failed her."

13

KALINDA

A host of servants rearranges the terrace into an outdoor banquet hall with low tables and candlelight. The sultan dines among his wives and courtesans, away from the rest of the attendees. Eunuchs stand guard around them, scrutinizing any patron who comes too close.

Prince Ashwin is seated at a table on the dais, and my competitors and I are invited to feast beside him. He saves the floor rug to his right for me, leaving the left one open. Princess Citra plunks down on it before Indah and Tinley have a chance.

While servants set dishes of food before us, down the short steps a toddler seated with the sultan's court screams and throws food at his nursemaid.

"Who is that?" I whisper to Ashwin.

"The heir to the sultanate. Kuval has a lot of daughters, but that is his first son."

Princess Citra must be fifteen years older than the young prince, yet her baby brother is to inherit the throne. Such dynamics seem unfair given the princess's loyalty to her homeland. The nursemaid picks up the screaming boy and paces with him out in the garden.

Citra scoots closer to Ashwin's side, drawing his attention. "What did you think of my token, Ashwin?"

"Ah . . . it was unexpected."

"Was it?" she purrs. Indah laughs at her from across the table. Citra scowls. "What?"

"You're exactly as your reputation portrays." Indah's gaze slides across the table. "All of you are."

"Oh?" Tinley sits forward, her light hair gleaming under the chandelier lantern. "What have you heard?"

"I'll start with you, daughter of Chief Naresh," Indah replies. "You cut your teeth on mahati bones and learned to fly when you were only four. At age eight you hatched Bya and have since spent most of your time on your falcon in the sky. Your proficiency is with the crossbow, you enjoy anything that has to do with heights, and you tug at your tresses when you're uneasy." Tinley swiftly unthreads her fingers from her silvery hair. "Ever since your father's second in command cornered you in the tanning hut, you distrust men. If you lose the tournament, you'll negotiate for better trade for your people. However, if you win, you do not intend to live with the prince. You'll settle in a mountain outpost and spend the rest of your days patrolling the empire's borderlands from the sky."

Ashwin stops chewing. "You wouldn't stay with me in the palace?"

Tinley shoots Indah a poisonous glare. "I haven't decided yet, Your Majesty."

I pick at my food with my fingers. The spicy sauces and dishes smell delicious, of turmeric and coriander, but I am too nervous dining with these women to put anything in my belly.

Indah swivels her focus to Citra, her next victim. "You have never left Iresh. You didn't even set foot outside the palace gates until you were fourteen. Your father is afraid you'll be killed like your mother was." I sit up straighter, and Ashwin stills, the flatbread in his hand forgotten. Citra's eyes and jaw harden. "You have one full younger sister,

Tevy, who shares your same mother, and you would do anything for her happiness. Your first love was with a palace servant when you were thirteen. Your father found out, castrated the boy, and sold him to another household. Since then, you invite public male attention often to punish your father."

Tinley snorts, amused now that the focus is off her. I spread my fingers out in a fan against my breastbone. How does Indah know all of this? From the other women's reactions, everything she says is accurate.

"You don't know anything about me," Citra seethes.

Indah leans back, unperturbed. "As for your reasons for participating in the tournament, you will do anything to avoid being given in marriage to an old, fat man. You even tried to run away once, but you were caught and the sultan's kindred beat you before his court."

Citra's face flushes. "Enough."

I would console her if she would allow it. Citra's relationship with her father is none of our concern.

"And what of Kalinda?" Ashwin asks, engrossed in Indah's game.

"I know the least about the kindred," Indah replies, switching her attention to me. I block the urge to cover my face. "You're an orphan raised in a Sisterhood temple of the Parijana faith. Your people believe you're Enlil's hundredth rani reincarnated, though you won your rank tournament on account of your opponents conceding. You have no particular weaponry skill, as your strongest offense is your faith in the gods."

"Why does she wish to win?" Tinley asks. Clearly this supper game has become a means for her to study her opponents.

"Glory," answers Indah. "The kindred wishes to uphold her reputation as a fierce sister warrior."

Glory? I tamp down a guffaw and wait for Indah to reveal more about me. Something in regard to Deven. Or Hastin. Or Tarek. She sits back, finished, but my nerves stay locked on high alert. Indah knows more about me than a stranger should, and I sense she is holding back.

Tinley stabs a hunk of boar meat with one of her talonlike finger-nails and shoves it into her mouth. "Kalinda, were you really claimed from a Sisterhood temple?" she asks, staring at me with her cloudy irises.

"Yes."

"You *killed* to wed the rajah?" Tinley's tone drips with disapproval.

Ashwin pushes food around his plate. Although he understands why I defeated his mother, it would be callous to speak of her death in his company. "I didn't want to," I answer.

"I would never kill for a man," Tinley says, shoving more meat into her mouth.

I tip my chin up, lifting my chest. "We didn't fight for a man; we fought for a better life."

"Their reason isn't so unlike your own for entering the trial tourna-ment, is it, Tinley?" Citra asks, tapping her painted nails against her wine chalice. "We all want the life that goes with the throne."

Tinley glares at Citra as she picks up a piece of flatbread and tears it into bite-size pieces.

"Don't they have Claimings in Paljor?" Indah asks, her voice inex-plicably chipper.

Tinley answers Indah, ending her stare off with Citra. "We have temples of the Parijana faith as Tarachand does, but only for the breth-ren. The women don't preside in the faith. As for the Claimings, we have none. We're betrothed from infancy." Tinley smacks her lips, gaining a look of disgust from Citra, and adds, "My intended died last year, but you already knew that."

"I thought it would be impolite to share," replies Indah.

Tinley huffs, for Indah's other descriptions have already surpassed rudeness.

"What about you, Indah?" Ashwin asks.

"She isn't going to say anything insulting about herself," Citra replies, her glower unyielding.

Indah raises her hands, palms out. "I'm a Virtue Guard for Datu Bulan, come from Lestari." The datu is the ruler of the Southern Isles. His stronghold, the city of Lestari, is located on the largest island. "My mother birthed me in healing waters and raised me on milk and honey. I learned to walk on our island's sandy beaches and spent my childhood fishing on the southern seas. My weapon of choice is the trident, which works to spear big fish and irritating supper patrons."

Citra utters a stale laugh.

Tinley sets her chalice down hard, nearly spilling her wine. "Indah, you *didn't* say anything bad about yourself."

"She didn't have to," I say. "Indah is arrogant, offensively honest, and too observant for her own good."

Indah laughs, a light tinkle like clinking shells. "Kindred, you sound like my father."

"He must be a wise man," inserts Ashwin.

Citra lowers her pointed glare, remembering we are in the presence of the prince. "Let me serve you some more, Your Majesty." She ladles him another helping of sauce, even though his plate is already swimming in it.

Indah observes the celebrators across the terrace, fishing for more secrets. I nibble at my food, my thoughts hooked on what she said about being a Virtue Guard.

"Are any other Virtue Guards in Lestari?" I ask her.

"Yes, we're the last sovereign to work with bhutas. Datu Bulan has one of each serving on his high council."

"Even a Burner?" I ask.

Indah tilts her head, cataloging my curiosity. "The datu retains all four to maintain balance. We work in conjunction with him and his advisers. Our Burner Virtue Guard is one of the most powerful Burners in the world. Though there could be others we don't know about . . ."

I arrange my features into disinterest, my pulse charging. *Oh, yes. Indah knows more than she pretends.*

Citra tries to spoon-feed Ashwin, but the food falls down his chin and into his lap. When she moves to clean it, he waves her away.

"Burners aren't welcome in Paljor," Tinley says, chewing with her mouth open again.

Indah sips her wine. "Our people don't live in fear of Burners."

"You live on *islands*, surrounded by *water*," replies Tinley.

"We also aren't afraid of a few burns." Indah slides a glance at me.

I drop my hands below the table. Did she see the healing boil on my palm? She must sense I am hiding something. I would like nothing more than to shoot fire over their heads and boast about my powers as they did, but I cannot let my people find out who I am.

Musicians set up drums and two-string chordophones on the walkway over the stream. The drummers strike a low beat, and the sultan's courtesans rise to dance in the garden. Citra tugs on Ashwin's hand. He tries to anchor himself to me, but I have no interest in battling the princess for a dance with him.

After they go, Indah bends across the table toward me. "I'd like to speak with you alone, Kindred."

I would rather return to my chamber for the night, but I am interested to hear what she has to say. Tinley is so fixated on her food she does not care that we leave her at the table alone. Indah and I move away from the music and cross the garden to a banister near the cliff. A dark figure follows us, a tall man with a sleeveless tunic and short baggy pants. His hair is long at the back and shaved on the top of his head and around his ears. A blowgun hangs at his waist, the short bamboo pole sticking out of his leather belt.

Indah catches me staring at him. "That's Pons, my personal guard."

Pons stops behind us, his stance protective, attentive. Longing for Deven draws my gaze over the cliff to the dim lights of the encampments. *Great Anu, please heal him.*

"Your assessment at supper was entertaining," I say to divert my thoughts from Deven. "How did Citra's mother die?"

"She and Vizier Gyan were near the Tarachand border when Rajah Tarek launched his eradication of bhutas. A battle ensued, and she was caught between the imperial soldiers and the rebels." Indah faces the terrace, studying the sultan and his wives. "The sultan hoards his wives and courtesans like gems to stow away in a treasury. In my nation, women and men are free to choose their own fate. Who we wed isn't tied to our godly devotion."

Lestari is a republic nation. Why would Indah give up her freedom to wed Ashwin? "You didn't say what you stand to gain from the trial tournament."

"Neither did you." Her gold eyes take me in. They are nearly the same color as Brac's, only paler. "I think my initial assessment of you was off. You're content to stay in the shadows, aren't you?"

I answer with a guarded smile. Indah will have to find out about my past with Tarek and Deven from someone else. I will not be supplying her secrets.

"Datu Bulan was impressed with your success in the rank tournament," Indah notes. "He was not invited to attend your wedding, but we heard word of it. We were shocked to learn of Tarek's death. He has lorded over the continent for years. Now that he's dead, many wonder what's become of the Zhaleh."

Alarm spikes through me, but I manage not to react. "I have no idea."

"Datu Bulan feared the fall of Vanhi meant Hastin seized the Zhaleh as well, but our informants reported that the warlord has been hunting for it . . . and you."

"I cannot imagine why."

Indah folds her arms loosely across her chest. "I can tell you're lying. Your heartbeat sped up. I can feel the blood pumping faster through your veins."

Indah senses the water in my blood moving through my body. Remarkable and terrifying. Since she can detect my lie, I opt to say nothing.

"The Zhaleh belongs in Lestari, protected by our Virtue Guards," she presses. "We want to help Prince Ashwin, but Datu Bulan won't provide aid to the empire unless the Zhaleh is safe with us."

My pulse hums faster despite her monitoring it. "Then you've wasted your time coming here."

I start to walk away, and Indah calls after me. "You cannot protect the book alone, Kalinda. Only Virtue Guards can guarantee its security."

I pass Pons in the shadows and speed up. I hasten out of the garden, past the celebrating guests, and into the palace. Partway down the corridor, I pull off my veil and then turn into my chamber. Natesa's antechamber door is closed; she must have turned in for the night. I haul out my sketchbook. The Zhaleh is still hidden inside, but for how long? Indah cannot be alone in her search. Everyone knows Tarek had the book, and now that he is dead—

My chamber door flings open, and Ashwin marches in. "Are you all right? I saw you leave the feast in a hurry."

I lay the book in my lap and conceal it with my hands. "I'm fine. Indah said something that worried me."

"Was it about the Zhaleh?" His directness blindsides me. Ashwin sits beside me on the bed. "Brother Shaan told me you brought it from home. Do you have it?"

Brother Shaan trusts the prince enough to tell him about the book, so I might as well show him. I remove the Zhaleh from the sketchbook facade and set it in his lap.

Ashwin rests a tentative hand over the weathered cover. "It's real." He opens the book and peruses the pages. "I appreciate all books and texts, but this . . . The Zhaleh has existed since Anu bestowed godly powers on the First Bhutas." He reaches the back of the book, farther than I sought. The final page has symbols all over it, runes.

"Can you read them?"

"A few." Ashwin runs his fingers over the marks. "This means 'evernight,' this means 'smoke,' and this here means 'awaken' or 'rekindle.'"

My skin bristles in alarm. "This is the incantation to release the Voider."

Ashwin pulls his finger away from the page, as if touching it alone will transfer evil onto him. "I dare not read more, for once the incantation is started, it must be completed. I don't know if this belief is true, but I've heard the invoker will go mad with desire to finish the spell."

"The incantation is a curse?"

"From what I can glean, it is sort of a prayer, but not to the gods."

"Then to who?" I question.

"Not who, *what*. When the day was made, so was the night. When man was made, so was his shadow. The Void dwells in darkness, and life dwells in light. The Voider cannot cross over to where light reigns *unless* he's invited. But once welcomed, everything the gods created would be consumed by evernight."

My nerves tingle from heightened awareness. The shadows between the lanterns grow sinister fangs.

Ashwin goes on in a hushed tone. "It's said that the Voider can call to those in the light, tempting them with the promise of a favor. From what I have read, it isn't a favor as we know it. Whatever the person who releases the Voider desires most is the bargain the demon must fulfill. Even knowing the dangers, having your heart's wish granted is an enticement many cannot resist."

My heart's wish is to start a life with Deven independent of the rajah's reign, but I would not unleash a demon to attain it. "A heart's wish won't mean much when the world is ending."

Ashwin closes the Zhaleh and offers it to me. "Desperate people can be deceived. A mirage tricks them into believing cool waters await them, but when they bring a drink to their lips, they draw in sand."

I hold the Zhaleh, a plan to hide it forming in my mind. I will need a contingency arrangement should something happen to me during the trial tournament. I offer Ashwin the oil vessel. "The Zhaleh and vessel are both needed to release the Voider, so we'll hide them apart. You take the vessel, and I'll take the book."

Ashwin studies the small container with a troubled frown. "How many bhutas died to fill this?"

"Tarek needed a thousand drops of blood, one each from a thousand bhutas."

Ashwin's fist slowly curls around the vessel, and he slips it into his pocket. "I should return to the feast."

"Citra is probably wondering where her dance partner went," I tease.

He grimaces. "Are all kisses so . . . wet?"

"No." I laugh and then my heart pangs, thinking of Deven, my first kiss.

Ashwin's demeanor sobers. "I'd like to know what you're thinking."

"No, you wouldn't." I shift away from him, and the corners of his mouth turn downward.

Ashwin rises to leave, pausing at the door. "Kalinda? Don't tell me where you hide the Zhaleh. I may not be strong enough to resist the call of the Voider. I'm still of Tarek's blood."

"Brother Shaan wouldn't have told you about the book if he was worried." I push a reassuring smile at him. "You shouldn't be afraid of becoming your father."

Ashwin's gaze pulls inward. "Unfortunately, I should."

I tiptoe into Natesa's darkened antechamber and stop beside her bed. Her sleeping face looks peaceful without her typically cross expression and sarcastic smirk. When I knew her at the temple, Natesa dreamed of marrying a rich benefactor. She was livid when Tarek picked her as his courtesan. Does she have nightmares about the Turquoise Palace? Do visions of Tarek disturb *her* sleep?

I have not thought to tell her of my own nightmares. I trust Natesa—she would not be here otherwise—but I have only ever confided my deepest fears in Jaya.

I shake Natesa's shoulder gently. When she does not stir, I jostle her harder.

She groans. "You better be on fire." Lamplight streams through the open door, falling across her groggy face. "It's the middle of the night. I need at least eight hours of sleep, or I'll have puffy eyes tomorrow."

"I'm sorry for waking you, but I need your help."

Natesa pushes herself up to sitting, her dark hair wavy around her. "Do you really need me *right now*?"

"Yes." I lower my voice even more. "I need your help hiding the Zhaleh."

***

I pace the width of my bedchamber the following afternoon. The colorful inks and charcoals beside the untouched parchment taunt me from the corner of my eye. I pause to finger the tops of the ink jars. Red, yellow, blue . . . I could try them. Just one drawing . . .

I yank my hand back and pace again.

"Would you sit down?" Natesa asks, brushing polish over her nails. After a yawn, she adds, "You're making me anxious."

I *am* anxious. No one knows what I can expect for skill demonstrations this evening. Not even Opal and Rohan have heard anything. The sultan is not revealing any more about the trial-tournament proceedings. All I know is that I am to meet my competitors at the mouth of the Morass at sunset.

Across the room hangs a tapestry of the jungle. Within the verdure are an elephant, a tiger, and a dragon cobra curled near a rock, as well as crocodiles sunning on the riverbank. The dangerous creatures are symbols of Ki's majesty and power, a harrowing reminder that this is her land and I am a mere visitor. I draw my daggers and aim at the tapestry. I release the first dagger. The pointed end cuts through the cloth, impaling the wall. A fair hit. I grip my second dagger and toss it next. The blade lands below the first.

"Would you fetch me a drink of water, please?" Natesa asks, lying stretched out on my bed.

"You're my servant, not the other way around."

"I seem to remember you waking me in the middle of the night. I have puffy eyes to prove it."

"You promised not to speak of it," I remind her. Last night, after an hour of debating the best place to hide the Zhaleh, we hid the book under loose floor tiles in her antechamber. Should someone come sneaking around for it, we agreed they would search my room. Natesa is nearly always in our chambers, so she will guard the book.

She flashes her hands at me and fakes a pout. "I have wet nails."

"Fine. Give me a moment to finish." As I retrieve my blades, Tarek's figure appears in the dimness out of the corner of my eye.

I've missed you, love. He reaches for my hair, his eyes smoldering with need.

Pain lashes up my arm from the rank marks on my hands. I rip a blade from the wall and throw it at him. The dagger turns end over end through Tarek, and he vanishes. My dagger hits a potted tree in the corner, rustling leaves, and falls to the floor.

"Kalinda?" Natesa joins my side, staring at the accosted tree. "Did I miss something?"

I hold still, waiting for my pulse to calm. "I thought I saw a . . . a lizard."

"Hmm. That's enough practice for now." Natesa wraps her arm around me and directs me to my bed.

I lie down, numb with confusion. Tarek has never visited my mind in the daytime. Could there be legitimacy to my nightmares? Do the gods consider our marriage binding?

My memory replays the image of Tarek in the shadows. Only now that I think about it, he looked different. His eyes blazed like coals disintegrating into the night, and when he reached for me . . . the backs of my hands burned.

The sun sinks into the treetops. Standing with my competitors at the Morass, I try to dismiss the notion that every creeping creature lurking in the trees is waiting to draw me into the jungle's gullet.

A small crowd of onlookers gather to hear what our skill of demonstration will be. Princess Citra holds herself with confidence, at ease in this wild land of her heritage. Indah and Tinley peer anxiously into the foliage. I seek out Ashwin. He is the only attendee who cares what happens to me. Although he is preoccupied with the sultan, my nerves are steadier with him near.

The sultan addresses us from the front of the crowd. "Welcome to skill demonstrations. The purpose of this preliminary contest is to provide competitors the opportunity to display their abilities to all of the foreign dignitaries and courts. At the sound of the gong, competitors will go into the jungle and search out the most deadly thing the Morass has to offer. Dangerous animals, plants, and insects dwell here. Each competitor must find and capture one lethal living thing from the jungle. This demonstration will test their weaponry skill, tracking and hunting ability, and orienteering."

The Morass is not somewhere I wish to spend the day, let alone the night. I try to avoid things that want to kill me.

"One more rule." Sultan Kuval's mustache twitches with delight. "Competitors must return to the palace throne room by dawn with their deadly offering or be disqualified."

The old buzzard is changing the rules. By tradition, skill demonstrations are regulated, to the point of allotting the same amount of time to each competitor for her performance. Adding the possibility of elimination is unheard of. But protesting the alteration is pointless. The sultan and my competitors will think I am a bellyacher if I complain. Moreover, this does not change my plan. I will still be in and out of the jungle as fast as I can.

Sultan Kuval directs the servant manning the gong. "Ready your mark."

Indah bends into her knees, preparing to run. Citra draws her machete and sends me an arrogant grin. Her father handpicked this skill demonstration to suit her. Tinley straightens the strap of her quiver, filled with bolts for her crossbow.

The gong sounds, vibrating across the open space. My competitors tear off in separate directions. I draw my daggers and sprint into the dense trees.

Beneath the leafy canopy, grayness coats everything, thick as the steaming air. I dart through the cloying mists, water rattling in my lungs. Soon, I can no longer hear the sounds of civilization, and I pause to catch my breath.

Strange noises echo all around me. Above me, a macaque peers down from a low bough. Its persistent stare itches at my nerves. Monkeys can bite when provoked, but they are not considered dangerous. I am here for the most lethal predator I can find. The king of the Morass.

I walk away from the macaque and trudge into a swamp, wading up to my knees. Fireflies zip past me, brightening flecks of light. The shielded sky dims to pervasive dark. My thighs burn as I wrench my feet from the muddy waters. I would fashion a torch of some kind, but everything is soaked and green, unfit for burning.

When I finally leave the bog, something wiggles against my leg. I bend down and brush against a slimy, fat body. "*Agh!*" Hopping up and down, I pluck the leeches off my ankles. Blood spills from my skin where they fed from me. Leeches are deadly in large numbers, but I can do better. I toss the bloated pests aside and move on.

Not too far ahead, the trees open to a quiet clearing, and I come to a halt. Moonlight shines down on old stone pilings. I follow a dilapidated, crumbling wall to the structure's darkened main entrance set between two pillars. The ancient ruins extend underground and into the hillside. These must be the remains of an archaic temple, abandoned long ago. Predators could be holed up inside, but I step away, my footsteps cautious. I will not trespass on sacred ground.

Something behind me snaps. I pull my dagger and whirl around. Before I see anything, the ground beneath me buckles and lifts me backward.

Citra's shadow splits from a copse of ferns. She raises the ground beneath me again, and the avalanche shoves me toward the temple entrance. I stumble on the sliding dirt dragging me into the ruins. I grab the lip of the door and hang on. Citra sends forth an incessant stream of rocks, pelting my arms and face.

"You've found the most deadly thing in the jungle," she says.

"Your father didn't mean our opponents."

"My father underestimates me. He thinks I'm unfit to rule, but I'll show him how worthy I am after I take your throne."

She pummels me with more dirt, pushing me farther inside. My grip on the doorjamb lessens, my beaten knuckles aching.

"This was Ki's sanctuary," Citra yells over the barrage. "Under these ruins lies a labyrinth of tunnels. Even if you find a way out, you will not return to the palace by dawn. Do me a favor—don't return at all."

She throws a storm of rubble at me. I grip the doorway, soil seeping into my nose and stinging my eyes. Larger rocks hit my wrists and arms. One of my hands slips. Holding on with my final grip, I reach for my powers, but a landslide sweeps me into the ruins.

Citra seals the door, and I am locked in the dark.

14

Deven

I part my eyelids at the creak of the cell door. The Aquifier healer comes in carrying a lamp. He is followed by a man with a haunting face. I blink fast, questioning my sight. Rajah Tarek . . . except he looks as he did when he was younger.

While growing up in the Turquoise Palace, I would sneak glances at His Majesty from behind my nursemaid's skirts. His domineering presence and lust for cruelty petrified me. Rajah Tarek controlled my mother's life and sought to destroy all bhutas, including my brother, who was forced to hide his powers. When I finally stood against Tarek, my years of loyal service as his soldier meant nothing.

"Captain Naik, I've come to view your progress."

The stranger's voice is higher and smoother than Tarek's. *Prince Ashwin.* I did not get a fair look at him when he came for Kali the other night, but his voice matches my memory.

The Aquifier moves behind me and runs his hands down my back, over my still-healing wounds. I hiss at a brief flare of pain, my skin stretched thin. The prince frowns—a show of compassion or culpability?—and occupies the stool beside my cot. *Great skies, he looks like his father.*

"Well?" the prince asks the healer.

"Captain Naik has recovered remarkably fast, but he still has scars."

"Continue your sessions until they're gone," says the prince, "including the one on his shoulder."

The one on my shoulder is where I was struck by an arrow while escaping execution. An arrow Rajah Tarek ordered his guards to fire.

"It's an older wound, but I'll do my best, Your Majesty."

I wait for the Aquifier to leave and then speak to the prince. "I don't mind scars."

"I cannot decide if you deserve them or not. Did you betray Rajah Tarek?"

"I already confessed to the vizier."

"I want to hear from *you*," he says.

This boy has placed himself between Kali and me like a stone wall. His concern about my injuries—wounds *he* caused—means less than nothing. I remove all emotion from my voice and report my answer. "Rajah Tarek caught me trying to steal the Zhaleh and presumed I was working for Hastin."

"You weren't?"

"No." I planned to exchange the Zhaleh for the warlord's help in getting Kali and me out of Vanhi, but the prince does not need to know that.

"Kalinda credits you for escaping Vanhi. I'm grateful for your loyalty to her."

I slam my teeth together. The scars on my back were not caused by his civility. "I didn't do it for you."

"Even so, I am in your debt. I hope someday soon Kalinda will become my kindred. I thought it fair to let my intentions be known."

At the finish of his words, the wall between Kali and me grows taller and thicker. "Are you in love with her?" I scrape out.

"Are you?"

I boost my chin, unwilling to answer. "Why are you here?"

He sits nearer to me. A gold cuff on his wrist reflects the brassy lamplight. "I don't want hard feelings between us. I need your support and leadership with my soldiers."

"*Your* soldiers don't recognize you as their rajah, and they believe I'm a traitor. They won't trust me again."

"They may trust you after I exonerate you." His certainty rivals mine—a blood-borne arrogance stemming from generations of rajahs.

"Why do you need me?" I ask, holding to my defiance. "You have a yard full of soldiers out there."

"Kalinda trusts you." Prince Ashwin studies me, trying to understand what Kali could possibly see in a battered soldier. "Sultan Kuval has overextended his authority. I have tried to dismantle these encampments, but Kuval knows he maintains control so long as he detains my people and soldiers. He says he will provide aid once the trial tournament is through, regardless of the outcome, but the quickest way for him to cow me is to extort his hospitality."

"You don't think he'll honor his word?"

"I won't know until the trial tournament is through. By then it will be too late. No matter the outcome, my men must be ready to march on Vanhi. As it stands, I have an army but no commander. You have three days to ready them."

I bark a hollow laugh. Three days to redeem myself? I have no command over these men. "Even if I could regain the men's trust, *I* don't trust *you*."

"I don't need you to trust me. I need you to obey." His hard voice shrinks my scowl. I was a soldier too long to defy my ruler without suffering regret. "My coming here to visit you wasn't simple. Opal and Rohan are diverting all sound and standing watch, and I had to bribe the healer not to tell anyone I came. I won't have the opportunity to visit you again. I need you to rally the men. Prepare them for every possible outcome, and I will promote you to general."

I exhale a tight breath, aghast at the ease with which he negotiates. This is what the prince does. He bribes people with promises he does not intend to honor. How much control can he truly have when he is surviving off the generosity of the sultan? "You cannot remove Hastin from the Turquoise Palace without help from a bhuta army."

"I am aware."

His neutral tone riles me more. "Then what are you going to do about it? You want *me* to earn the allegiance of your men. Don't you think that at some point *you* should earn their respect on your own merits, without Kali or me?"

Princes Ashwin chuckles. "I admire your straightforwardness, Captain Naik. I know you don't like me yet, so do this for Kalinda. We both know she's the true face of the change coming to Tarachand."

The prince professes to have good intentions for Kali, but I cannot muster the trust needed to fall in line behind him. He has the power to save the empire—or be the ruin of us all. Kali is directly tied to his actions. If Prince Ashwin falls, she will go down with him. Like Rajah Tarek, a noble's rule ends in death. Kali is tied not merely to her throne but to this boy prince who could get her killed, either in the tournament or from his inexperience as a ruler.

My voice toughens. "Exonerate me, and I'll do what I can."

"Thank you," Prince Ashwin replies. "Naturally, this cannot go beyond us. Please don't tell your men about your orders."

Winning over the loyalty of the men in three days will be beyond difficult—it will be nearly impossible, especially without telling them I am acting under the prince's orders. But I cannot risk someone snitching on me to the vizier. "You have my word."

"Again, I thank you." The prince stands and tugs down his tunic, a disquieting movement I saw Rajah Tarek perform countless times.

My angry voice strikes out at him. "You can keep your thanks and tell me this—did you order me lashed?"

Prince Ashwin pushes back with a stern frown. "Does it matter if I did?"

"It matters to Kali."

Redness crawls up his throat. My actions are insubordinate. Skies, I could be lashed again for my belligerence. But to my amazement, the prince's expression tempers with sympathy. "I'm sorry for what happened to you. It was not done on my command."

His regret humbles me to a place of reflection. *Good Anu, I think I believe him.* "Then who gave the order?"

"I don't know." His face sharpens with aggression. "But I promise when I discover who it was, they will pay."

The prince slips out, and the glowing lantern he left does little to cast away the shadows of my uncertainty.

15

KALINDA

Darkness smothers me. The air is thinner and enclosed inside the ruins. I lie on my back and stare into nothing. I cannot see my hand in front of my face.

My hand.

I push my powers into my fingers. They cast a pale glow, uncovering walls strangled by vines and an uneven rocky floor buckled with tree roots. After getting up, I wrench a dry root free. I cup the top of the wood and shove my powers into it. A small flame sparks. I blow on the flame, and my breath caresses the new embers into a blaze.

The torchlight brightens the caved-in entry. The rock pile is too high and packed thick, well within the doorframe. I have to find another way out.

Extending the torch in front of me, I hazard my way into the ruins. The floor slopes, leading me into the trenches. Every few steps I pause and listen for sounds above my thumping heart. Water drips nearby, but the rowdy jungle noises are absent. The corridor breaks off into dark doorways. I choose the path in front of me over and over again, maintaining a line. I lose track of time, but at least an hour, maybe two, passes before I enter a large room.

Torchlight opens up the area, which has not seen sunlight in a long while. Moss blankets the floor, and fungus sprouts from rotten branches. The ceiling is so high I cannot see it beyond the circle of light.

The hairs on my bare arms bristle as I cross the cold room to a wall mural. The land-goddess stares out at me. A gigantic dragon cobra swathes her strong shoulders. Ki is magnificent, nearly the whole height of the great chamber.

The mural continues, transitioning from thriving jungle foliage to a scene at a mountaintop. Jagged peaks with snowy tips and gray rock fill my sight. The depiction of the Alpanas—home—chokes me with longing. On the top of the summit, perched like a bird of prey, is a blue-black snakelike monster. Below it, legions of warriors shoot arrows at the beast. The great serpent blows fire into their ranks, burning them to ashy silhouettes. The mural is lifelike, and as an artist I admire the painted detail. I close in on the sinister serpent, the First-Ever Dragon. The demon Kur is rarely depicted in portraits, but I remember once seeing a sketch of his blue-black scaly form.

Deep breathing rings out behind me.

I spin around. "Who's there?"

The echo of my voice answers, and then silence, broken only by my drumming pulse.

Turning my back to the wall, I cross carefully to the center of the room. Four stairs lead me up a dais. The circle of my torchlight brushes against the base of a throne. I approach the old stone chair, bringing the light nearer. The back of the seat is fashioned into the head of a dragon with its jaw open, poised to devour its occupant. The rest of the dragon's serpentine body winds around the heavy feet. This was Ki's throne. I can imagine her ruling from here, deep in the heart of the jungle she dominates. But why does a dragon decorate her place of power?

Ki's throne room is belowground, where her territory meets the demon Kur's. Perhaps Ki came here to visit Kur, and the story of their being lovers is true. I cannot think of another reason why she would rule from a throne shaped into the symbol of a demon.

Breathing sounds again, closer.

I thrust the torchlight out in front of me. "Show yourself," I demand shakily.

The air stirs behind me. Nothing emerges from the blackness, but the hairs on my body rise. Something lurks in the dark. In the Void.

In front of me, behind the throne, two blue eyes blaze. I cannot see what they belong to, but they smolder with a fire that is strange to mankind. They are more darkness than light, like what remains after a star collapses.

The rank marks on the backs of my hands burn. Wincing in pain, I nearly drop the torch, but I maintain my grip on the light. Whatever creature dwells in this shadowed lair burned me—and it is not of this world.

I force my knees to bend and my feet to move. I back up and follow the wall around the chamber. All the while, the blazing blue eyes watch me. Behind the dais, a doorway leads to an antechamber. I crest the threshold and run. My footfalls resound off the walls and come back to me, as though I am being chased. I push myself faster. The antechamber empties into a corridor. Then another. The hallways weave endlessly, and soon the floor inclines. I climb into warmer air and pause for a breath. I see no signs of the soulless creature following me, but I press on.

Before long, exhaustion drags my pace, and my torch burns low, near to extinguishing. *No, don't go out.* I will never find my way out of here without light. I scan the ground with the dying torch to find its replacement and see dead roots near a short alcove. I crouch over the roots and wrench on the loose wood.

Something hisses.

I freeze with my arm outstretched. A black snake lifts its head level to my face and spreads its neck ribs into a flat, wide hood. I recognize the viper's diamond markings from the popular depiction of Ki. A dragon cobra.

The torchlight goes out.

Gods above.

Another hiss pierces my chest. Darkness conceals the cobra, but it is near. I slowly pull back my arm. Resting both palms on the ground, I brighten my fingers to a glow. In the dimness, I distinguish the shape of the serpent before me, coiled to strike. I dare not reach for my dagger while in its striking distance.

Ever so slowly, I shift my body weight from my arms to my knees. The dragon cobra stands higher and waits for me to move again. For an excuse to strike. Venom hides in its fangs. Another sort of danger hides inside me.

I push more light into my hands planted on the ground. The dirt around them smokes, and the cobra recoils from the awful burning smell. I quickly grab the snake behind the head. The viper's jaws unhinge, opening to bite, and its body whips against my arm. I scorch its neck, pushing in the full heat of my powers. Its leathery skin around my hand turns dry, and the cobra's body slackens. I drop it and withhold my inner light. Shadows sink through the world.

It's dead. It's gone.

I wait for my heartbeat to calm and then light my hand with my powers. The cobra lies still before me. Beside it, an ember burns in the dirt where I created the smoke. The small light is not intimidating like a campfire or a full flame, but it is still nature-fire, born of me. I scoop up the ember in the dirt, cradling it in my palm. I can sense its light fading. As I am fire, and fire is me, I am responsible not to let it go out.

I call to the ember with my powers, not pushing but singing and coaxing. *Come to me. Bring me your warmth. Show me your light.*

The ember brightens. I call to it again, encouraging it to grow, and a flame juts up. I pull away the rotted branch and touch the end to the tiny flame. The fire licks at the wood hungrily and soon feeds.

I gawk at the torchlight. I controlled nature-fire.

The cobra's corpse lies at my feet—the something deadly I need to complete the skill demonstrations. After setting aside the torchlight, I cut off the snake's head with my dagger so no one can tell I scorched it to death and then sling the viper's body over my shoulder and set off with my torch.

I follow the sloping floors up for a long while. Exactly how much time has passed since I was locked inside the ruins, I cannot say, but my feet and legs ache from walking. The vines grow thicker and greener along the walls. Roots burrow across the ground. I lunge over one and slow to inspect the wall they tunneled under. A crack zigzags across the solid stones. I lower my face, and fresh air kisses my cheek.

At last. I drop the dead cobra and prop up the torch for light. I kick the crack in the wall hard. A handful of pebbles crumble, widening the fracture. I plunge my blade into the crack and pry off more stones, working until the fissure grows to a hole the size of my fist.

Dusky light filters inside. I slam my elbow into the wall, and the crater expands. Still, it is not big enough. My legs quake with exhaustion. Perspiration drips down my back and face. My fatigue implores me to rest, but this is the way out.

Beyond this wall is Iresh. Beyond this wall is Deven.

I search for something hard and pick up a stone. Using it as a hammer, I beat the outlet, opening the gap as wide as my hips. I toss the dead cobra out the hole and pull my upper body through. A sharp edge slices my underarm. I ignore the pain and wiggle out to my hips. One final shove, and I fall outside, panting. Lying on my back, the sky lightens before me.

Dawn has passed. I am out of time.

No. Citra will not *win.*

I push up to my knees. The jungle looks the same in every direction, so I climb atop the temple ruins and explore the skyline for the palace's golden dome. Like a coin glinting in a pond, it appears in the sky. My whole body aches, but I have a ways to go yet. I scurry back down to the ground, toss the dead dragon cobra over my shoulder, and hike east.

~~~❦~~~

My late arrival to the Beryl Palace, filthy and blood speckled, garners me an armed escort from a pair of entry-door guards to the throne room.

The hallways are fragrant with the scent of mango rice, a local breakfast dish. My stomach grumbles in hunger. I will eat *after* I finish this. The guards stop before the grand entrance to the throne room. Sultan Kuval is speaking to the full hall. I march inside without an invitation. My powers remain with me as I pass through the threshold. Unlike the war room, the throne room is not lined with toxic plants. When I am halfway down the main aisle, the sultan pauses midsentence. Ashwin is seated opposite him on the dais. He sees me, and relief shoos the worry from his expression.

My competitors are lined up along the west wall with their "something deadly" from the Morass. Tinley holds a basketful of poisonous white currants. I cannot fathom how Indah managed it, but she blindfolded and tied down a crocodile longer than a fishing boat, at least sixteen hands long. Behind Citra, fettered to a stone pillar, a full-grown tiger prowls the length of its short chain. The striped cat growls when I pass. I avoid Citra's hot glare and put on a smile just for her. She did not think she would see me again.

I reach the dais and sling the dragon cobra off my back. The decapitated viper lands near the sultan's feet. Its unique black diamond markings are easily identifiable. Several people gasp. The sultan regards me coolly.

"My 'something deadly,' Your Majesty."

"You're late. You may leave my throne room."

I lower my voice so only he, Ashwin, and I can hear. "I missed the deadline by no fault of my own. I was sabotaged."

Ashwin's posture snaps straight, but Sultan Kuval reveals no surprise. His lack of response fires my temper.

"You knew Citra planned to trap me in the temple ruins."

Sultan Kuval's voice lowers to a threatening rumble. "Have a care, young Kindred. You tread on treasonous ground."

"You don't want me in the tournament, so you ordered Citra to stop me."

"I'll have you imprisoned if you dare slander me further."

"The truth is not slander," I say louder, fury boiling through me.

"You're disqualified from the tournament," he shouts, his face red against his white mustache. "Leave before you humiliate yourself even more."

I stand my ground, pressing my feet into the floor. "I've come too far to leave now." The sultan gapes, and murmurs ripple behind me. "You can cheat . . . you can send your bhutas after me . . . you can try whatever you will to encourage me to quit . . . but I will not concede!"

Shocked whispers fire off around me.

"Her hands and feet."

My fingers and feet burn brightly with my powers. Smoke rises around my sandals, and I can feel the hard stone beneath me. I rein in my soul-fire. My hands and feet return to their normal appearance, and the smoke disperses, but I am too late.

The sultan reels on Ashwin. "She's a *Burner?*"

Ashwin's face turns pasty.

Gasps rise to shouts of alarm. I draw back a step. I burned my sandals off my feet and seared footprints into the floor before the sultan's dais. Dread knocks me to my knees. *I've defaced his throne room.*

The outcries continue. People scatter away from me as though *I* am fire, wild and destructive. Ashwin rubs his forehead with stunned dismay.

I look to him for understanding. "I . . . I didn't mean to . . ."

"Detain her!" commands Sultan Kuval.

Guards wrench my arms behind me and bind my hands with snakeroot. My powers shrink to a dim, useless light. I am so washed from weariness and mortification I do not protest. They lug me down the center aisle amid the audience's fearful cringes.

From the door, I glance back at the dragon cobra lying dead at the sultan's feet and wonder what the snake did wrong besides being exactly as the gods intended.

16

DEVEN

A bright stream of light falls across my face, waking me. Two bhuta guards step into my cell. "Vizier Gyan wants to speak to you," one says.

"Why?"

He kicks the leg of my cot. "Just get up."

Meathead.

I rise slowly, allowing my body time to adjust. The Aquifier came once more last night and healed the last of my scars; even the arrow wound is gone. But the memory of the pain lingers.

Shielding my vision, I step out into the sun. The guards lead me to the quad where the other prisoners are gathered. I spot Yatin, his head higher than the sea of men like the peak of a wave. Worry puckers his brow. *Not a comforting sign.*

Vizier Gyan waits near the pole where I was lashed. The guards leave me there, facing the glares and confused frowns of my fellow soldiers.

The vizier holds out a letter. "I received a message from Prince Ashwin. He requested that I read it to you all. It says: 'I have made a gross error. I was made to believe Captain Deven Naik betrayed his post of command. In truth, there is no more loyal, dedicated soldier in all the empire. So it is with the utmost remorse that I offer my apologies to the captain and exonerate him of all incriminations.'" The vizier folds the letter shut. "Captain Naik's title is reinstated. He'll join you in the general population."

Several men murmur about the announcement to one another.

Vizier Gyan leans into my side and grumbles in my ear. "I don't know why the boy prince changed his mind, but I will be watching you. Step out of line once, and I'll lock you up and bury the key." He tugs down his long sleeves and clips out of the quad.

Yatin pushes his way to me. "Good to see you, Captain."

"Same to you." I smile a little, disbelief filling me up. The prince kept his word. I have been exonerated.

An older soldier with a square chest and rangy legs comes up to us and bows. "Captain Naik, I'm Lieutenant Eko. I served as Prince Ashwin's temple guard and accompanied the prince and Brother Shaan here to Iresh. The bedroll added to Manas's and my tent must be for you."

I school my annoyance. *Of course I'm bunking with Manas.*

"I'm in the same tent," Yatin says quietly, setting aside some of my annoyance. "We'll show you the way."

I follow Yatin and Eko to the final tent in the outer row, near the south wall. Eko throws back the flap, and I duck inside. The interior is sparse, with one bedroll and blanket each for six men. Condensation drips down the walls from the damp air, and noisy mosquitoes dart about.

Yatin swats one away from his bushy beard. "Your bedroll is near mine. Manas and Eko are across the tent from us."

Eko scratches an insect bite on his arm. "The latrine is near the eastern outer wall, but it's nearly full, and the guards aren't motivated to dig another. Don't be late to the dining tent, or you won't be served meals. And stay away from the water barrels near the gate. That drinking water belongs to the guards."

Manas appears at the open tent flap. "I don't care what they say about you, Deven. You're still a traitor."

A sudden coldness hits my core. I remember when he was a twelve-year-old boy with knobby knees and a squeaky voice. He is still smaller in size than me, but the start of a beard buds along his chin, like a lamb sprouting his first woolly coat. My friendship with Manas is over, but I will take indifference over his blatant hatred.

"I'm willing to settle this in the sparring ring," I say. Sparring is a customary practice for two men needing to sort out their differences. Manas and I may need more than the typical three rounds.

"The kindred isn't here to save you this time," Manas replies, sneering.

"Then you'll have no one to blame but yourself when you lose."

Manas moves to strike me, but I duck out of reach, and Yatin simultaneously thrusts out his arm, blocking him. "No one out there trusts you," Manas snarls.

"I'll duel any man who steps forward." None of them despises me as much as Manas does, that I know of.

Manas relaxes his pose and grins hard. "I'll spread the word."

Eko watches him exit with a frown. "I'm afraid the prince hasn't gained allies by releasing you, Captain."

"You don't seem to mind," I say, considering Eko with cautious interest.

"I have the benefit of having served His Majesty for many years. If Prince Ashwin says you're loyal to the throne, you are." Eko bows in farewell and ducks out of the tent.

I sit on my bedroll and stretch out my legs. I have been in camp ten minutes, and I am already fatigued from the tension.

"Manas will be a problem," I say. "How did he even escape Vanhi?"

Yatin takes a seat beside me and bats at the mosquitoes. "Brother Shaan brought him with him. Why did the prince exonerate you?"

"I have no idea."

Yatin studies me while scratching at an insect bite on his chest. I do not like to lie, especially to Yatin. I once asked him why, with his gentle nature, he did not join the Brotherhood instead of the army. Remembering his answer brings a slight smile to my lips. *After growing up with five older sisters, the army was familiar. I was used to being told what to do.* He has never disobeyed my orders. I trust him with the truth of why the prince vindicated me, but with Galers stationed about camp, I cannot tell who could be listening. I would rather lie than endanger us both.

Manas opens the tent flap. "Ready to duel, *Captain*?" He jeers at my reinstated rank.

Wait until he finds out I'll be a general.

I rise, my back pain gone, but the healer said the taut sensation, like calloused skin, could stay awhile. Manas leads me to the quad. A large circle has been drawn in the dirt, a temporary sparring ring. A dozen men line up to fight.

"You said you'd battle any man who steps forward," Manas remarks, smirking.

"Are you first?" I ask.

"I never said I was going to fight you." He hands me a staff. "I'll let them have that pleasure."

Coward. He never could beat me in a fair fight.

The first man in line picks up another staff and steps up to me. A bhuta guard strolling by does not interfere. He wears a yellow armband marked with a land symbol. Our bamboo staffs are twigs against his Trembler powers.

I enter the ring. Much of our early soldier training occurred in a sparring circle. In addition to fighting skills, we learned self-control, respect for our opponents, and how to win and lose with humility. Gripping my weapon, I brace for a beating. I will deliberately lose enough duels to appear demoralized but not enough that I will be seen as a weakling. By day's end, I will be bruised and sore, but my comrades' resentment will be appeased. Soldier to soldier, there is no greater equalizer than defeat.

Manas signals the start of the duel. My opponent attacks, and my quest to regain their respect begins with the first blow.

17

KALINDA

The guards dump me in an empty antechamber far away from the throne room. I rest my forehead against the cool tile floor, the frightened cries of the sultan's court still booming in my ears. I search my mind for something else to think about and find the image of Deven cringing from my glowing hands.

Sultan Kuval throws open the door and stomps in, Ashwin on his tail. I stay lying on my side, the toxic snakeroot binding my hands behind me, and stare up at them.

"You deceived me," bellows the sultan. "She's a *Burner*." He spits my god-given powers at me, like I am the dead dragon cobra I flung at his feet.

"Kalinda isn't dangerous," Ashwin replies. "She's Kishan's daughter."

"Kishan was an idealistic fool. He was always lecturing others about unity and the need for Virtue Guards. I will tell you what I told him—I have no place for Burners in my nation! Burners are soulless children of the Void."

I have heard this slander before. Rajah Tarek twisted the truth of bhutas' godly origins and told his people we were demons. That was a lie, yet Sultan Kuval is not condemning *all* bhutas, only Burners.

"Kalinda stays," Ashwin counters, leaving no quarter for dispute.

"Then she must take the neutralizer tonic to suppress her powers." Sultan Kuval tosses his hands in the air. "You saw what she did to the floor of my throne room. Burners are reckless!"

The neutralizer tonic is the liquid form of the noxious plant around my wrists. My nose scrunches in disgust, recalling the bitter tang of the concoction. I drank neutralizer tonic to reduce my fevers long before I knew the so-called remedy for my bhuta powers was toxic.

"Kalinda won't poison herself," Ashwin says, standing taller and towering over the stout rajah. "As a Burner, she is well matched to her opponents."

The sultan expels an ugly laugh. "Don't you see? Kalinda has conspired against us! She's an informant for Hastin."

"She disagrees with Hastin's regime," Ashwin counters. "She's risking her life for a chance—only a chance—to defeat him." *But I am deceiving him. I haven't told him that I killed his father.* "Kalinda escaped sabotage and caught the most deadly viper in the Morass, a tremendous testament to her courage and skill. She *will* fight in the trial tournament."

Sultan Kuval's mustache twitches against his cheek, which is red from anger. "It's your empire falling to ruins." He glares down at me, as though he wishes to kick me like he would a disobedient mutt, and then storms out.

Ashwin kneels beside me. He undoes my bindings and flings the snakeroot across the room. His arms come around me, and he helps me sit up. I lean against him, a headache pounding against my temples.

"I'm sorry," I say.

"Don't be. With bhutas as your competitors, the sultan and his court would have found out eventually."

I rest my head against his sturdy shoulder. He stood up for me against the sultan, and he was brilliant. "Why does Kuval think Burners are demons?"

"That was his bias speaking. A Burner killed Citra's mother."

I release a weary exhale. "Indah neglected to mention that detail."

"His wife's death isn't a subject the sultan likes to speak about."

"I imagine not." I have no hope of ever winning Sultan Kuval's support, but he is not my primary concern. Now that my secret is out, it will not be long before word reaches the encampments. "What will our people think when they hear what I am?"

Ashwin wraps his arm tighter around me. "Burner powers are feared above all else, so you'll be the contender favored to win. Our people will love you all the more and thank the gods for sending you."

His answer is kind but unconvincing. "The Janardanians think I'm a monster. They fear me, but you don't."

"I do," he whispers. "I fear the hold you have on my heart."

"Ashwin—" I start to move away, but he holds me near him.

"You're no monster, Kalinda. I've met a monster, and you're nothing like him. I'm ashamed of Tarek, ashamed of how the rest of the world perceives the empire and me on account of him. But I am not ashamed of you."

Ashwin's soothing scent, aloe vera oil, invites me closer. He dips his chin nearer to mine, so our lips are only a dandelion's length apart. Our sides press together, his warmth searing into me. His dark eyes turn liquid with affection, and his jaw softens with trust. He combs his fingers through my loose locks. "Your hair is like woven twilight."

A recollection of Tarek's intrusive hands stroking my hair slams me. *Enough of this.*

I push from Ashwin's hold and rally the strength to stand. He rises with me, steadying me on my rickety legs and bare feet. He tries to pull me close, but I step from the circle of his arms and totter for the door.

"Kalinda?" Ashwin asks.

I do not stop. Tarek may be dead, but his memory lives on in my shadow. I cannot outrun him, but I have to try.

Ashwin calls after me again, his footfalls close behind me. I round a corner and see Opal hurrying our way.

"Prince Ashwin," she says. "Brother Shaan needs you."

Her urgency causes me to pause.

Ashwin hastens past me to Opal. "What is it?" he asks.

"Civilians in the encampment have fallen ill." Apprehension furrows Opal's brow. "Some of the ailing aren't expected to recover."

I nearly double over from guilt. I helped Hastin take over Vanhi and run these people out of their homes. They are here, and falling ill, because of me. "I'm coming along," I announce.

Opal's gaze sweeps to me. "My apologies, Kindred, but the sultan has insisted that you stay away from the encampments."

So Sultan Kuval *did* hear our people chanting my name. "I'm here to offer my support to the prince. I'd like to go, if he'll have me."

Confusion lingers in Ashwin's expression from my hasty exit moments ago, but he dismisses his hesitancy with a perfunctory nod. "Kalinda will join us."

———※———

Opal fetches me another pair of sandals and then carries Ashwin and me down to the encampments on her wing flyer. The afternoon sun warms the humid air, and the wind rushing over me wicks away the sweat beading across my upper lip. We land and go to Brother Shaan, waiting for us near the entry gate to the civilian camp.

"Your Majesty," he says, bowing. "Five dead after dawn, another two this hour."

Ashwin mashes his lips together. "When did the sickness start?"

"Yesterday, but it's spreading quickly. The healers believe the local mosquitoes carry a scourge. Our people aren't accustomed to the strange climate."

I arch my chin to see inside the camp. Sick tents have been set up away from the main housing. People swing fans, shooing away the bugs, yet the insects hover like vultures waiting to feed off a sky burial. The ailing people fill the sick tents and lie on bedrolls around them.

"I need to go in and offer my condolences to the grieving families," says Ashwin.

A Janardanian commander blocks the gate. "No one may go in or come out, Your Majesty."

Ashwin takes a charged step forward. "My people are *dying*."

"Those are my orders."

Ashwin digs his thumbs into his tear ducts, collecting his frustration. The same anger burrows in my bones. I will snap if something is not done.

"Can we pass out lemon-eucalyptus oil to ward off the insects?" I ask.

"We're in short supply," replies Brother Shaan, "and collecting the resources to concoct more ointment would take a fortnight. The trial tournament will be over by then."

I watch the residents swaying the fans. The breeze brings coolness to the clammy heat but also disturbs the hovering mosquitoes. "Can we station Galers around the camp? A constant draft could push the bugs away."

"I don't have approval for that," the commander says.

Ashwin drops his hands from his face. "Do it."

The commander holds the prince's defiant stare. A warning passes from Ashwin to the soldier, silent but tangible. The commander shifts away and murmurs to his men. A bhuta guard with a sky symbol on his armband whips up a wind, summoning a hearty gust that sends the mosquitoes off to the jungle.

Ashwin chops out orders. "Brother Shaan, you'll oversee the camp in my stead. I'll speak to the rest of the guards about setting up shifts for the Galers."

The prince marches to the guardhouse. I am astonished that the Janardanians are heeding his commands. Perhaps they fear the illness will spread to the city. Or maybe they are beginning to view Ashwin as a legitimate ruler.

A group of refugees meanders over to the fence to stare at us.

"Opal told me you revealed your powers," Brother Shaan remarks.

I turn my back to the onlookers. "Do the people know?"

"They will soon. When they do, I'll tell them it's a rumor started to defame you. That should give them time to adapt to the idea."

I twist my fingers in the pleats of my skirt. "I don't like lying to them."

"They must prepare for what's to come. No matter who wins the tournament, Ashwin will wed a bhuta. His children will be bhutas. The next heir to the Tarachandian throne *will* be a bhuta."

"So long as it isn't a Burner," I mutter.

Brother Shaan lays a consoling hand on my shoulder. "Undoing their prejudice will take time. Have patience and faith."

Faith will not undo my actions. I glance at Ashwin to ensure that he is still out of hearing range. "Why didn't you tell the prince how Tarek died?"

"Your support gives Ashwin the confidence to rule, and he gives you hope for a peaceful empire."

"Your being right doesn't justify lying to us." I pull from Brother Shaan's grasp. "You should have told me when the rest of my party arrived."

"I meant to tell you later that night. I'm sorry. I didn't know Deven would get hurt." Brother Shaan's remorse files down the sharpest edges of my anger. "I wanted you to have time alone with the prince. Both of you were wounded by Tarek. Only you can truly understand how deeply. You have every reason to trust each other."

Across the way, Ashwin still speaks to the guards. My confidence in him is growing, and I am coming to rely upon his support. Telling him the truth about Tarek's death can wait until after the tournament, when our people are free.

The crowd peeking over the fence grows. More than my presence is drawing attention. I look a fright in my filthy training sari with the dry blood on my arm. "I better go," I say.

As I cross back to Opal, waiting at the wing flyer, I pass the gate for the military encampment and long for a glimpse of Deven. Seeing no sign of him, I fend off my disappointment and turn away. *Anu, let him be safe.*

Opal flies me back to the palace. As we circle over the gardens, I spot Tinley below, grooming her mahati falcon, Bya. The great bird stays still as the Galer brushes its beak. When we land, the falcon squawks and ruffles its feathers. Up close, the mahati is even more striking, its red-orange feathers blazing in the sunlight. Tinley pets her bird and speaks in a low, soothing voice. She does not treat Bya like a beast with a master but as a dear friend. The falcon nudges Tinley in the shoulder with its beak, and she tosses it a scorpion to eat.

"Doesn't the stinger hurt him?" I ask, listening to the crunch of the scorpion being devoured.

"Her," Tinley corrects. "Bya's female."

"She has a beautiful name."

Tinley is not warmed by my compliment. She turns her back to me and says, "Slag."

Opal sets a hasty pace away from Tinley, and I rush to catch up. I do not recognize the term "slag," but, given Opal's reaction, I doubt Tinley intended her use kindly.

In the palace corridors, guards stiffen when they see me, and servants cower. A group of the sultan's courtesans, escorted by eunuch guards, makes an abrupt about-face. As they scurry away, I overhear one of them mutter "slag," and the others titter.

"What does 'slag' mean?" I ask Opal.

She answers in haste. "It's a distasteful term for a Burner. My mother taught Rohan and me never to use it."

I sniff once, feigning a lack of interest, but the offense stings. I have never heard a derogatory term for the other bhutas. Are Burners despised so much? I drag my sore feet to my bedchamber, impatient to bury my head under my blankets and muffle out the world, but Opal halts before the threshold.

"You have a guest," she says, lowering her brows.

Before I can ask who is inside my chamber, Indah opens my door and smiles.

18

DEVEN

Gods, it's hot. The absence of a breeze is stifling. Lieutenant Eko offers me a wet cloth for my face. I dab the rag against my bloody lip where I was hit by a staff. Manas scowls at Eko and me from inside the dining tent with the other soldiers. *Friendly as usual.*

Midday meal comes to a close. I hardly touched my mushy rice, leaving it for Yatin to finish. My whole body is sore from sparring.

"You take a beating well," Eko says, sitting with me.

"I've had practice."

"General Gautam was your father," he notes. "I was surprised to hear of his death."

Interesting that I say I'm used to a beating and he mentions my father. Did Eko know the general as I did? The general tortured me for information about the rebels before he died. I remember the general bleeding out on the dungeon floor, but I suffer no powerful ache or loss. Everything I understand about honor and respect, I learned from my mother and other sister warriors. My father does not deserve my sorrow, only relief. He can no longer torment anyone.

"The circumstances were complicated," I answer.

"They often are." Eko squints up at the hillside. The gold dome of the Beryl Palace gleams in the sunshine. Below the impressive structure, a gigantic sign has been erected with four names written in bold letters.

Indah of Lestari
Citra of Janardan
Tinley of Paljor
Kalinda of Tarachand

They posted the rank board for the tournament. I fasten my gaze onto Kali's name. *Did I really tell her she had to compete?* The memory rings hollow through me. *Yes, I did.*

Eko wipes at his forehead. His cheeks turn pink beneath his gray beard, burning in the heat of the day. "Manas told me you're the kindred's personal guard."

"I was. I no longer serve in that capacity."

He scratches his cheek, working through a puzzle. "Are you married? Have any children?"

"No."

"Me neither, but I was in love once. A young woman came to sell sunflower seeds to the brethren at the temple. After spending all my coin to buy her wares, I mustered up the courage to visit her in the nearby village. Her father sent me away and told me not to come back. He had arranged a marriage between her and the village blacksmith. I thought I wouldn't see her again, but the next fortnight she came to the temple peddling her seeds, and I asked her to marry me."

When Eko started his story, I did not anticipate caring. "What did she say?"

"I was too late. She had wed the blacksmith two nights earlier." Eko takes back my rag and dabs away sweat on his upper lip. I gulp down a lump of regret. His story did not end the way I hoped. "I won't pretend to know your circumstances, Captain, but I know what it is to have fate stacked against you."

Manas must have told him about Kali and me. No offense to Eko, but our relationship is none of his concern. "The Brotherhood temple must have been an undemanding post."

"Most of the time it was, unless the rajah came to visit." Eko swipes at his forehead, his flushed cheeks darkening to scarlet. "I've seen a man whipped twice in my life. Once was you, and the other was the last time the rajah visited the prince . . ." Eko trails off and rests his head in his hands. "I think I've had too much sun."

I lay my hand on his back—his skin burns through the thin cloth of his tunic. I signal for Yatin, and he comes right over.

"Eko needs to lie down," I say.

We help Eko cross camp to our tent and lay him on his bedroll. I test the temperature of his forehead. He is feverish, his clammy skin sticking to mine.

Manas bursts inside the sweltering tent. "What did you do to him, Deven?"

"Nothing. He's fallen ill. Fetch a guard."

Manas opens his mouth to argue and then sees his friend's ruddy face and darts out.

I sit back on my heels, listening to Eko's labored breathing over the buzzing mosquitoes. Yatin reflects the same grim expression. We have seen sun sickness before. I had it myself the first time I crossed the Bhavya Desert. I fell off my camel during training and hit the sand like a stone. Yatin hauled my sorry rear back to Vanhi. Eko's fever is too high for sun sickness. I do not know *what* this is.

Manas returns with a guard and a healer. The guard snaps at us to leave. Yatin and I wait outside with Manas. He holds himself tense, wringing his fingers.

The guard steps out of the tent, leaving Eko with the healer, and tromps off for the guardhouse. Moments later, a gong rings, calling all prisoners to the quad. The healer could be a while, so Yatin and I join the men. They are already there, mumbling about why we have been summoned. Vizier Gyan stands near the gate, talking with the guard who left Eko.

Something is not right. Our captors are more troubled about Eko than I assumed they would be over one sick prisoner.

Vizier Gyan enters the quad wearing his usual long-sleeved tunic that hangs past his wrists to his knuckles. He must be accustomed to the heat, as he does not sweat in the warmer clothes. A land symbol I did not see before is sewn on his jacket collar. He's a Trembler? The only other Trembler I have met is Hastin. Last time I saw the warlord, he dropped boulders on a group of palace guards, crushing them to death. I cannot decide which is more fearsome, Burner or Trembler powers.

"An illness is sweeping the civilian camp," the vizier announces, drawing a collection of sharp breaths from us prisoners. "We thought it was contained, but a man in this encampment has fallen ill. We'll quarantine him from the general population. If you detect the beginnings of a fever in yourself or another man, report it immediately."

"How are our families?" one of our men asks. "Are they all right?"

"We have no other news," replies the vizier.

The men are not satisfied.

"My wife and children are in there!"

"We deserve to know if our families are well!"

Vizier Gyan signals for silence, but the demands multiply. My own fears expand. Mother and Brac will arrive any day. Vizier Gyan will confine Mother to the civilian camp, and given that Brac would not entrust his Burner identity to outsiders, he will be sent here with me. Skies, it would be good to see my brother, but I do not want him or my mother imprisoned. Neither camp is safe.

The guards step in to break up the distressed men, hauling off the loudest shouter. Upon seeing him dragged away to confinement, the rest of the protesters ramble off.

But there is nowhere to go. We are all trapped inside this cesspit together.

151

19

KALINDA

Indah holds my door open. I shove down my agitation at finding her inside my chamber and step past her. After a quick inspection, nothing appears out of order. Pons is stationed near the balcony, in full view of the room and the gardens. Longing sweeps over me. *That's where Deven would stand if he were here.*

"Kalinda, your guests asked to wait for you to return," Natesa says, her high voice nervous.

"I hope you don't mind," Indah adds, settling on my raised lounge. "Your servant offered us tea."

Stick to truths. She can sense liars.

"I'm happy to entertain a visit, but I'm in sore need of a bath." I hold out my dirty skirt as proof.

"This will only take a moment." Indah pats the seat beside her. I join her, expecting this will be brief. Natesa hovers near the teapot and pretends not to eavesdrop.

"So you're a Burner," Indah remarks, an observation without condemnation. "I should have guessed. Your eyes flash when you're irritated." She laughs. "Yes, like that. My mother's eyes do the same thing."

"Your mother is a Burner? Didn't you say she's an Aquifier?"

"My *father* is an Aquifier; I said my mother birthed me in healing waters. She's the datu's Burner Virtue Guard. She'll be pleased to hear of your powers. Burners are scarce, even in Lestari. My mother has not said so, but she wished I, her only child, would inherit her abilities." Indah's tone carries no resentment, merely acceptance. "I admire your restraint, Kindred. If you hadn't revealed yourself, I wouldn't have guessed your secret. Even Pons heard nothing. Your Galer guards are skilled at misplacing sounds."

"Pons?" I ask, glancing at her guard in the balcony doorway.

"Pons is a Galer. He was born in a village south of here. His parents brought him to Iresh when he was a child." *He* must be Indah's collector of secrets. "I hope you don't mind that, after I left the throne room this morning, I researched your heritage. I was fascinated to hear your mother was Rajah Tarek's first-ever wife, Yasmin, and your father was the former bhuta ambassador Kishan Zacharias."

I shield my dissatisfaction. "Who told you that?"

"Your servant. She's quite sociable."

I cut a censorious glance at Natesa, who stares a little too attentively at the teapot. "Natesa isn't my servant; she's my friend."

"My apologies. Your *friend* told us how Rajah Tarek claimed you. An incredible story with a tragic ending." Indah taps her fingers against the back of the lounge. "Some might think it's strange Rajah Tarek was murdered and yet you escaped."

"The warlord invaded the palace, and I was fortunate to get away. That's what happened."

"I believe that is *part* of what happened." Indah's lips curl upward knowingly, her golden eyes shimmering.

She's enjoying this. Pons may be her informant, but she relishes the challenge of unburying secrets. I dread her next question will be about the Zhaleh, so I present a fatigued smile. "I should wash up now."

Indah rises fluidly, in one motion. "Thank you for the tea."

Pons goes to her and escorts the entrancing Aquifier out the door.

"No woman should be that beautiful." Natesa checks her reflection in the mirror glass. "The gods should spread their beauty around to the rest of us."

I sink back into the cushion. "How long were they here?"

"A couple minutes. Indah walked around but didn't touch anything." Natesa fixes the kohl at the corner of her eye. "I'm sorry I talked about your heritage. She acted like she already knew."

"I understand. Indah can be persuasive." Though I cannot say what she is after. Has she come to Iresh to participate in the trial tournament or to find the Zhaleh?

Natesa dabs lip stain onto her lower lip. "I was concerned when you didn't come back last night. I was ready to ask Opal to find you when Indah showed up and told me you'd returned."

I tamp down my surprise at Natesa's worry for me. "Sorry. I should have sent you a message as soon as I arrived at the palace."

"It's all right." She brushes more rouge onto her cheeks. "Indah said something interesting while she was here. Did you know women are considered equal to men in Lestari? They can even wear trousers. Can you imagine?"

More freedom *would* appeal to Natesa. Her dream is to become an innkeeper, but women cannot own commerce establishments in Tarachand. "Perhaps when we're through here, you can go to Lestari."

"Only if Yatin comes with me." Natesa glances out the open balcony, hoping for a glimpse of her husky soldier. "I think he'll want to."

"Of course he will. He cares for you."

She stares unseeingly at the sky. "My first night at the palace, Rajah Tarek summoned me to his chambers. Before he touched me, he said courtesans aren't made for love but for lov*ing*."

Revulsion scalds my mouth. Does Tarek's damaging reach have no end? I assumed Natesa's pride was impenetrable. She was orphaned at a young age and worked hard to rise above her loss. For her to believe she is unworthy of love bothers me a great deal.

"I told Yatin what Tarek said," Natesa goes on, her attention locked in her memory. "Yatin said if anyone treated his sisters that way, he would gut them. I have never seen him more upset. He hurt on my behalf." Her focus returns, hooked to the horizon. "Knowing he's out there, imprisoned . . . I cannot stop worrying."

Her anxiety rakes at my own. Deven is so close, yet our last moments together have pushed him far away. Perhaps the gods will return his good fortune now that we are apart. Some good has to come from how terribly I miss him.

I plaster on a smile for Natesa. "Yatin and Deven will look after one another."

"And we'll do the same for each other," she says, extending her hand to me.

Jaya and I used to hold hands and squeeze them to say *I love you*. Natesa deserves to find happiness, but reaching for her would be a betrayal to Jaya. I am not ready to let Jaya go. I follow Natesa's gaze outside and pretend not to see her outstretched fingers.

Two heartbeats later, she walks away.

———✦———

After sleeping through the rest of the day, I wake in the night with an insatiable urge to draw. I light a candle and open the colorful inks. An hour later, I finish painting the peacock. The bird that is native to Vanhi was the most vibrant thing I could think of to draw. I would carry on, but my out-of-practice hands ache. It has been too long since I have created something beautiful.

I set aside the wet parchment to dry and bend forward to blow out the candle. The mesmerizing colors cause me to pause. Brac said my soul's reflection can be seen within nature-fire. What could mine be? A tigress? A mother bear? A falcon? I lower my gaze eye level to the root of the flame, its golden tip flickering.

As I concentrate on the heart of the fire, something swirls in the burning blue center and then ascends upward. A scaly face with gleaming eyes, a long snout, and two wiry whiskers manifests in the flame's yellow offshoots.

The dragon snaps at me with pointy fangs.

I reel back, and the face disappears.

It takes me a moment to comprehend what I saw. My soul's reflection is *a dragon*?

But dragons are evil . . . My soul-fire sings to . . . a *demon*?

The hour is late. My imagination must be exploiting my exhaustion. I rub my weary eyes, scrubbing the fiery dragon from my vision, lean over the candle, and blow out the flame.

Mountain air, thick and crisp as chewing ice, hangs like an icicle in my chest. Jaya wraps her arms around me, her cheek pressed to my upper arm. "I'm glad we're home," she says.

The Alpanas rise above us, cutting into the sky with snaggily teeth. I clasp my hands over Jaya's. "I've missed this. Missed you."

We look out over the boxy garden where Deven rakes weeds from around the barley plants. A straw hat shades his dark eyes and bearded jawline. He sees us watching and waves.

"You can still have this," Jaya says.

"It won't be the same without you." I take in her pretty round face, tiny chin, and wide nose. Her shining smile could scatter rain clouds.

"You could release the Voider and ask him to bring me back."

I still my wistfulness and answer sadly, "I cannot do that, Jaya. The Voider would destroy everything. I'd be bringing you back to a fallen world."

"The Voider doesn't want to rend the sky from the land. Those are lies."

"How do you know what it wants?" I ask, gazing at her more closely.

She leans toward me, and I recoil from the sudden craze in her eyes. Her voice grows deep and raspy. "Because I *am* the Voider."

Jaya's face and body melt away into a coiled dragon cobra at my feet. Before I can flee, the viper strikes my shin. I sink down, holding my bitten leg, and shout for Deven. He comes running, but as he approaches, his shape changes.

When he reaches me, Tarek kneels at my side. "Shh, love." He pulls me into his lap and pets my hair. The viper's poison is paralyzing, trapping me in Tarek's arms. "We will always have each other."

I scream and sit upright, a flame bursting from my hand. Natesa jumps back from leaning over me. My heatwave barely misses her and hits the tapestry of the jungle across from my bed. The thick cloth ignites and burns outward in a circle. Natesa rushes over and beats the fire out with a broom. I press a hand over my sprinting heart and search for Tarek and the cobra. Both are gone.

Natesa throws open the balcony door to dispense of the smoke and then props against the broom, out of breath. Smoke hazes the distance between us. The tapestry has a huge hole scorched in the center. "You scared me into my next life," she says.

"I'm sorry." I bury my face in my clammy hands. The burning viper bite on my leg and Tarek's arms around me is still sharp in my mind. "What time is it?"

"Dawn. I came to wake you. Your first trial starts soon."

I cannot face my competitors shaken. These nightmares must stop. I throw back the bedcovers, tug on my robe, and hurry out the door. I reach Brother Shaan's chamber and knock. No one answers, so I go down the hall to Prince Ashwin's door. Rohan is there, standing guard.

"Kindred, what's wrong?"

"Have you seen Brother Shaan?"

"Not yet today."

I knock for Ashwin and wait. My knee jogs impatiently. I need to speak to Brother Shaan before my dream fades.

Ashwin answers bare chested, his hair ruffled. "Kalinda."

My face heats from his unabashed stare roving over me in my thin robe. I duck my chin to hide my blush. "I hope I didn't wake you. I need to speak with Brother Shaan. Do you know where he is?"

"He's supposed to come by shortly to report on the camps. You're welcome to come in and wait for him." Ashwin opens the door wider, revealing more of his bare golden chest. I slip past him inside and leave Rohan in the corridor.

"Sorry for the clutter." Ashwin tidies up books lying across the table and chairs, clearing a spot for me. "Mint tea?" he asks, gesturing to a steaming cup.

"No, thank you." I scan the texts stacked everywhere, looking anywhere but at his shirtless torso. "Have you read all of these?"

"Most of them when I was younger. I was lonely without them around—I had shelves full of books in my room at the temple—so I borrowed these from the sultan's library."

I scan the heaps of books, marveling at how well educated he must be. "You must have read a lot growing up."

Ashwin's tone turns reflective. "Tarek said I read too much. He thought it was a waste of time. But during his last few visits, he requested I read to him. He said it made him happy to listen to me share something I enjoy. He was happy because I was happy." Ashwin rubs the sad tilt of his lips. "Sometimes I still read aloud to remind myself he wasn't a total monster."

I understand why Ashwin romanticizes people. He saw a glimmer of goodness in his selfish father, which taught him not to discount anyone's potential for decency.

I show him the ink on my fingers from painting last night. "I retreat into my artwork when I need a moment's peace."

"You used my gift," he says, his demeanor brightening.

"I don't believe I thanked you."

"You're welcome." He waves at a chair, and we sit beside each other at the table. "Tinley and Citra asked me to ban you from the tournament. I won't, of course."

Their request comes as no surprise, yet their derision hurts. I fold my arms across my chest, and Ashwin notices the scar on my forearm.

"From your rank tournament?" he says, sipping his tea.

"The duel with your mother," I explain. Ashwin frowns at the mention of Lakia, and my gaze jumps to his bare shoulder and the tops of scars. "How did you get yours?"

"Rajah Tarek found out I'd been sneaking out of my room to the temple's roof. He was concerned the villagers would discover who I was, so he whipped me to deter me from doing it again." Ashwin rests his elbows on the table, waves of remorse rising off him like the steam from his teacup. He twists the gold cuff on his wrist. "My caretaker, Brother Dhiren, was punished for not protecting me. Tarek had him executed."

I rest my hand on Ashwin's shoulder, absorbing his guilt as strong as my own. He reaches up and clasps my fingers. This near him, I am aware of his toned arms and flat stomach, his skin warm against mine. He smells of linen and mint, of sleep and fresh tea. His dark hair waves freely around his face, brushing the back of my hand. Ashwin is appealing in a way his father never was. Tarek was vile, but Ashwin . . .

I pull away. "I should go."

He reaches for where my hand was seconds before. "You don't want to speak to Brother Shaan? He'll be back soon."

My nightmare of Rajah Tarek is foggy now, replaced by the image of his handsome son. "Another time," I say, and step out the door.

20

KALINDA

I meet my contenders and their parties at the base of the waterfall. Citra and Tinley sling glares my way but stay distant. Off to the side, Pons speaks to Indah. Their closeness would draw attention if he were not her guard. What secret is he relaying to her now?

We surround a lagoon that feeds into a stream. The picturesque cascade does nothing to ward off my nerves. I fiddle with the pleats of my sparring sari, the skirt tucked between my covered legs. My competitors and I are all dressed in warrior apparel and strapped with weaponry. Natesa insisted that I bring both of my daggers *and* a khanda. I did not argue the added weight of the sword; I must be ready for whatever trial the sultan has prepared for us.

Sultan Kuval stands near the lagoon, Ashwin beside him. He and our guards, Opal and Rohan, are my support. Brother Shaan is still supervising the care of the refugees. Ashwin looks dashing in an all-black tunic and trousers with silver embroidery and a dark turban. I have tried to put the image of him shirtless from my thoughts, but it sneaks back in as he smiles at me from across the audience.

Gods above, don't get distracted.

"Welcome to the trial tournament," announces the sultan. "For the first test, each competitor will have five minutes to complete a challenge of valor. To begin, Indah will represent the water-goddess Enki, Bearer of the Seas."

Indah steps forward with her trident, her dewy skin shimmering in the sunlight, and joins him at the base of the pool.

"Contending against nature requires valor," the sultan continues, "a total submission to the gods, and faith in one's god-given abilities. For Indah's test, she will stop the flow of the waterfall."

The Lestarians murmur, the pitch of their low voices distressed. This will be no easy feat for Indah. My insides churn like the base of the waterfall. What task does the sultan have planned for me?

Donning a steely expression, Indah steps on the placid edge of the lagoon and floats on a mist across the pond, stopping outside of the spray where the waterfall feeds into the pool. I allow myself to enjoy the tranquil sight of Indah in her element, anxious as to how she will force nature to bend to her authority.

A gong rings, and the sand timer is turned upside down. Indah's five minutes begin.

The Aquifier holds out her trident in front of her with one arm. As she raises the weapon, the streaming water above us narrows. Her arm gradually goes up, and the waterfall shrinks. When the flow is half of when she started, Indah's feet break the surface of the lagoon. Her arm shakes to maintain her grip on the trident. The cascading water pushes her down, but her weapon continues to hold the falls up. She submerges to her knees.

My amazement at her feat so far leads me to cheer silently. *Come on, Indah. Succeed against nature. Against the sultan. Against this arduous trial. Enki, strengthen her.*

Indah grasps her trident across her chest with both hands and raises it to her chin. The waterfall is nearly gone; the rock face glistens with dampness. In one last exhibit of strength, Indah jerks the trident above her head, and the remainder of the cascade seals off.

Her arms give way, and Indah plunges under the surface. The water gushes down on the lagoon in an explosion that sends us viewers back a step.

The gong sounds, signaling the end of her time.

Indah breaks the surface, the waterfall gushing around her. The audience applauds, and her party shouts her name in congratulations. Indah swims to the bank of the lagoon. Using her trident as a staff, she pushes to her feet. Sopping wet and grinning, she reminds me of a bird after a bath. I cannot help but smile. Pons hauls her against his wide chest in a hug, soaking his clothes.

"Indah advances to the next trial." Sultan Kuval's announcement ends the Lestarians' celebration, quieting us all, and he goes on. "Princess Citra will now represent the land-goddess Ki, Mother of the Mountains. For her trial, Citra will sculpt a stairway into the cliff and climb it to the top."

The crowd mumbles about the complexity of the challenge. I presumed the sultan would give his daughter a less complicated task, but building a staircase to the rise of the cliff and scaling it in five minutes will not be simple.

The princess, however, is undaunted. Citra blows Ashwin a kiss and glides to the cliff to the right of the waterfall. Her impervious arrogance astounds me. Did her father forewarn her of the challenge, or is she impossible to intimidate?

The gong sounds, and the sand timer is flipped over.

Citra throws out her hands, and a stairway forms in front of her, etched into the stone wall. She starts to walk up the cliff, building more staircases to climb. The princess pushes herself into a jog, and stairs materialize to match her swift pace.

Halfway up, Citra throws out her hand to create another staircase, but nothing appears. She skids to a stop on the edge of the last stair, her arms windmilling. Sultan Kuval freezes, and the people gasp. I press down on my pounding heart while Citra continues to teeter. As she falls forward, she carves another staircase before her and lands on it. The audience releases a collective breath.

The sand timer is nearly out. Citra has done well so far, but I would not be sad if she failed her timed test and was eliminated.

Before catching her breath, Citra stares up the cliff, searching for the summit. She pulls herself up and doubles her speed, carving steps beneath her as she sprints upward. More zigzagged staircases guide her to the top. She sets foot in the palace garden high above as the gong sounds.

Applause fills the basin. Citra leaps down the wall from switchback to switchback until she lands on the ground. She strides over to Ashwin, her hips twitching, and offers him an orchid she picked while in the garden above. He accepts her gift with a bow.

A girl darts away from the viewers and slams her arms around Citra in a hug. I recognize her from the declaration ceremony as Citra's younger sister Tevy.

"Princess Citra advances to the next trial," Sultan Kuval declares, puffing out his chest.

Indah slow claps beside me. "What a surprise," she drawls.

"What do you mean?" I question.

"Who do you think stands to gain the most from a union with Tarachand?"

"Every sovereign stands to gain something."

"But only one shares the largest border with the empire. Should that border close to refugees . . ."

I wish Ashwin were near enough to hear, but he is still raining praise on Citra. "The sultan said the border will remain open," I say.

"Things change. Do you have a friend by the name of Brac?"

A thread of worry spools at the back of my throat. "Yes. Why?"

"Pons heard something on the wind before the trial started. He said the sultan intercepted a letter that arrived for you this morning. Brac and his mother have been held up at the border and cannot get through. Sultan Kuval has barricaded all roadways leading into Janardan."

"Are you certain?" I glance at the sultan. He beams proudly at his daughter.

Indah follows my gaze, and her brows crimp downward. "My informants are trustworthy. And so am I."

She could be endearing herself to me to get the Zhaleh, but she profits nothing from this lie. Matching her stare, I sense her certainty. Brac and Mathura are not coming.

"Your friends are camped near the border checkpoint," Indah says in a hushed tone. "They're safer there than in the encampments, but it does make one wonder about the sultan's intentions to honor his word . . ."

She saunters off, casual in her decimation of the fragile treaty between Tarachand and Janardan. What does the sultan gain by stranding our people at the borders? I cannot conceive what he ultimately wants or what he will do if Citra does not win the tournament.

Ashwin meets my gaze across the crowd and frowns. He can tell I am upset. I wipe the concern from my face and resolve to speak to him later. I must concentrate on the trial now.

"Tinley will now represent Anu, God of Storms," decrees Sultan Kuval.

Tinley goes to his side, and the crowd hushes. Overhead, black clouds rush across the sky. A gust rustles the long reeds near the lagoon and plucks loose petals from the wild orchids. Two people come into view high on the cliff, Galers manipulating the wind. A crash of thunder startles everyone, and then a lightning bolt sends me ducking.

The sultan shouts over the blustery weather. "Tinley will now disperse the storm. Turn the sand timer!"

A lightning bolt illuminates Tinley's determined face. She places two fingers in her mouth and whistles. Another crash of thunder sends spectators dashing to the bottom of the cliff and under an overhang that provides shelter. The dark clouds unleash a steady stream of raindrops. I cram under the overhang with the others. Ashwin squeezes through the crowd to my side.

"This is madness," he remarks.

A screech barrels across the sky, and Tinley's falcon, Bya, swoops down. Tinley jumps on Bya's back, landing in her woven saddle. The mahati flaps its fire-colored wings, and they pitch upward, speeding into the storm.

"*That's* madness," I reply.

The great bird and her rider streak across the dreary sky, dodging lightning bolts. Bya fights to stay upright, but the strong gales knock the mahati around like a dancing leaf. Tinley, her hair white as the August moon, shoots a bolt into the storm with her crossbow. A patch of blue opens where the bolt disappears.

The audience sounds its awe; I cannot tear my gaze away.

Tinley fires three more bolts, and the sky around her opens farther. Her falcon swings around, leaving a circle of clear blue. As Tinley arms her crossbow to shoot again, the gaps in the clouds collapse to a gray wall. In seconds, her progress is reversed.

A thunderclap rattles straight to my feet. I shield my face from the lashing wind. Two soldiers hold down the hourglass timer. The sand is nearly half gone.

Thunder rages after Bya, but the falcon's wings slice through the gray. As Tinley and Bya drag a ribbon of blue across the stormy abyss, a lightning bolt strikes. Bya dips, and Tinley slides out of her saddle. The crowd gasps. I lay my hand over my mouth in alarm. Gripping the mahati's neck, Tinley struggles back into her seat and steers Bya directly into the storm.

With her feet planted in her saddle, Tinley stands and releases bolt after bolt into the massive thunderhead. The bolts bring along with them a flash of cleansing winds. The zipping gusts sweep across the sky, dicing up the storm and opening the firmament to mellow blue.

Bya banks right and then flaps her wings, pushing away more of the perilous clouds. The sand timer is nearly finished. *They're going to make it.*

Tinley stands in the saddle with her crossbow armed. She and Bya streak upward into the last thunderhead, and a lightning bolt strikes down. An earsplitting scream fills the sky.

The falcon is falling. Twisting. Turning end over end for the land. Tinley holds on to Bya's back, trying to rouse her. But the great falcon is in a free fall.

The spectators go still. Sultan Kuval's mouth opens in shock, stunned by the sight of this mighty bird spiraling to her doom.

"Do something!" Ashwin shouts.

Opal and Rohan run into the field and stretch out an airstream between them. The swirling vortex smacks my face with brisk gusts. The two position themselves under Bya and throw up their wind. Like an invisible net, the swelling current catches the falcon and slows her fall. Opal and Rohan dig their heels into the ground and slowly lower their arms, bringing the bird and her frightened rider to safety.

Bya lands in a heap of fiery feathers. Her outstretched wing tip splashes in the lagoon.

Tinley hops off the falcon and peers into her glassy eyes. "Bya!"

The falcon does not respond; her wing smokes where the lightning struck. Indah rushes in and lifts a whip of water from the lagoon. She tosses the airborne stream at the falcon's wing, dousing the last of the embers. The Paljorians cry mournful sobs that bruise the soul.

Tinley wraps her arms around the falcon's neck, burying her teary face in Bya's feathers. The sky has returned to blue, mockingly so. No thundercloud or lightning can be seen on any horizon.

Indah slides her healing hands over the bird's injured wing. "Water bless the sky. Sea reflect the clouds. Blue of the sky shine in the heart of the sea."

She repeats the healing prayer, and each time she finishes, my despair grows.

Ashwin goes to Tinley and touches her back. She cries with her face in her hands. He turns her around and enfolds her in his arms. She lays her face against his chest, sobbing so hard her hair shakes like wheat stalks rippling in a breeze. Ashwin seeks me out with wet eyes and holds Tinley tighter.

Overhead, a rain cloud gathers and pours lightly over them, a patch of misery in an otherwise cheerful sky. Finally, Indah stops her strings of prayers and steps back from the falcon's injured wing.

Citra shields Tevy's face from the devastation, gripping her sister against her. A silent tear runs down Citra's cheek. She brushes it away before anyone else sees.

Sultan Kuval saunters over to me and slicks down his white mustache. "Tinley failed to complete her trial," he says.

"Have you a heart?" I hiss. "She's lost her best friend."

"She has also lost the tournament. Should you fail as well, Citra and Indah will move ahead to the duel, and your people will be one day closer to better living conditions and remedial care."

His bribe sets my teeth on edge. "I won't fail my trial on purpose."

"I didn't imply you should. I'm merely providing you consolation for when you *do* fail." He strolls away pompously, his hands tucked behind his back.

I glare past him at bamboo-woven riverboats drifting upstream into the lagoon. The bows and sterns of the long, narrow vessels curve out of the water with a regal rise. Gold leaf covers the sides of the first canoe, the imperial boat.

Sultan Kuval lifts his voice. "We'll now adjourn to the riverboats for Kindred Kalinda's trial."

One by one the audience members flock to the water's edge. Citra parts from her sister, leaving Tevy to return to the palace with her eunuch guards. The Paljorians stay with their competitor. Tinley pulls away from Ashwin and clings to Bya, weeping into her side.

I walk toward them. Bya is even bigger up close, her fiery feathers breathtaking. My heart wrenches hard. I cannot believe this guardian of the sky is gone. I stop beside Ashwin and Tinley, press my palms together in prayer, and dip my chin.

"May Anu welcome Bya to the Beyond, and may she find peace and contentment flying the forever skies."

Tinley's swollen eyes take me in with reserve. I bow in farewell, and Ashwin and I leave her and her people to mourn.

Ashwin helps me board a riverboat beside Rohan and Opal. As our boatman paddles us out of the lagoon and down the narrow waterway, I stare at Tinley clutching Bya.

If she can fall this far, I can too.

Our boats slide down the stream, out from under the low-hanging trees and into Iresh. We glide past bamboo huts and those people along the water's edge. They wave when they see Sultan Kuval and Princess Citra. Soon their cheers draw a large crowd, until the muddy banks are packed shoulder to shoulder. Some run alongside us, matching the speed of the parading vessels.

The waterway widens and empties into the River Ninsar. Spectators gather along the waterfront between rows and rows of bobbing fishing boats. Our vessel drifts into an open slip, and Rohan jumps off to tie the line. Ashwin and I follow Sultan Kuval to the end of a dock. There a gong and sand timer wait. Bhuta guards are stationed along the riverside, and a dinghy is tied to the end of the pier. Out farther in the river, a barge is buoyed. I swap a questioning glance with Ashwin—*What are we doing here?*

"We've come to our final trial of valor for the day," says the sultan. "Kindred Kalinda will now represent the fire-god Enlil, Keeper of the Flame."

I join the sultan's side, my back to the river.

"Due to the dangerous nature of the kindred's powers, her trial will be held here. At the sound of the gong, we will release a burning arrow to light the barge in the middle of the river on fire. She will have five minutes to row out to the barge and extinguish the flames. The boat is tied to buoys that are anchored to the riverbed to ensure it does not drift away. Aquifiers are on standby should there be any danger of the fire spreading to shore."

Thorny fear rakes at my belly. They want me to tame nature-fire. I coaxed an ember into a flame once, but that hardly qualifies me as a master Burner.

Ashwin comes to my side. "Kalinda, you don't have to do this."

"True, Prince Ashwin," the sultan says loudly. "The kindred may concede."

The onlookers whisper to each other. They must think I am a monster *and* a coward.

"I'll go."

I lay down my khanda, climb into the moored dinghy, and pick up the oar. The sultan gestures toward shore, and a guard there lifts a bow. Another soldier lights the pointed end of the arrow on fire. With the tip burning, the arrow flies out over the water and strikes the flat-topped barge. Flames overtake the boat, and trepidation blazes through me.

Ashwin leans over me from the dock above. "Have you lost all sense?"

"This is why you brought me here, isn't it? This *is* the trial tournament."

"Gods, Kalinda," he says, terror shaking his voice. "I'll give you your freedom. Just don't do this."

"I'm not doing this for my freedom. I'm doing this for the empire."

The second I utter the words, they are true. I am kindred to the Tarachand throne, and our people must come first. Before my needs, and even before Ashwin's. Everyone I love has been affected by the empire's divide. Brac and Mathura are stranded at the border, and Deven and Yatin are imprisoned. Deven predicted this moment was coming long before I did. He saw what I must do to free us. I can play the sultan's game. I can face fire for Deven and the others I love. I can set aside my fear for my people. I can—I *must*—fight for peace.

The gong sounds, ringing down on me.

Ashwin says the Prayer of Protection. "Let the sky lead you, the land ground you, the fire cleanse you, and the water feed you." He unties the dinghy from the dock and tosses me the line. As I paddle out, he stays crouched on the dock, his troubled gaze watching me go.

Spectators observe me from the waterfront, drawn from their huts by the smoke and light of the fire. A few boat lengths later, the heat of the inferno hits me. I stop rowing and slip over the side of the dinghy into the cool river. The small boat bobs away. I swim the final distance to the barge and hoist myself up on deck.

Flames flicker over everything, slithering tongues of yellow, orange, and red. A burning segment of the wheelhouse breaks off and splashes in the water. The fire hisses like a disturbed den of vipers and then extinguishes to smoke. I am tempted to jump back into the water, but the memory of Brac's last lesson stops me.

You have nothing to fear. You are fire, and fire is you.

All fire starts with a spark. A tiny ember like the one I cajoled to life in the temple ruins. I brought fire life—maybe I can take it.

I push to my feet, heat singeing my face and hands. I close my eyes and search for my inner star. A single, perfect light in a velvet night. Brighter, bigger, hotter than nature's flame.

Summoning my soul-fire to protect me, I open my eyes and stretch out my hand. My fingertips touch the yellow rim of the fire. Instead of pulling back, I pull the heat in. The flame unravels from the blaze and twists around my finger, dancing like a child around a campfire. I watch the flame coil down and link together on my hand like a ring. Fear eludes me. We are made of the same essence. I am fire, and fire is me.

The flames spread at my back, blocking my way to the water.

Don't panic. They're friends too.

No, not friends. Servants.

I am the greater fire.

Water douses the flame, wind feeds the flame, land cups the flame, and I . . . I rule *the flame.*

I step forward, and the flames part in front of me, revealing a charred path. Smoke billows away, clearing a place for me to breathe. I enter the sea of fire.

Warmth slams my face and rises through my feet. My inner star shrinks from the wildness of nature's inferno, but my powers protect me like a shield. Another step, and more fire parts. I take one footstep at a time, charming the flames as I would a cobra.

Shh . . . I'm welcome here. We're the same.

At the center of the barge, the blaze surrounds me and shoots over my head like a halo. I cannot see the shore. Within the firestorm, where life ends and new life begins, the veins on my arms glow so brightly I *am* flame.

The fire forms into serpents, wingless dragons made of luminous tendrils. Their beauty transfixes me. I do not wish to part with this humming power, this reflection of my soul. But I must nearly be out of time.

I stroke a fingertip down a fiery dragon's long, scaly back. When I reach the tail, I pull my hand away and blow on the thread of flame ringing my finger. *Rest, dear one.* The flame vanishes to smoke. Now for the others.

I throw out my arms and the fire curls away, receding out of reach. I pursue the heat and exile more flames. They shrivel to a dusting of ash and embers.

Working in a circle, I shrink more flames, banishing them to cinder. As I blow out the last flare, on the far side of the barge, the blaze has nibbled down the taut ropes that connect the boat to the anchored buoys. The fire has nearly bitten its way through.

I hurry over to extinguish the burning ropes, and two things happen at once.

The gong rings, a muted bell of failure.

And the nearest rope snaps.

Instead of swinging back at the barge, the burning rope launches for land. Onlookers along the waterfront dart away from the blistering whip lashing the sky. The rope strikes several boats tied along shore, and the fire leaps onto the vessels. The Aquifiers on standby summon streams of water from the river and throw geysers at the early flames, but the blaze jumps from one wooden watercraft to the next, chewing up canvas sails. Within seconds, smoke hazes the breadth of the city dock.

The rope on the other side of the barge is still on fire. As I run for it, I trip on a burned hole in the deck and fall. The second rope snaps, flinging back at me. I duck, and it lands in the water. With my hands and face deep in ashes, the barge beneath me groans. The side where the ropes broke dips into the river. Water rushes up on deck, gushing my way. I search the surface for the dinghy, but it has drifted downriver. The fire-damaged deck beneath me begins to lift as the other half of the barge tips downward into the water.

Pushing to my feet, I scramble across the slanted deck. The creaking and groaning mount to a roar. As the floor buckles, I reach the bow and leap into the river. I submerge in the dark cold. Water becomes my sky and my land. A portion of the barge lands with me. I try to swim out of its path, but a fragment of broken wood tangles in my hair and drags me downward. The barge sinks nearby, sliding past me with deadly grace.

I cannot reach my hair to detangle my braid. I kick for the surface, but the debris is locked against my head, towing me under.

My lungs burn for air. I fight to wrench free . . . Darkness turns me inside out, filling my sight. I open my mouth to gasp, and water fills me.

As I choke, a hazy light materializes before me. A young woman floats closer from the deep, her white robe trimmed with pure light. I recognize her sweet face.

Jaya.

My best friend reaches for me, but I have no strength to gather her in a hug. Her arm passes around me, and she tugs my hair free.

"Swim, Kali," she says.

I paw through the water weighing me down. Jaya drifts away, fading into the deep. I strain to see her vanishing light.

She is leaving me. She is breaking my heart all over again.

I open my mouth to call to her, and a powerful current charges at me, dragging me away from Jaya's glow. I break the surface, and arms grasp me. A hand cups my forehead.

"Blood is water, and water is mine."

The water in my mouth and nose clears out, like raindrops wicked away by a beam of sunlight. I collapse forward, coughing. Indah holds me upright, both of us hovering over the river.

"Gather your strength," she says. "They need help onshore."

Indah floats us toward land on her mist. Smoke obscures the shoreline, and flames flash like glowing spikes. The fire runs the entire length of the city's waterfront.

We reach the muddy riverbank down from the dock, and Indah lets me go. I fall hard on my bottom, my legs and arms waterlogged. Indistinct shouts surround me. All of my senses are muddled.

Slowly, I comprehend Citra and a group of Tremblers are heaving dirt upon the flames and sinking the burning boats. Indah joins the Aquifiers dousing the blaze. Everyone rushes to stop the fire from spreading inland. I used most of my powers to extinguish the barge. But I grab what is left, don it like armor, and walk to the blazing boats.

A flame leaps at me. I throw my hand up, and it curls away like a disobedient dog's tail. I focus on the next flame, and the next, but I might as well be trying to catch fleas. This fire has more fuel than the contained barge fire; it is nearly impossible to get in front of.

My hands shake. I sink to my knees, preserving the strength to stand, and shrivel more flames. Several more return in its place. *I cannot win this.* My soul-fire is shrinking and weakening my shield. Heat breaks through, drying my lips. Smoke chokes me. I am drowning again, this time on flame's breath.

A breeze encases me, and I inhale sharply. Rohan stands at my side, summoning a clean wind that flows around us.

Indah comes into sight beside us, with Pons. She throws water, hissing flames to embers, while Rohan and Pons maintain breathable air. I collect the last of my soul-fire and command the fiery destruction to bow to me. The flames dip, kneeling at my feet. Citra crosses to us and stamps out the last of the blaze with a mudslide.

Rohan pushes away the smoky air with a slingshot of wind, and my eyes clear of the burning sensation.

Indah looks up at Pons and grins. "You have soot on your face." She taps his nose, and he grins at her.

Rohan stamps out cinders beneath his feet. I taste ash in my mouth and feel gritty soot inside my ears. Citra rests on a pile of rubble. Her usually flawless hair lies limp around her dirty face.

Opal's wing flyer swoops down from overhead. Before the craft comes to a full stop, Ashwin jumps off and runs to me. I meet him halfway, and he grabs me against him.

"I saw you on the barge." His voice is muffled, his mouth pressed to the side of my head. "You walked into fire."

"I guess I did," I reply, just as amazed at myself. "Are you all right?"

"I'm fine." He leans away, and his shock evolves to marvel. "When you vanished into the fire, I panicked. Then I saw you inside it, shining like a star."

"I'm glad you aren't hurt either."

Sultan Kuval marches up the shoreline, a fleet of soldiers at his heels. Citra clambers to her feet. "Kindred Kalinda!" the sultan shouts. "You are an abomination. Look what you did!"

More smoke clears, exposing the wreckage around me: the ruined boats and dock, half sunken and charred beyond repair. The reality of the sultan's blame silences any defense of my actions. Everywhere I go, I leave a trail of ashes.

"Disqualify her, Father," Citra demands. He would not guess that moments ago we were battling alongside each other to put out the fire. "She didn't pass her test."

"She did." Ashwin wraps his arm around me, and I lean into him. *Let them see us united.* "Kalinda's trial was to extinguish the barge fire. No one mentioned the buoy ropes."

Sultan Kuval roars. "This would not have happened if Kalinda weren't a—"

"I do hope you're going to say the aftermath of the fire would have been worse without the kindred's aid," Ashwin warns. "Anything else would be disrespectful, and after showing great valor by risking her life twice today—once to pass the perilous trial you forced upon her and again to save your city—she deserves your appreciation. Or if you cannot muster gratitude, at the very least you can manage silence."

Sultan Kuval sucks his bared teeth, and Citra's mouth falls open. Before they can utter another vile word, Ashwin pulls me closer, and we walk away.

21

DEVEN

Cries sound outside the tent. Yatin does not stir from his nap. He is like a hibernating bear; he can sleep through anything. I bat away more annoying mosquitoes and step outside.

Smoke billows over the city skyline. Not long ago, a thunderstorm came out of nowhere and drenched us. Yatin and I took cover in our tent, but my clothes are still damp from the rain. My suspicions double. These odd natural occurrences must have to do with the trial tournament.

On the hillside rank board, Kali's name remains, along with her three competitors. Is Kali up against her own kind? Do they know she's a Burner?

Bhuta prison guards jog past me. Apprehension quickens my pace as I follow them to the gate. Most of the guards file out. Only two bhutas stay behind—even the towers are empty. From the symbols on their yellow armbands, they are Tremblers, not Galers.

This is the chance I have been waiting for. I have memorized how many guards are on duty on average—twenty. How many prisoners—approximately five hundred. How many guards are bhutas—about half. The guards change shifts at noon and midnight. Twelve-hour stints mean they are worn out at the end of their watches. Tired men make mistakes.

I stride up to a man I sparred with the other day, the one who landed the hit to my mouth. My lip has mostly healed, but it hurts when I smile. Not that I have had much to smile about lately. I tug on his sleeve and lead him around a corner so we are hidden from the remaining guards.

"Have you seen Manas?" I ask.

"Last time I saw him he was sulking outside the sick tent."

"Go get him and then wake Yatin. Tell them to meet me by the latrine."

He reclines against the outer wall, in no rush to obey. "You aren't my captain."

I lean into his face and drop my voice to a growl. "If you bear any love for our homeland, you will do as I say." He cringes from me. "Go quickly."

The soldier rushes off, and I round the corner. The other men and guards are captivated by the plumes of smoke in the distance. I stroll past them to the deserted east end of camp. The latrine area is the only place I can guarantee privacy. But skies, it stinks.

While I wait, the smoke continues to pour into the sky and frustration builds inside me. I cannot shake the nagging worry that Kali is in trouble. I slam my fist against the high prison wall, wishing I had the power to knock it down. Kali is out there fighting, and I cannot help her.

The soldier I sent on my errand shows up near the tents alone. He shrugs and hurries off. Manas must have refused to meet me, and I doubt he woke Yatin.

Great gods, do I have to do everything myself?

I stalk to the opposite end of camp, my angry strides eating up the muddy ground. Manas sits cross-legged across from the sick tent, brooding. He has been waiting to see Eko, but only the sick are allowed inside. Ten more men have fallen ill since yesterday.

I prowl up to him. "Get up."

He sits forward, resting his elbows on his knees. I oppose violence as a means of garnering cooperation, but I do not have time for his snit. I grab him by the scruff of his shirt and haul him to his feet.

"Take your hands off me!" he says. I shove him into the dead end beside the sick tent and block his exit. "I don't have to listen to you."

He tries to skirt past me, but I hold him back. "I am your commanding officer, and I've had enough of your insubordination. Explain yourself. How did you escape Vanhi?"

"Brother Shaan brought me with him."

"How did you escape Hastin?"

He casts me a petulant glower. "What do you care? You left me."

"Are you working for Hastin?"

Manas scoffs harshly. "You're questioning *my* loyalty?"

I grab him by his shoulders and shake him a little. "Answer me."

"Hastin had his daughter winnow me." His upper lip curls in repugnance. "You don't know what it's like to have someone reach inside your body and take part of you away."

I release him, my hands falling at my sides. I have not forgotten the frosty emptiness I felt when Brac parched my soul-fire, but telling Manas I understand will only prove his spite. Manas has reviled bhutas since he was a boy, when a Galer killed his family and wiped out his village. He has acted out in fear and hatred since then.

"Bhutas are a disease," Manas drivels on. "Prince Ashwin believes they should be exterminated."

His mention of the prince sharpens my focus. "What do you mean?"

"Eko told me the last time Rajah Tarek visited the prince at the northern temple, they discovered his instructor was a bhuta. Upon the rajah's order, Prince Ashwin executed the filthy demon." Manas sneers at me. "I warned the prince that Kindred Kalinda is one of them."

"Lower your voice," I say, glancing around.

"You think I don't want to tell everyone she's a traitor?"

I grip Manas by the front of his shirt again but restrain from decking him. "Do not speak ill of our rani in my presence, Soldier. What did the prince reply?"

"He told me not to say anything. He said he would take care of it."

Manas would relish sharing specifics of the prince's promise to "take care of" bhutas with me, so this must be all he knows. I let him go and stalk out of the dead end.

Smoke plumes pour like a fountain of death into the distant sky. Prince Ashwin knows Kali is a Burner. Maybe he lied about his affection for her. Then why the tournament? If I am right about her competitors being bhutas, the prince will marry a bhuta regardless of whether or not Kali wins.

Unless the trial tournament is a ruse. But for what? Why did Prince Ashwin lure Kali here? What could he stand to gain from trapping his people?

The Zhaleh. Does the prince know Kali has the book? Did Brother Shaan tell him?

I stalk to my tent, my thoughts consumed by razor-sharp fears. I should be with Kali. My duty is to protect her. But that is not the worst of it. I love her. *I love my queen.* Yet I let my shortsighted jealousy of her marriage to Rajah Tarek come between us. I let *the boy prince* come between us . . . and perhaps my own insecurities. The fate of the empire is important but not more important than Kali. I throw open the tent flap and duck inside. Yatin is still sleeping. I jostle his shoulder.

"We have to go," I say in a low voice. "Kali's in trouble. I've been watching the guards' shifts. I think we can—"

Yatin rolls over. His face is red and his forehead slick with sweat. I press the back of my hand to his cheek. His skin is burning, and the pitch of his breathing is shallow. Yatin was well this morning. His appetite was less than usual, but he had no fever.

I slump down onto the ground. *We aren't going anywhere.*

On a muttered prayer, I step outside to call for a healer. Several banging noises draw my gaze upward. Civilians in the neighboring encampment are casting stones at the rank board. Kali's name remains on the list, but Tinley from Paljor has been taken down.

Vizier Gyan comes the other way, flanked by several bhuta guards returned from the city. "Captain Naik, come with us," says the vizier.

"Why are they throwing stones at the rank board?" I ask.

The vizier drops his voice so no other prisoners can hear. "The civilian refugees have learned that Kindred Kalinda has been lying to them. She's a Burner."

I hold myself perfectly still, my stomach pitching. Our people were taught to abhor bhutas, and now the strongest remaining symbol of the empire—their chosen contender in the trial tournament—is a Burner. Their enemy.

"Will you tell my men?" I ask, fearing a riot. The soldiers will rage when they hear their beloved kindred, their champion rani, has deceived them.

"We both know that would be unwise," Vizier Gyan replies. "Neither of us wants an uproar."

He does not have to convince me; I will protect Kali's identity for as long as possible. "One of my men has fallen ill. I need help moving him to the sick tent."

Vizier Gyan checks on Yatin and then calls two guards. Together we heave Yatin off the ground. He is so large we need a fifth man to carry him across camp.

Manas waits outside the sick tent. I pass by him while lugging Yatin inside. The ailing lie on bedrolls across the floor. My insides sour at the reek of vomit and excrement. As soon as we set down Yatin, the other men leave. No healer is here to ask after Yatin's condition. Maybe I missed him outside.

On my way to the tent door, Eko grasps my ankle. He lies on the floor, his color green and his beard crusted with dried vomit. He tries to speak, but his words are indecipherable.

I crouch down and tug his blanket up to his chin. "Lieutenant, you should rest."

Eko parts his chapped lips and groans, a painful cry of misery. The injustice of this soldier, who served dutifully for years, suffering without aid incenses me. Eko gave everything to the empire. What has the empire given him in return?

Eko drops his head to the side, struggling to breathe. I reach for him, and he clasps my fingers with the meaty hands of a seasoned soldier. I grip Eko tighter to tether him to mortality, but his nostrils flare, and his chest pumps hard to draw in air.

I have seen death before and heard the sounds of life's final struggles. The fish that flaps wildly against the bank. The struck deer that runs off with the arrow. Before death, everything becomes louder, faster. And then all falls silent.

"Stay with me, Eko," I say, but his grip weakens in mine. He gargles out one last exhale and goes still.

I pull away, sitting among the other ailing men. The Janardanians have the resources to help, yet they leave my soldiers to fester in their infirmity. Prince Ashwin is as much to blame as the vizier. He is doing nothing to stop the spread of illness and protect his people.

Great Anu, I don't know what to do. How do I fight this?

Vizier Gyan opens the tent flap. "Captain Naik, that's long enough."

I bow my head. "Gods, bless Eko's soul so that he may find the gate that leads to peace and everlasting light." After I finish the Prayer of Rest, I drape the blanket over his face. Stepping out, I face Vizier Gyan with clenched fists. "Where are the healers?"

"They're helping in the civilian encampment."

"My men are *dying* in this bug-infested cesspool. They need remedial care."

181

From across the way, Manas turns ashen. He stands up and calls, "Eko?" One of the guards pushes him back, but Manas shouts past him. "Eko!"

Men leave their tents to view the commotion, trickling in from all over camp.

"Tell them to return to their tents," Vizier Gyan orders. His guards begin to disassemble the onlookers.

I step closer to the vizier and drop my voice to a cold snarl. "You think you're weakening our ranks, but you're strengthening us."

"I'll give you time to think about who's in charge here before I have that word with you." The vizier signals to a guard. "Lock him up."

A Galer seizes me and pushes me out of the crowd. As I am forced away, the men glare at Vizier Gyan. Finally, they see that *I* am not their enemy here.

The hut comes into view, and my urgency rises. I have to send a message to Kali before I am locked away. Prince Ashwin said Opal and Rohan are listening to the happenings in camp, but so is Vizier Gyan. He will probably decode anything I say, regardless of how I conceal my meaning. Still, with what I learned from Manas about Prince Ashwin, I will not make this easy on him. This message is for Natesa and Kali, the people who care about Yatin and who will do something, not the useless boy prince. When we are almost to the cell, the right words come to me.

"Tell little lotus the bear is sick!" I yell.

"Shut him up," says Vizier Gyan.

The Galer grasps the back of my neck, and his invisible hand of power dives into my lungs. The air is sealed off from my mouth. I cannot breathe. My empty lungs burn for the sky. The Galer guard lets me go. I stumble forward into the cell and fall to the dirt, wheezing.

Vizier Gyan's shadow fills the doorway. "Defy me again, Captain, and I will grind your bones to dust." He slams the door and locks me inside. I curl up on the ground and wait for the agony of the winnowing to pass.

22

KALINDA

A warm bath does not rid me of the scent of smoke or wipe away the ghostly image of Jaya floating in the deep. Natesa leaves me alone with Opal to go and burn my clothes. Riddled with singe marks and holes from shooting embers, my sparring outfit is a total loss.

With hair damp from my bath, I stare at my untouched supper. I should renew my strength, but I cannot muster an appetite. Longing pangs through my chest like a lost echo. Did I really see Jaya? Or did I imagine her?

I did not dream up the aftermath of the fire. All those destroyed boats. All those frightened people glaring at me and blaming me for burning down their livelihoods.

Rohan slips inside my chamber. "Where's Natesa?" he asks.

"She'll be right back. Why?"

He shrugs and comes to the table. "Probably nothing. Are you going to eat this?"

"Help yourself."

He sits beside me and digs into my plate.

Natesa comes in with the empty laundry basket and spots Rohan eating my food. "That was for Kalinda."

"I told him he could have it," I say.

Rohan flashes Natesa a disarming grin and eats more papaya. He chews twice and then says, "I heard something strange today. Natesa, what does Yatin call you again? A nickname of some sort?"

"Little lotus," I reply.

Rohan takes a bite of flatbread. "That's what I thought. Would the message 'Tell little lotus the bear is sick' mean anything to you?"

I lock gazes with Natesa. She sets down the basket, her body tense. We puzzle through the message at the same time. Natesa is "little lotus," so "the bear" must be . . . My insides plunge.

"Who sent the message?" I ask.

"I'm not allowed to say," answers Rohan.

Natesa marches to him and snatches his plate away. "Tell us."

"Prince Ashwin said not to talk about what I hear in the camps. I couldn't find him, so I came here. I didn't think it meant anything, honest." Rohan reaches for his plate, but Natesa swings it away.

"Tell us everything," she demands, "or I swear to the gods I'll throw your supper out the window."

"Wait! Captain Naik sent the message. The sickness has spread to the military encampment. Some of the soldiers have fallen ill. One of them has died."

"Is it Yatin?" Natesa asks, near to breathless.

"He's alive but unwell."

She lowers the plate in disbelief. Two slices of papaya slide off to the floor.

Rohan takes back the dish before she drops it too. "No one's supposed to know. Prince Ashwin doesn't want anyone to panic."

My nerves crackle with alarm. "Is Deven sick?"

"I don't think so," Rohan answers.

Natesa presses her palm to her stomach. "We have to help Yatin."

"No, no, no." Rohan throws up his hands. "Didn't you hear me? No one can know I told you."

"Who else could have heard Deven's message?" I ask.

"Any Galer who was listening, I suppose," says Rohan.

By now, Vizier Gyan must know the meaning of Deven's message. Deven must be terrified for himself and Yatin. Why did Ashwin not tell me Yatin is sick or that the illness has spread to the military encampment?

"Kalinda, we have to go down there," Natesa insists.

"I don't think that's a good idea," I reply. "Any attempt to interfere could worsen the situation." We must find another way to help Yatin. A single solution comes to mind—but it will cost me. "Rohan, I need you to take me somewhere."

He casts a pining glance at his food and then drags himself to me at the door.

Natesa rushes to follow us. "I'm coming with you—"

"Stay here in case Ashwin or Brother Shaan comes by. Tell them Rohan is escorting me on a walk." I grasp her hands firmly. Natesa gnaws her lower lip. "I promise I'll help Yatin."

"Where are you going?" she asks.

"To visit a friend."

———⊰⊱———

Indah answers my first knock.

"May I come in?" I ask.

After a heartbeat of hesitation, she opens the door. Pons is seated at a table near the hearth, eating supper with her. The intimacy of their meal causes me to pause, but neither laments the interruption. He rises without complaint. Indah trails him with her gaze as he goes into the corridor to stand guard with Rohan.

"I apologize for interrupting," I say.

"We were nearly finished." Indah invites me to sit with her at the table in the chair Pons vacated.

The layout of her chamber is exactly like mine. Her trident is propped near the door, and a shell necklace hangs over the bedpost. Much of Indah is still a mystery, but after today at the river, being competitors is not all there is between us. We respect each other, and that is a firm enough foundation for trust.

"Thank you for what you did. I have to admit I was surprised."

Indah crosses her curvy legs. "We aren't enemies, Kalinda. We're competitors, but we're also both sister warriors. In Lestari, women don't turn their backs on each other."

"Did you . . . Did you happen to see anything unusual in the river? A light perhaps?"

She drops her head to the side in question. "No. Should I have?"

"No, I, ah . . ." I push aside my memory of Jaya's spirit. "That isn't why I've come. My people are falling ill in the encampments. One of my friends, a guard, is sick. Can you spare an Aquifier to care for him?"

Indah leans back in her seat. "I'm willing to help, but the datu's aid isn't free. You know what he'll ask for in return."

"I do, and after seeing all four bhuta powers work together to put out the fire, I believe the Zhaleh will be safer with Virtue Guards. Tell Datu Bulan that once the tournament is over, I'll go to Lestari with you and bring the book to him myself."

Indah lays her palm flat on the table, taken aback. "I—I will tell him."

"Do you know I speak the truth?" I ask, and she nods twice in succession. "Then you know I'll honor my word. Please, send a healer to Yatin right away."

"I'll offer our services, but I cannot guarantee the vizier will accept."

"I understand and will appreciate any effort you make."

Indah runs her fingers up and down her water cup and studies me. "Your people in the civilian encampment saw the smoke over the city and asked about the fire. The guards told them you're a Burner."

I go still, my chest screwing tight.

"Your people responded . . . unfavorably." Her voice holds no delight but sympathy. "They threw stones at the rank board to strike down your name."

Her words wallop me like the stones my people cast. *I knew this could happen. Tarek taught them to hate bhutas. Hate me.*

But the people loved me. I was their champion.

I was an imposter, a treacherous kindred who murdered their rajah and hid behind the warlord's insurgence.

I was trying to help. I didn't mean to hurt them.

The outcome is still the same. They are suffering due to me. Yatin is sick thanks to me. I am fire, razing everything in my path.

I bury my regret and stand to leave. "Please inform me of Yatin's condition as soon as you hear."

"You've made the right decision." Indah boosts her assurance with a taut smile. "This is best for all our people."

I am no longer in the position to determine what is good for anyone. I have been wrong too many times. It would be arrogant of me to assume I can watch over the Zhaleh as well as four Virtue Guards. The book is better off in Lestari, far away from me.

Prince Ashwin is not in his chamber, but Opal rests on the lounge. I dismiss Rohan to finish his supper and settle in to wait for the prince's return. Books are still scattered about Ashwin's room, piled on every surface. I scan the religious texts and notice *Enlil's Hundredth Rani* among them. A shiver runs down me, as I think of Tarek's belief that I am Enlil's rani reincarnated. With the revelation of my powers, I doubt our people believe I am the dead favored queen now.

I turn my attention to Opal. "When will the prince return?"

"I don't know," she says, sitting up and stretching from her nap. "He's gone to request more aid for the encampments, but after today . . ." I grimace and slide my gaze away from her. "Kindred, the dock fire wasn't your fault."

The people of Iresh don't think so.

"Please don't call me kindred," I answer softly.

Opal sighs at my back.

Ashwin comes inside and slams the door hard. "Opal, find Brother Shaan and—" He notices me, and his whole body slumps, shedding his anger. "Kalinda, I didn't know you were here."

"May I have a word, Your Majesty?"

His chin ticks sideways at my use of his formal title. "Of course. Opal, you're excused."

I wait for Opal to leave and close the door before I speak. "Why didn't you tell me the illness has spread to the military encampment?"

"I heard about it upon our return from the river and went to the sultan straightaway. I waited two hours for a ninety-second meeting with him." Ashwin runs a frustrated hand through his disheveled hair; he looks as though he has been doing that for hours. "Kuval refuses to increase his aid. All of his help is going to the ailing civilians. He thought that's what I'd want."

"Is it?"

"I wish I knew." Ashwin unbuttons his jacket with swift jerks. "The Galers' constant wind wards off the mosquitoes, but people are still falling ill. The death toll has risen to fifty. Children are among them." He removes his tunic jacket, revealing a thin undershirt, and tosses it onto the bed. The jacket slides off and falls to the floor in a heap. Ashwin grips the back of a chair to steady himself. "The sultan told me he closed his border to more refugees. He says our people are safer there, but they're *my* responsibility."

I share his dissatisfaction. I hate not knowing if Brac and Mathura are all right. "Indah told me. She also said the people know I'm a Burner. They reacted as I feared."

His voice softens some. "They'll come around once you win the tournament."

I find no deception in his reassurance. He believes the people will adore me, or perhaps he cannot comprehend how they could *not* adore me.

I pick up his jacket from the floor and hold it close. "You're already more a rajah than Tarek ever was."

"*You* will make me a better one." Ashwin steps to me and lays his fingers over my almost-faded rank mark on my hand. "You give me the strength to stand up for myself and our empire."

Knowing it is dangerous to hope, I push out my squeaky voice. "Did you mean what you said on the dock about setting me free?"

"You've been free since Rajah Tarek died." Ashwin squares himself to me, his stare insistent. "I spent my childhood trapped in one room; I will not trap one person to me for the rest of her life." His finger strokes mine. "I ask the gods every day why I was born into this disaster. I didn't choose this fate either, Kalinda."

"Rajah Tarek—"

"Chose you out of hundreds of temple wards. He could have had anyone for his final rani, but he saw something in you. Tarek may have been flawed, but in this he was completely inspired." Ashwin's gaze meanders over my face, savoring every feature. "All I ask is that when you look at me, you see *me* not Tarek."

"I do see you, but there's more to consider."

"You mean love," he replies, lowering his forehead nearer to mine. His velvety-brown eyes engulf my sight. "I have no experience with women, so I cannot convince you that my affection is real. But I can say that we will rule as equals and achieve great good together. Promise me you'll think about it."

His lips hover over mine, taking nothing. He has given me a choice—more than I have ever had—but everything I do leaves a ripple. I cannot tiptoe across the pond of life without leaving huge, life-changing wakes. I must stop thinking of what was or what I hoped would be. Deven let me go. I should quit holding on to something that no longer exists.

I have been running since I left Vanhi, running from Hastin, from Anjali, from my mistakes. My time running stops now.

"I promise," I say.

Warmth fills Ashwin's expression. He turns his head and brushes his lips against my cheek, a whisper of a caress. "I understand your heart won't change overnight, so, for now, consider what's best for the empire." Fervent intent coarsens his voice. "I will do anything for the good of my people."

A scalding tremor skitters down my spine. Ashwin's fervor reminds me of Tarek's. I am uncertain which is more troubling: my nightmares of Tarek or the part of him that I discern in his son.

23

DEVEN

In the middle of the night, as I am falling asleep, two large men grab me from my cell and lead me to the guardhouse.

Vizier Gyan is seated within at a writing table that faces the door. He jots something down in a book and waves at an empty chair without looking up. I enter and sit across from him. The walls are barren, though hung over the desk is an ornamental imperial khanda with a beryl-jeweled hilt. The writing table is organized to perfection, not an ink quill out of place. In case the vizier is observing me, I steal glances at the stocked armory in the corner, a lock dangling from the closed door. Khandas. Crossbows. Machetes. Enough weapons for a small army.

The vizier shuffles his parchments aside, squaring the corners into precise angles. My interest turns to a book before him. Runes I cannot read mark the cover. More experienced brethren of the Parijana faith can understand runes, but I did not study with the Brotherhood long enough to interpret them myself.

"Captain Naik," he says, lifting his chin. "Now that you've had time to contemplate your place here, I have some questions for you. How close are you to Kindred Kalinda?"

I hesitate. Why ask me about Kali? "I am—*was*—her guard, sir."

"She broke into your cell on your first night here because you *were* her guard?"

"I cannot speak to her reasoning."

Vizier Gyan clasps his hands in front of him, his sleeves inching up slightly. He wears his usual long-sleeved tunic jacket with untailored cuffs. Odd. He is fastidious about the orderliness of his writing desk, yet his sleeves hang too long. "Prior to my telling you, did you know she's a Burner?"

"I . . . I'm not sure I understand. Do these questions pertain to the trial tournament?"

"I'm conducting the questioning, Captain." The vizier reclines in his chair, casual in his control. "Did you know Kindred Kalinda is a Burner?"

His surliness when he says "Burner" makes me wish Brac were here to singe his nose hairs. "Yes."

"Did she conspire with the bhuta warlord Hastin to murder Rajah Tarek and infiltrate the Turquoise Palace?"

"No."

"Then why did she run from Vanhi?"

"As you said, Hastin and his rebels invaded the palace. She feared for her life and ran."

"*After* she killed Rajah Tarek," he says. My eyes expand in shock. "You needn't protect her. I know she covered her body in poisoned lotion and seduced Tarek to his death."

My gut turns to serrated ice. Who did he hear this from? I never questioned Kali about her wedding night or let the details enter my mind. I cringe at the image of her with Rajah Tarek in *that* way. "I cannot speak to rumors, sir."

"Sultan Kuval's first-ever wife, my *sister*, was killed by a Burner. My brother-in-law believes Kalinda is inherently evil. Like fire, she's driven to destroy. Yesterday, during her first trial, she burned down our docks. Two innocent fishermen lost their lives."

I steal a moment to absorb this. Kali would never intentionally hurt anyone, but her actions tend to inadvertently cause trouble.

Vizier Gyan rests his forearms on the table. "Have you had any contact with the kindred since the night she came here?"

"No."

"One of the Lestarians came to my gate this evening and offered his healing services to your man, Yatin. Your little outburst about 'the bear' reached someone."

Praise Anu, Kali or Natesa heard my message and arranged help for Yatin. "I don't know what you're talking about."

Vizier Gyan exhales an irritated breath at my buttoned smirk. "Captain, why did Prince Ashwin absolve you of treason?"

"I don't know." I wrestle the urge to shift in my chair. The vizier is trying to rile me. I have employed the same tactics while interrogating soldiers, poking at them until I find the one weakness that becomes their downfall.

Vizier Gyan purses his lips thoughtfully. "Are you aware of how close Prince Ashwin has become with Kindred Kalinda?" I force impassivity into my expression. "They spend a lot of time alone together. Yesterday morning she was seen leaving his bedchamber in her nightclothes."

"Is that a question?" I ask coolly.

"Kalinda is endeavoring to wed the prince."

"She's his for the taking. He has first rights to her."

Vizier Gyan's smile twists. "Does that anger you, Captain?"

I lock my jaw. Any response I give will be warped and used against me.

"You met the kindred at the Samiya Temple where Rajah Tarek claimed her and escorted her from the temple to Vanhi. There, you were instated as her palace guard, and, later, you were accused of spending the night with her. You were sentenced to execution, but she freed you from the dungeon and helped you escape. You returned for her the very same evening Rajah Tarek was killed."

An itch starts at the back of my mind. Where did he hear this from? "Your informant has it wrong. If I was of value, would I be here while the kindred is out there, as you said, endeavoring to wed the prince?"

"I don't care so much who weds the prince. I'm more interested in an item the kindred stole from Vanhi."

He's after the Zhaleh. I should have guessed from his circling questions that he has no interest in Kali but in what she is protecting.

"You were caught with the Zhaleh and sentenced for treason," he presses. "Where is it?"

"I don't know. Rajah Tarek had the book for years. It must still be hidden in Vanhi."

Vizier Gyan's stare turns frigid. "The kindred gave me the same answer, nearly word for word."

"Then it must be true," I retort. "Hastin could have it."

"Captain, we both know the warlord doesn't have the Zhaleh."

I narrow my eyes at Vizier Gyan. Has he been speaking with Hastin? Is the warlord the one who fed him information about Kali and me?

"Tell me where the Zhaleh is, and I'll release you to the kindred," he says.

I would like to comply with him more than I will allow myself to consider. "I don't know where it is. That's the truth."

Vizier Gyan inclines forward in his chair. "Day after tomorrow, the final two competitors will duel in the arena, and my offer will expire. I need a better answer by then."

"My answer will be the same, *sir*."

"All right." He musters a cryptic grin. "You may return to your housing."

The guards lead me to my tent; the other men are already asleep. I lie down beside Yatin's empty bedroll and listen to the buzzing mosquitoes. I need to warn Kali about the vizier's interest in the Zhaleh, but I cannot chance sending another bizarre message Gyan can easily decode. The prince's suspicions about the sultan were correct. Regardless of the tournament's outcome, I doubt Sultan Kuval will allow Kalinda, a Burner, to retain her throne and free us.

The only way my men and I will escape this prison is by fighting our way out.

24

KALINDA

I wake in the middle of the night to the sound of ragged breathing. A startling awareness barrels down on me. I am not alone. My bedchamber is dark, my doors to the balcony closed. A soupy thickness clots the air. The darkness presses down upon me like an iron curtain.

Something brushes past the side of my bed. My heartbeat hammers inside my skull. When Jaya appeared to me underwater, she was light, true, and warm. This is the antithesis—a pressing, cloying chill. I experienced this pervading despair one other time, in Ki's throne room.

I slip my hand under my pillow for my daggers. Whatever is here exhales across my face. Its breath smells of rubble and ruin, loss and sorrow. The scent permeates my senses, squeezing my heart and spinning my mind into places I never wanted to return.

I am blindfolded in the Claiming chamber.

Rajah Tarek inspects me, a predator circling his prey.

An invisible force tugs at my hair. I grasp one of my daggers, but the backs of my hands burn, and I drop it.

Don't test me, love, says a voice directly over me.

The words are Tarek's, but the tone is different, a raspy hiss.

"Who are you?" I ask shakily.

Its breathing stays over my bed, blowing the scent of charred rubble across my cheek. *Your husband. Have you forgotten me already?*

Two blue eyes appear above me, burning like azure flames. I twist to reach my daggers, and when I turn back with blades drawn, the malevolent presence has disappeared.

I collapse against my pillow. Fears expand like a paper lantern inside me, strangling the remnants of a scream. I can still smell ashes and the char of burned skin.

And Tarek's spirit lingers, like an invisible chain forever linking our souls.

I hold myself still and grip my daggers close. They cannot cut the dark, but having them pressed over my thudding heart provides a comfort that almost convinces me I am safe.

The next morning, I receive instructions from Opal to go alone to the south gate of the tiger paddock. Natesa has been gone since I woke—she is probably off doing laundry—so I dress in my training clothes, braid my hair, and run out the door.

Raindrops sprinkle on my head as I turn down the dirt path. Citra and Indah wait for me at the gate to the paddock. Sultan Kuval stands off to the side, scowling at my late arrival. No one else is here but us.

"Today," he begins, "you will face a deadly opponent of your choosing in a test of fortitude."

"Is the weather part of the challenge?" Indah asks, holding out her palm to watch the raindrops patter on her skin.

"This is the start of the wet season, so you can thank Anu for the weather," the sultan replies. "As this trial is about fortitude, you may use your weapons, but you may *not* rely upon your powers." He holds up a vial of neutralizer tonic, water steeped and boiled with poisonous white baneberry and snakeroot.

"I won't take that," I say, repelled by the memory of the vile drink. I am not too keen to ingest anything Kuval would give me either.

The sultan's lips spread in a cutting smile. "You may concede the tournament and leave at any time, Kindred."

He'll never give up, will he? I widen my stance to prove that I am staying.

"I'll drink it first," offers Citra. She takes the vial from her father, swallows a swig, and passes it to Indah.

Indah sniffs the tonic and wrinkles her nose. "How long will the dosage last?"

"The effects will fade by tomorrow," answers Sultan Kuval.

Indah sips her part. I watch her closely for an adverse reaction, but she appears unchanged. She passes the vial to me.

I have not taken neutralizer tonic since I came into my powers. But seeing as the sultan gave the same vial of poison to his daughter and Indah, I drink my portion. I grimace at the bitter flavor, and immediately, my soul-fire shrinks, hunkering down like a cowering pup.

"When the gong rings, you will all enter the paddock and separate to find a package left for you—you will know yours when you see it. Retrieve your package, and deliver it through the gate near the tower at the far side of the paddock within ten minutes." The sultan lifts the door lever. "Be on watch. My tigers haven't fed in days."

The sultan's vague instructions acerbate my nerves. How are his tigers opponents of our choosing? I never volunteered to fight a man-eating cat.

A gong rings across the way, and the sultan opens the gate. I cannot see any spectators or tigers in the rain-soaked flora. Citra is the first inside, followed closely by Indah. I go last, and Sultan Kuval shuts the door on me, rapping my heels. Though he cannot see me through the fence, I glare over my shoulder at him and then face the rainy forest. My competitors are gone.

Ten minutes. Plenty of time to become a tiger's meal.

I creep through the underbrush and promptly lose sight of the fence. Raindrops glisten off everything, pooling at my feet and drenching my thin clothes.

A shriek nearby sets my hairs on end. I follow the sound about fifty paces and stop. Citra stands before me with her machete drawn, confronting a huge orange-and-black-striped cat.

The tiger growls and paces before a banyan tree. Above them, a girl hangs upside down from the branches. I blink to see her better through the rain. Citra's sister Tevy has been tied up in the tree. She is gagged, soaked, and shivering. Citra has to pass by the tiger to reach Tevy. I draw my blades and step forward to help her and her sister.

The tiger growls at me.

"Go away, Kalinda," Citra snaps.

I leave my gaze on the large cat. "I came to help."

"This is a competition, you dolt. Find your own package."

The sultan's instructions return to my mind. *Find a package left for you—you will know yours when you see it.*

My heart shrinks. If Citra's package is her sister, could mine also be someone I love? Praying Citra can help Tevy before the tiger helps itself to them both, I back away and run. I leap over roots and fallen logs, searching for anyone or anything familiar. I would call out, but what name should I shout? Is my package even a person?

As I am forced to circumvent a bamboo thicket, I come upon the far gate. A four-legged observatory tower butts up to the fence line. High above me, the spectators watch, a leafy roof shielding them from the rain. Ashwin sees me and scratches his nose . . . and continues to scratch. What is he doing? *He's pointing west.* That must be where I can find my package. *Gods bless you, Ashwin.* I revolve and sprint back into the trees.

Time flows like sand through my fist. I sprint the width of the paddock, my side aching. I spot the west fence through the foliage and slow. The trees thin to a grassy expanse, and in the middle, I spot Natesa kneeling, tied up and gagged. Nothing else is around her.

I step out of the trees. She shakes her head. At the same time, something hisses near my feet.

A dragon cobra bedded down in the high grass to escape the rain. A dozen more snakes hide from the weather in the protective grass between Natesa and me. The closest dragon cobra lifts its head and spreads its flat hood. *You will face a deadly opponent of your choosing.* The sultan meant the deadly thing we took from the Morass. I should have realized his meaning when I saw Citra with the tiger. But, gods' virtue, how can I defeat these vipers without my powers?

The dragon cobra beds down again to evade the rainfall. My time is running out, but I cannot rush and risk Natesa or me getting bitten. I harness my concentration and step forward on light feet. Slowly, so slowly my muscles ache and quiver, I tread carefully across the field.

The vipers express little interest in me as they take cover. *Thank Anu for the rain.* I am almost to Natesa when I nearly step on a camouflaged snake. I sidestep to avoid it, but the startled dragon cobra jerks its head up. After a tense, still moment, the agitated dragon cobra lies down in the grass again. I traverse the remaining distance to Natesa and cut her bindings free.

She yanks the gag from her mouth. "Have you lost your mind? Why didn't you burn the vipers into their next life?"

"I don't have my powers for this trial."

"Buzzards," she curses. "How are we going to get out of here?"

"We backtrack the way I came." I hand her my second dagger and lead our way across the field, wary every step.

We arrive at the trees, and Natesa bends forward, panting. "I wanted to kill you while I waited in that field. I still want to strangle you, but I'm also happy to see your face."

"And I yours. We have to get to the far tower before the gong sounds. Let's go."

We race into the trees, jumping over heaving roots and dodging low-hanging branches. Mud puddles nearly unsettle our footing, but we make good time across the paddock. As I spot the peak of the observatory tower through the canopy, a scream comes from my right. I stop, and Natesa waves me forward.

"Come on!" she says.

"That could be Indah. You go to the gate. I'll meet you there."

"I don't think so." Natesa juts out her chin. "You're stuck with me."

I smile a little, astounded that being stuck with Natesa causes me gladness.

"Why are you staring at me like that?" she demands. "Do I have eye kohl running down my face?"

I take her hand in mine and squeeze. "You look perfect."

"All right," she responds, lifting a bemused brow.

I release my grip on her, and we sprint toward the origin of the scream. About a hundred strides later, we exit the trees to a pond. Natesa and I skid to a halt.

The water is alive. A monstrous crocodile thrashes its tail and splashes near the bank. Indah dodges its snapping jaws, defending herself with her trident. Above them, Pons is tied to a tree bough.

"Is it too late to change my mind?" asks Natesa.

"Distract the crocodile. I'll help Indah."

Indah stands up to her ankles in the water, helpless in what is typically her domain. I slosh into the pond to her. She eludes the crocodile's lunge and bumps into me. We fall into shin-deep water and then push to our feet and run for the bank.

"Watch your step!" Indah cries.

Another crocodile rises up from below the surface. Indah and I stand back to back, each facing a reptile sliding closer. *They're smiling at us.*

Natesa swings down from a tree on a vine, a broken branch in hand, and whacks one of the crocodiles on the head. The monster slips back into the pond and disappears. On Natesa's backward swing, the other crocodile bites down on her bough and pulls her into the pond beside us. She lifts the branch like a staff.

"Get Pons," I tell Indah.

She wades out of the waterhole. While Indah climbs the tree to Pons, Natesa holds the crocodile at bay by swinging her branch. I keep an eye for others, guarding her blind side. Indah reaches Pons and cuts him free, and they clamber down. As they run for us, a smaller crocodile bursts from the water and snaps at them, catching Indah's foot. The Aquifier falls to the ground, trapped in its jaws. Pons picks up her trident and stabs the crocodile through the head with the three pointed ends.

Natesa and I retreat from the bigger crocodile, edging over to them. Pons lifts Indah into his arms. Her ankle is a bloody mess. I yank the trident from the dead crocodile, and Natesa guards our retreat.

In the cover of the trees, I guide the way to the gate. We have to hurry to beat the timer and get Indah to a healer, but carrying her over the uneven terrain slows Pons.

"Go on," he calls out, cradling Indah closer. "We'll be right behind you."

Her foot drips blood, and the color drains from her face. Pons will care for her, but leaving them feels wrong. She saved my life.

Natesa tugs my arm. "Kali, come on."

"We'll send help," I promise Pons.

I vault over roots and duck under branches, pushing myself faster than before. Natesa and I clear the trees. The lookout tower is ahead. Guards open the gate, and the crowd in the observatory gasps. A tiger appears down the way. Natesa beelines through the gate. I pause, gripping the trident and waiting for Indah and Pons.

Come on. Come on. Come on . . .

"Kali, get in here," cries Natesa.

The tiger prowls toward me. The guards wait anxiously to shut the gate, but I cannot leave Indah and Pons to emerge into the pathway of the tiger. I pace away from the gate, parallel to the fence, and the guards close my exit.

Pons crashes out of the foliage with Indah. The tiger whips its head around and snarls.

"Over here," I call at the cat, waving the trident.

The tiger returns its eerie yellow eyes to me and slinks nearer. From the corner of my vision, Pons strides closer to the gate. I hold the wildcat's attention, wishing I had my powers so I could singe its whiskers and give it a fright.

Pons and Indah arrive at our exit. The guards open it, and they slip through to safety.

I shuffle back the way I came, getting closer to the fence to avoid the tiger's steady prowl. When I am paces away from freedom, the great cat maneuvers a step ahead of me, placing itself between me and my escape route.

The gong rings, signaling the end of the trial.

I think nothing of it or of the blasted competition. I hold the tiger's golden gaze, staring into feral hunger, and jab the trident at the beast. I do so repeatedly, stepping cautiously with every stab, until I reach the gate.

Guards stand ready with armed bows. Another guard opens the door slightly. I nudge up to the divide. The tiger spreads its whiskers and growls. The door opens wider. A hand grabs the back of my clothes and pulls me through. I fall backward, and the guard slams the gate shut. The archers release arrows around the tiger, spooking it, and the cat runs into the trees.

Natesa drapes a blanket around me. "You like to scare the sky out of me, don't you?"

"How's Indah?" I ask, bending over to collect my breath.

"She'll be all right. Pons carried her off to see another Aquifier."

The spectators start down the stairs from the observatory tower. Sultan Kuval arrives on the landing first, and behind him follow Citra, wearing a gloating grin, and Tevy wrapped in a blanket.

Sultan Kuval stands over me and speaks, his voice like thunder. "Kindred, you failed to complete the trial in the allotted time frame and are hereby disqualified."

"What?" I clutch my blanket closer. "The assignment was to deliver my package to the gate in time. Natesa was out of the paddock before the gong rang."

Citra gives a quick, dismissive snort. "The instructions were to pass through the gate *with* her."

My gaze darts from Citra to the sultan. "I don't remember that rule."

"What you heard or didn't hear is no longer our concern," Kuval rejoins. "You're out of the tournament."

My mouth gapes open, hoping I have heard them wrong, but the sultan and princess loom over me with mocking smirks. I drop my head to conceal my gathering tears.

I'm finished. I'm really out of the tournament.

Ashwin comes down from the tower with Tinley and sees me sitting in the rain. "What's the concern here?" he asks.

"My sincerest regrets," says the sultan, his tone anything but genuine. "The kindred failed to reach the gate before the allotted time and has been eliminated from the tournament."

"Sultan Kuval," Ashwin says, drawing out his name with exaggerated patience, "we all saw what happened. Kalinda arrived with Natesa on time."

"But the kindred did not pass through the gate with her servant, as was the rule." The sultan seals his decision with a perfunctory jiggle of his double chin.

Ashwin extends a hand to him in appeal. "If you would please consider—"

"The rules stand. Indah and Citra will compete in the final trial. Tomorrow we will hold a rank duel at the amphitheater, and they will battle for your first wife's throne. We will reconvene then." Sultan Kuval thrusts out his thick chest, collects his daughters, and directs them away.

Ashwin's shoulders and head sag. He cannot go against the sultan's ruling without invalidating the entire purpose of the trials.

Tinley steps up to me after witnessing our exchange with Sultan Kuval. "You're brave, Kindred. Your face-off with the tiger was compelling." Raindrops sparkle like crystals in her white hair. "I'm returning to Paljor before the worst of the wet season arrives. I'm having Bya brought home for a burial." Tinley trains her milky eyes on me. "Thank you for the prayer on her behalf. Let me know if someday I may repay you." She offers Ashwin and me a full, elegant bow and strides off.

Natesa kneels in the mud and hangs a loose arm around me. "You *were* brave."

"I couldn't leave Pons and Indah behind," I whisper. My chin trembles, and tears fog my sight. I am one kind word away from them pouring down my face.

Ashwin stands over us with his hands deep in his pockets, his expression bleak. "Kalinda—" His caring tone undoes me.

I press my face into Natesa's shoulder and cry.

25

DEVEN

The grave has to be six feet deep, the guards said. As quickly as we dig, the hole fills with rainwater. Even so, the three other diggers and I somberly shovel mud into a slippery pile while the guards observe our progress from under the eaves of a tent.

Why must we bury the dead in the rain? The Trembler guards could excavate a grave with the crook of a finger. But that would be too easy, and they are entertained, watching us labor.

Gradually, the hole deepens. I shovel alongside Manas and the other two men until the grave is finished. We lean our shovels against the outer wall, and a guard orders us to drop the bodies.

The deceased are wrapped in bedrolls, their stocking feet sticking out, since the guards stole their boots. I imagine Yatin's big feet hanging out of a bedroll and scrub away the miserable thought. I wish I had the power to heal him, but at least an Aquifier is tending to him. He will be all right. I repeat it to myself, *He will be all right.*

We roll the first body to the rim of the grave, sliding through the slick mud, and push the dead man over the edge. He hits the bottom with a splash. The next two men land with empty thuds that hollow out my chest. We reach the last man, and I recognize Eko's shape under the blanket. Manas stands back to wipe his face, wet from rain and tears. The rest of us heave Eko into the hole.

The guards command us to leave the grave open. I suspect the vizier anticipates the illness will claim more lives. The four of us stare down at our dead comrades in silence. I am the highest-ranking officer, and so it is my duty to offer a prayer.

I recite the Prayer of Rest while the others bow their heads. "Gods, bless our comrades' souls that they may find the gate that leads to peace and everlasting light." At the closing, Manas sniffles. On impulse, I add, "And let Eko know, wherever he may be, that he is missed."

The gong rings for midday meal. I squint up through the rain at the nearest tower. It's noon; shift change. The Galer on duty will swap places with a new one. Both men will be preoccupied for a couple minutes while the previous Galer gives his report.

The men set off for the dining tent, but Manas lingers at the grave site.

"I'd like to speak with you," I say.

"I have nothing to say to you."

Gods, grant me patience.

"I'm trying to prevent us from losing more comrades. Please, Manas. We don't have long. The guards will be eavesdropping on us again soon." He does not lash out with a rebuttal—progress?—so I go on. "I've been monitoring the guards and the gate. I have a plan to break out, but I need your help organizing the men."

"Why do we need to break out? The prince said we'll be released after the trial tournament."

"That's what Sultan Kuval told him, but I don't think the sultan means to let us go. Think about it. Would you release your enemies' soldiers into your imperial city?"

Manas goes quiet. I am taking a risk, confiding in him. The vizier's informer could be another prisoner in camp. Manas could be reporting to Vizier Gyan for Hastin, but the chance is slim. Manas hates bhutas. I cannot picture him serving one.

"When the time comes to leave here, we'll have to work together," I say. "I cannot do this alone, and if you back me, others will too."

"What if Kalinda wins?" Manas asks. "Aren't you afraid of her, of what her Burner powers can do?"

"I fear her the same way I do the gods—out of respect." Manas scowls at my explanation. He cannot separate his emotions so easily, but for this to work, he will have to try. "Helping me is helping the prince *and* Kalinda. Can you accept that?"

Manas returns his attention to Eko's body and answers with reluctance. "Tell me your plan."

"We need weapons, not those measly staffs, but blades. We'll start by disarming the bhuta guards right before their shift change. Fewer are here then, and they are tired."

Manas frowns at me. "How will we overpower the bhutas?"

Bearing in mind that this shift change is nearly over, I speak quickly. "The last tournament trial is tomorrow. I wager the duel will draw a big crowd, including Janardanian soldiers. The vizier will most likely cut back on the guards here, leaving fewer men to call for help. While the tournament is going, we can overwhelm the guards, gain access to the guardhouse, and open up their small armory. We'll use those weapons to get out the gate. I saw a larger weapons bunker between the two encampments. Once we break it open, we'll have all the khandas we need."

Manas rocks back on his heels with an incredulous look. "Then what?"

"We get our people and march out. They're better off heading back to Tarachand than dying here."

A guard without a yellow armband comes into view near the tents. Fortunately, I recognize he is a Trembler, although I am certain a Galer will be back on duty momentarily.

"You there," the guard shouts. "You're missing midday meal."

I speak to Manas from the side of my mouth. "Remember what I said."

As I stroll away, he shoves me in the back.

"Liar," he seethes. I reel around to face him, hurt tearing through me. He shoves me in the chest harder and pushes me back a step. "You think you have friends in the palace, but no one cares you're here. You're nothing to the kindred. Nothing." His malice winds me. Manas leans into my face and snarls. "Prince Ashwin should have whipped you to death."

"Break it up," the guard says, tugging us apart.

"Stay away from me," I order Manas, my voice unsteady, and then stomp ahead of him into the tents.

I slip between two tents and wait for my heart to stop exploding. I am a fool for confiding in Manas. This is the last time I let him betray me. Seconds later, he swaggers past and pretends not to see me, but a smirk graces his lips.

That son of a scorpion. He did not turn me in. He is on my side. His outburst was to throw off the guard. Still, his accusation that Kali does not care for me tore deep. Why hasn't she come to see me? Is it true she is fighting to wed the prince? Or is she firm in her conviction to free our people?

Movement on the hill draws my gaze upward to soldiers altering the rank board. The second trial must be through. The guards take down Kalinda's name, leaving Citra's and Indah's.

I blink rapidly, my optimism stuttering to a halt. Anu would not let Kali lose. Her fate is to save the empire. I sent her away so she could fulfill her godly purpose. She *cannot* lose.

Other men notice Kali's name has been stricken from the rank board, and their murmurs fan out through camp. Not knowing she is a bhuta, they express concern for their kindred. They know, like me, that Kali would not lose without giving everything she has to the competition.

Great Anu, let her be safe.

The devastated voices around me mount, the sound of hundreds of hearts collapsing all at once. I lower my chin, flexing my jaw muscles against rising tears. The Janardanians have stripped away more than Kali's name. They have stripped away our hope. The foreigner who wins the throne will not care for the good of our families.

"Captain Naik, your presence is requested in the sick tent."

Two guards wait before me. My chest crowds with panic. I can only think of one reason why they would call me to the quarantined area.

I hurry past them. First Kali and now Yatin? The gods would not be so cruel.

At the far end of camp, more sick tents have been erected and roped off. The white canvases are marked with deep-red crosses stained into the side with black currant juice. A man in a long blue tunic and shortened trousers waits outside a tent for me.

"Captain Naik," the stranger says, "I'm caring for Yatin. He's asked for you."

The healer opens the flap, and I duck inside. Improvements have been made since I was last here. Lanterns hang from the overhead bamboo poles, and mosquitoes swarm the lights like snow flurries in a blizzard. The tent is packed with men lying on floor mats. The sick cough and shake with chills. I crouch down over Yatin while he sleeps. Sweat coats his forehead.

"I've made him comfortable with a sedative," the healer explains. "He's young and robust, but he's very ill. You should be prepared for either outcome."

I can think of two outcomes, recovering or perishing, but I will only accept the first as Yatin's fate. The healer sets a basket of supplies down near us and goes to check on another patient. A familiar vial nestles within the basket—the neutralizer tonic that blocks bhuta powers.

The healer carries it with his remedies. I do not think. I pocket the vial and then take hold of my friend's hand.

"Yatin."

"Deven," he rasps. He sounds as though the desert is lodged in his throat. I reach for the ladle in a nearby water bucket and trickle a drink over his lips. Yatin opens his clenched hand to reveal a small silver object. "Give this to Natesa. Tell her I wish . . . I wish she could have met my sisters—" He breaks off in a coughing fit and drops the ring.

I pick it up and examine the lotus flower design on top. I cannot bring myself to consider the circumstances that would cause me to give Natesa the ring for Yatin. I push it back into my friend's palm. "Give it to her when you're better."

Yatin holds the ring out, his arm quivering from the exertion. "Please. Just in case."

My nose burns with restrained tears. *If I take the ring, it will make this real. And this cannot be real.* "You hold on to it. It'll remind you what's waiting for you when you're better."

Yatin closes his hand around the lotus ring and rests it over his heart. Wheezing on shallow breaths, he rolls his head to the side and rests. Yatin is strong, but what if the illness is stronger? What if his purpose is finished in this life and he is needed in his next?

His fist remains fastened around the ring. I am thankful that he has a tangible dream to hang on to. My thoughts pull in, recalling my own dreams, the life Kali and I envisioned together. What a dolt I was to let her believe I gave up on that, on us.

The healer signals from the door; my visiting time is spent. I pat Yatin's arm in parting. As I exit the tent, I slip my hand into my pocket. I have no pretty ring to hold over my heart, but I have the neutralizer tonic. I fasten my fingers around the vial and contemplate how this poison will help me get to Kali.

26

KALINDA

A hot bath washes away the mud but does not touch my numbness. I peel myself out of the cooling bathwater to dress, my wilted limbs drained of strength.

I have lost my throne. All this time I have thrashed and gnashed my teeth, trying to break free, but I am stripped bare of the only part of my life I was certain the gods had a hand in. The gods wanted Tarek to claim me. I fought that truth until I lost Jaya—and then I fought for her death to have meaning. I spilled blood to earn my throne. I held on to it with both hands as I searched for Ashwin. I wielded my rank against my enemies. I wore my nobility like a shield. I stood upon my throne to see into the future, dreaming of a better empire. Having my title taken is like tumbling down endless stairs. I am falling for an eternity, with no means of stopping.

You can turn to the Voider.

The errant thought sprouts from nowhere. I try to pluck out the terrible idea, but it grows roots.

The Voider can answer your heart's wish. It can set Deven and our people free from the encampments.

I shake my head, joggling the wayward thought away. I would never . . . And yet the temptation tests, teases, prods for an excuse to utilize the Zhaleh. Was Tarek led astray by the power of the Voider? Did it eat at his soul and rot his conscience?

Gods alive. I rub a sore spot between my eyes where a headache chips away.

One more day, and the trial tournament will be over.

One more day, and I can pass the Zhaleh on to the Virtue Guards.

One more day . . . and then what? The rank marks on the backs of my hands have nearly faded. I can barely see the number ones. What comes after they are gone?

I step out from behind my dressing screen, and Ashwin spins around.

"My apologies," he says. "I thought you were out." His cheeks flush upon seeing me in my robe, my damp hair hanging loosely down my back. He holds up my painting of the peacock. "I was admiring your artistry."

"I'm better with charcoals." I go to him and take back the painting.

"Will you show me?"

This is a ploy to raise my spirits, but I must admit, it is a good one. I settle on my bed and tuck a blanket around me. My powers have not yet returned from the tonic I drank before the trial, and I am cold. I pull my sketchbook into my lap. Ashwin sits beside me and watches me draw. When I finish, he inspects my sketch.

"She's beautiful," he says at last.

"Her name was Jaya. She was my best friend." I drew her soulful wide-set eyes and charming chin. What would she think of me losing my throne? When she saw me at the palace with Tarek, she said I was suited for the life of a rani. I hate to think that I have disappointed her, wherever her soul may be.

I set aside my charcoal stick and brush my fingertips clean. The soot has sunk into the lines of my skin, like my guilt over her death.

"I was thinking about your throne," Ashwin says, setting aside the sketch. "I see no reason why you should lose it completely."

"What do you mean?"

His blush deepens, but he maintains eye contact. "After I take my first wife, I may have more of them."

A laugh bursts out of me. "Are you asking if I'll be your *second* wife?"

"Only in name," he answers with all seriousness. "We would wed after I take my kindred. You would still be the one that I"—he swallows—"love."

I reel away from the enormity of that word. "Ashwin—"

"I don't need an answer now," he hurries on. "You have time to consider."

His earnestness astonishes me. I was not jealous of Tarek's other wives, and I would not be jealous of Ashwin's. But I have not been entirely honest with him. He says he wants to wed me, but he does not know what I have done.

"No matter what happens tomorrow, I would like you by my side." Ashwin leans in slowly, and instead of moving away, I go still. I am curious what will happen once our lips touch, if all it takes to fall in love is one kiss.

My thoughts jerk to Deven. Now that my throne is no longer mine, we can be together, yet Ashwin's proposal beckons me, tugging me closer. He can offer me something Deven cannot. Ashwin can give me a way to right my wrongs. Together we could rule the empire, unseat Hastin from the palace, and release the ranis and courtesans he has imprisoned. We could do a mighty good together, if I become his second rani.

My sketch of Jaya shines like a beacon in my side vision. I cannot fully avenge her death unless I ensure the empire becomes a peaceful place for everyone. Every person, bhuta or full-mortal, should have the opportunity to build the life they choose. I can enact change in the palace. As Ashwin's rani, I can make Jaya's dream come true.

The prince's lips meet mine. His kiss is tentative yet grasping with excitement. His arms come around me with unexpected might. His slight build holds strength, one not of size or heftiness but inner determination. A refusal to fail. My hands climb to his smooth-skinned jaw, and I wait for my breath to catch or my lips to tingle.

Ashwin's kiss is inviting, but it does not stir my heart. His kiss does not inspire dreams.

He sits back, his face rosy. His taste clings to my lips, neutral in flavor. Nothing about his touch entices me to seek out more.

He laughs breathily. "That was, ah . . ." He notices my reserved expression and sobers. "Did I scare you?"

What does he . . . ? Oh. He thinks his resemblance to Tarek upset me. Guilt throbs at my temples. I cannot have a lie between us any longer. His kiss may not inspire dreams, but his offer to take me as his wife is still a choice I need to consider for Jaya, for the people in the encampments, for those subject to the warlord's rule back home. Ashwin needs to understand who I am before either of us seriously contemplates a union.

I straighten and meet his gaze head-on. "Hastin did not kill your father," I state, articulating every syllable. "I did."

Ashwin goes motionless, except his face, which slackens in shock.

"I won my rank tournament so I could marry Tarek and avenge my best friend. He murdered Jaya, and I wanted him to pay." Hearing the conviction in my voice causes me to wonder if my revenge was warranted. What gave me the right to kill Tarek? Did I do anything except cause the empire more pain?

My explanation has caused *Ashwin* pain. He threads his fingers in his hair, abject in his acceptance of what I have done. "Why . . . Why did you lie to me?"

"I shouldn't have." Regret clogs my voice, making me sound small. "I was ashamed and afraid of what you might do. What you might think of me. I wanted to tell you, but Brother Shaan thought it best that you not know. He said you would trust me more."

"Lying to me?" His disappointment comes at me harder than if he railed.

"I thought the truth would be worse," I say, a weak excuse but true nonetheless.

"I haven't lied to you, Kalinda." His soft voice strains, his windpipe crushed by my betrayal. "I told you the truth from the beginning, even when it was difficult to share about my parents, even when I felt like a dolt for stating my feelings for you."

Ashwin gave me more than the truth, he gave me his trust.

"I'm sorry. I was wrong," I tell him.

He drops his head, removing me from his sight. "You think I take after Tarek and have no heart to break."

"No," I answer without hesitation. "I meant it when I said you're not like him."

Ashwin's voice rises with his gaze, both sharp and direct. "Yet you don't trust me. You still see him in me."

I flounder to reassure him. I cannot deny that I have seen portions of Tarek in Ashwin, attributes of an ironhanded ruler that unnerve me. If Ashwin looked like someone else, if he was anyone else's son, I would have been more apt to trust him.

His intense stare brightens with pain. "I didn't love my father, but I was foolish enough to love you."

I stretch out my hand to console him, but he pulls away and leaves, slamming the door. The echo of his angry parting lands heavy on my heart. I huddle my knees into my chest, cursing myself. Ashwin is innocent of Tarek's actions, yet I cannot work out how to separate the two.

Natesa edges in from her antechamber. "Is everything all right? I heard Prince Ashwin leave. He sounded upset."

I rest my chin on my knees, hugging them closer. "Ashwin offered to take me as his second wife. I told him I killed Tarek."

"That's an interesting answer to a marriage proposal." Natesa comes over and lies beside me on the bed, covering her legs with the blanket. "Do you want to wed Ashwin?"

"No . . . Maybe . . . I don't know. I want my *throne*." I groan at my indecisiveness. "That doesn't make sense."

Natesa contemplates my answer, the cozy ping of rainfall seeping in through the windows. "I used to wonder what it would've been like if I had been claimed as Rajah Tarek's rani instead of you, but the throne was always yours."

The gods intended that I be a rani, of that I am finally certain, but it infuriates me that they handpicked me to be the instigator of so much anguish. "I was the empire's downfall."

"You were our awakening." Natesa props on her side and captures me with her stare. "The empire was in a downward spiral. Rajah Tarek's rule was hanging by a thread. Whatever horrors follow you, you aren't responsible for his actions."

Her praise compounds my guilt. *Neither is Ashwin.* I hid the truth from Ashwin to protect myself, so our people would continue to believe that I was above Tarek's influence. But I am not untainted by Tarek. I am not wholly innocent in the dire state of the empire. And I cannot repair my mistakes that led to the collapse of Vanhi without Ashwin.

Natesa rolls onto her back and gazes up at the ceiling. "Priestess Mita used to say that the sky has two faces, day and night. But the night doesn't actually rule. Only when the sun turns its back on the world does night appear. You are light, Kalinda. You cannot turn your back on your godly purpose. Whatever choices you made, you made them with approval from the gods." She grips my hand in hers. "The sun may not be shining yet, but dawn's first ray is coming."

"Do you really believe that?"

Natesa sends me a wry smile. "Isn't our friendship proof enough of miracles?"

I snort a laugh and enfold her in my arms. "You're a good friend."

"I never thought I'd hear you say that."

"Neither did I," I say, pressing my cheek to hers. Natesa's face squishes in aversion at my affection, and I hug her harder. She half-heartedly pats my back in return, drawing another laugh from me.

The door opens, and Indah enters with Pons. Upon seeing Natesa and me together in a private moment, Indah pulls up short. "Should we come back?" she asks.

"No, come in." I am still in my robe, but I am past worrying about indecency. I am more concerned about how Indah is recovering. I climb out of bed and meet them in the sitting area. Pons helps Indah limp to the lounge. "How are you feeling?"

"I'm well, but it'll be some time before I can walk unassisted." Indah leans back in her seat, Pons standing behind her. "My people informed me that there was some confusion as to the rules of today's trial. I specifically recall Sultan Kuval saying we needed to deliver our package at the gate. He said nothing about us going *through*. After speaking with him, he has agreed that you finished before me. You're back in the tournament."

"What?" Natesa and I say in chorus.

"It wasn't without persuasion," Indah says, a wicked gleam in her eye. "Datu Bulan has allowed the Janardanians to fish in the southern seas at no expenditure. Sultan Kuval doesn't want to jeopardize their arrangement."

"I—I don't know what to say," I stutter out. "You gave up your place in the arena?"

"It wasn't really mine to begin with. You beat me to the gate. Pons and I wouldn't have made it out without you. We thank you for that." Indah beams up at her guard. Affection radiates between them, dazzling and whole.

They're in love. How did I miss seeing it before? The familiar way they speak to each other, their shared smiles, their intimate supper last night . . . It is so obvious now.

"Thank you," I say, my heart tugging in envy at their closeness. I wish I had a simple answer for what comes next. I may not feel for Ashwin the way I do for Deven, but if I win tomorrow, Ashwin will be rajah. And I will still be rani.

Indah shrugs off her good deed. "I may have done you a disservice. Citra was furious that her father admitted you back into the tournament. Her anger will bolster her hunger to win."

I nod, trusting Indah's caution. "Did you tell Ashwin?"

"I passed him in the corridor and notified him of the change." I observe her for an indication of his reaction. Was he glad to hear I will remain in the tournament? Indah's intuitive gaze intensifies on me, reading my insecurity. "He seemed distracted but pleased. He's worried about you. He was uncertain if you'd still wish to compete."

Ashwin is worried about whether or not *I* am willing to continue? I hurt him, and his concern is for me.

He is nothing like Tarek, nothing at all.

"I do," I promise.

"You better be certain," Indah says. "Because the people of the Southern Isles are also counting on you to defend your throne—and win."

27

DEVEN

Someone kicks me in the side.

"Get up," says a gruff voice.

I turn over on my bedroll, away from the guard's feet. "Meathead."

"What did you say?" he asks.

"Nothing," I mutter.

The guard rounds back to kick me again. I roll out of the way onto my knees and then push off the floor. Manas is awake and gone, as are the other men I bunk with.

"Is Yatin all right?" I ask. "Did he ask for me?"

"He's alive. Now *move*."

The guard prods me out of the tent and into the first rays of dawn. The rain clouds have cleared, and the stuffy morning air sticks to my skin. The whole of camp has been woken. I follow the line of men to the quad. The rank board on the dusky hillside has been altered, but I question my vision in the grainy light. Kali's name has been added to the board again, and Indah of Lestari's name is missing.

Kali's still in the tournament. We have a chance.

Vizier Gyan waits in the quad, flanked by his men. Since today is the tournament, I anticipated the grounds would be mostly clear of guards, but even more surround us. I look to Manas as to the purpose of this gathering, but he frowns, puzzled too.

"We have been informed of a schemer among you," announces Vizier Gyan.

Manas folds his arms across his chest in defiance. Other men shift on their feet, uncertain who the source is of this early morning roundup.

Vizier Gyan explains, "I've been monitoring everything in this camp, including what our visiting healers bring in and take out." My face turns to stone, shutting in my alarm. "Yesterday during our search we discovered something missing from one of the healer's baskets. Only one of you was permitted inside the sick tent while he was here." Vizier Gyan aims his finger at me. "Captain Naik, step forward."

I am not given the chance. Guards grab my arms and drag me before the vizier. They pat me down, find the vial in my pocket, and shove me to my knees.

Vizier Gyan holds up the neutralizer tonic. "Did you take this from the healer while in the sick tent yesterday?"

I stare straight ahead, regretting my impulsive choice to steal the vial. Anything I say could incriminate me further and possibly lead back to Kali. The vizier already suspects she sent the healer for Yatin. I will not give him a reason to interfere with her duel.

Vizier Gyan rests his hand on the back of my head. Pain explodes in my joints as my bones grind together, and then it stops.

"I will ask you one more time," he says. "Did you take this?"

"Yes," I squeeze out.

Vizier Gyan lets me go, and I fold over. Every bone in my body aches like he reached inside me and rearranged my skeleton. "What did you intend to use it for?"

I intended to pollute the guards' drinking water during the tournament today.

The grinding pain begins to fade. From my vantage point kneeling, I spot knife scars on the vizier's inner wrists under his long sleeves.

Bloodletting scars. I recognize them from the bhuta executions Rajah Tarek held often. Bhutas were bled from strategically placed cuts so they would suffer from blood loss, weakening their powers. Then they were bludgeoned to death with stones.

"I recognize your scars," I say. "Do your men know?"

Vizier Gyan's nostrils flare. He tugs down his sleeves and barks, "Take him to the cell."

The guards drag me to the one-room hut, my weak legs stumbling to keep up. *I am really tired of this cell.* Vizier Gyan follows me inside and slams the door, shutting out the guards. I rest against the wall, still recovering from whatever he did when his powers ground at my bones.

"Those marks on your wrists are bloodletting scars," I say, holding my aching arms against my sore rib cage. "Did Tarek order you executed?"

"Does that delight you, Tarachandian soldier?" he sneers.

"I never participated in any of the stonings. My brother . . . well, *half* brother, is a bhuta." The vizier's expression remains fixed in fury, so I press, "What were you doing in Tarachand?"

"My sister, the sultan's first-ever wife, and I were on a tour of the rice fields along our border when we were caught in the cross fire between imperial soldiers and bhutas fleeing Tarachand. A Burner killed my sister. I was captured by Tarachandian soldiers. Hastin stopped them before they stoned me to death." Vizier Gyan tries to bury his sorrow beneath his hatred, but I hear it in his voice, raw and raised like the scars on his wrists.

"You're working with Hastin."

Vizier Gyan flicks a speck of dirt off his jacket. "Hastin has grand designs to avenge our people. He desires to punish every last half-wit who hunted down and murdered bhutas. But his yearning for vengeance prohibits him from seeing the breadth of our opportunity. A throne tournament was the perfect distraction to finally strike back.

While the prince and the other nations have been in Iresh, I have been moving troops into Tarachand."

My lungs cave in on themselves. I saw the soldiers near our borders. They must be through by now. "Does the sultan know?"

"Kuval has ambitions to expand his rule into Tarachand. He thinks he can unseat Hastin from Vanhi and then use Citra to browbeat the boy prince into doing his bidding and increase his diplomatic power. But the better way is to secure the Zhaleh."

Does Hastin know Janardanian troops are in Tarachand's borders? Will he retaliate? I cannot determine how far the vizier's deceit has spread, but every unresolved offense since coming to Iresh suddenly makes sense. "*You* had me lashed."

"I assumed the kindred would run with you and the Zhaleh upon learning Prince Ashwin punished the man she loved. I had troops on standby to intercept her and take the book."

"You underestimated her."

"Every warrior has a weakness," he counters. "Kalinda will let her guard down—and I will be there. Rajah Tarek's empire will fall for what he did to my sister."

His surety unnerves me. He must have a plan in place to take the Zhaleh. "Releasing the Voider will destroy more than the empire. Janardan will fall too. The entire world will be lost."

"I have no interest in using the Zhaleh as a weapon. Instead of strong-arming Hastin with our armies, I will use the book to negotiate the warlord's exit from Vanhi. I do not wish to go to war." Vizier Gyan's antipathy carries stark honesty. "Kuval intends to send bhuta soldiers into battle, and more of *my* people will die. Bhutas are resigned to squander our powers or serve under Kuval's rule. I left my scars as a reminder of my sister's heart's wish—to set our people free. I will bring her dream to pass through her daughter."

"Citra won't win," I say.

"She will. Kalinda may have wheedled her way back into the tournament, but Citra *will* be champion, and I will ensure she gains the support of your people by giving them proper supplies and care. The refugees are so desperate for kindness they will love her despite her being a bhuta." I round my hands into fists, nauseated by his cunning. "Once Citra has the refugees on her side, she'll get rid of the boy prince and reign over the empire with me as her adviser. Bhutas will flock there for freedom."

The vizier will dismantle the empire and build a new kingdom on its ashes. "What of my people?" I ask, my queasiness spreading.

"The refugees will become slaves to the new empire, and I will turn you and your soldiers over to Hastin. He can execute you as he pleases."

I swing my fist at Vizier Gyan, but he opens a pit in the ground beneath me with his powers. I fall in it up to my chin, and the dirt squeezes around my limbs, trapping me.

Vizier Gyan stands above me, casting a shadow across his pit. "The duel will start soon. The amphitheater isn't far from here. If you listen closely, you'll hear my people celebrating your kindred's death."

28

KALINDA

I awake shivering.

Morning sunlight streams through the windows and balcony. My blanket is pulled up to my chin and my limbs are drawn in close to my heart, yet I am cold. I search inside myself for my soul-fire, but my powers elude me. I throw off the covers and stumble to the mirror glass. I try to push my inner light into my hands. They do not glow.

Natesa glides in, refreshed for the new day. She holds out a black training sari for my duel. "Good, you're awake. You leave for the amphitheater in an hour."

I swivel from the mirror glass, and even after I halt, my head continues to spin. "Sultan Kuval gave me neutralizer tonic yesterday before the trial. He said it would wear off by now, but I still don't have my powers."

"Slow down," Natesa says, laying out my clothes. "You took something from the sultan?"

"All of the competitors did."

My legs wash of strength. I rest against the vanity for support. The sultan poisoned me. Am I the only competitor he sabotaged? Or did he drug Indah as well? He would not impair his daughter.

I release a guttural moan. "Citra is going to crush me."

"You don't have *any* powers," Natesa asks, finally hearing me. *"At all?"*

Indah and Pons enter my chamber. Pons wears a navy tunic with a low-cut split collar and has recently shaved the sides of his head. Indah sports an aquamarine sari with dazzling gold beading that matches her lip stain. They came dressed in their finest, prepared to represent Lestari well in the tournament procession.

"We came to see if you need anything," Indah says, smiling. She reads our troubled faces and loses all cheerfulness. "What's the matter?"

"Kalinda doesn't have her Burner abilities," Natesa says, her palm over her mouth in horror.

"I haven't gotten my powers back after taking the tonic yesterday," I explain. "I think the sultan's poison is still obstructing them. Do you have yours?"

"Yes, my powers returned last night." Indah exchanges a puzzled frown with Pons, and then her eyes go wide. "My injured ankle. I bled the poison out."

The crocodile bite let her blood. Sultan Kuval gave the same tonic to Citra, but he must have warned her. By now, Citra will have let her blood to revive her powers.

Pons lays a supportive hand on Indah's shoulder, their frowns abysmal. They believe I have been sabotaged beyond repair.

I press down on my aching sternum. *Gods, gods, gods.*

"You're an Aquifier!" Natesa screeches at Indah. "You have to do something!"

"The only way to drain the poison is to let her blood," Indah replies, her voice regretful. "The recovery process takes hours. She would be in no condition to duel."

I slump down upon my vanity stool. Without my powers, Citra will bury me. I might as well be defenseless.

226

"There must be another way," says Natesa, pacing in front of me. Each time she passes by, my despair drops further.

She stops abruptly, and her chin snaps up. "What if you don't tell them? Let them *think* you have your powers. For all you know, the poison could wear off, and you'll regain them by the start of the duel."

I would prefer a remedy to bluffing, but Natesa's strategy may be the only answer. I cannot request a delay. Sultan Kuval will know I am stalling and tell me to concede, as he has done every other time I have protested during the trials. I have no other choice but to go forward with the duel. Whether I win or lose is up to the gods.

"This stays between us," I order. "Say nothing to Ashwin or Brother Shaan. I don't want to worry them."

Indah and Pons mutter in compliance, both tense and anxious.

Natesa throws up her gaze, suddenly aware of the time. "Skies above, you need your hair and makeup done before you go anywhere. I have a reputation to uphold."

I look in the mirror glass, my sallow reflection staring back at me. "Then you better get started."

Ashwin comes into my chamber as Natesa finishes painting my lips. Indah and Pons have already left for the procession. Now, nearly an hour after I woke, my hair is braided, my black training sari is pinned on tightly, and my daggers are strapped to my thighs.

I still have no powers.

Natesa gives me a hug. "Teach Citra what a true champion is. I'll be waiting for your return."

I squeeze Natesa back in thanks. She bows to Ashwin and then goes into her antechamber. I tuck away my worries and face Ashwin's nervous gaze.

"Brother Shaan suggested we arrive at the procession together so we appear united," he says stiffly.

I walk up to him and adjust his stand-up collar. His immaculate scarlet tunic and trousers are handsome. The black scorpion crest on his chest matches his turban. "We *are* united. I'm sorry, Ashwin. I was unfair to you when you deserved my honesty. I cannot promise you anything. Except that I . . . I would like to try again."

His face brightens with boyish charm. Is his smile sincere? Or does he see me as a murderess? The playful tilt of his head and the humor on his lips are so like Tarek. I cannot guarantee how close we can become when at times he reminds me of his father. My knee-jerk reaction may never go away.

"So you'll stay with me after you win?" he asks.

Ashwin's belief in my ability to triumph today corrodes my lesser apprehensions about us. We do not have time to discuss whether or not he forgives me now. His support of me is enough.

"I'll consider staying." That is the best assurance I can offer. First, I must honor my promise to return for Deven, and then I will know if he and I have anything left between us to hold on to.

"I was hoping you would wear this today." Ashwin hands me his gold cuff. "Brother Dhiren gave it to me. It belonged to his grand-mother. She was a sister warrior, like you."

The square cuff style is one a warrior wears to battle. I turn the piece of history over, running my fingers along the worn edges, dings, and shallow scrapes. This cuff has seen combat and bloodshed. I pray that today it will see victory.

I slip the gold cuff onto my wrist. Ashwin's wrist looks bare with-out it.

"I have a good luck charm too." He lifts a thin chain from around his neck. The oil vessel hangs at the end like a pendent. "I'm wearing it as a reminder of those we've lost. Is that morbid?"

It would be if I wore the vial, given it contains the blood of my people, but Ashwin is honoring the fallen. I tuck the vessel back under his tunic. "Protect it."

Ashwin takes my hand in his and then reaches for my other one. He holds them up and rubs his thumbs over the backs. "Your rank marks have faded."

On the day I need them most. *I will win them back,* I vow. But apprehension clamps down on me. Memories from my rank tournament plagued my sleep last night. Blood and screams and death.

Ashwin lets my hands go and skims his knuckles across my cheek. "You're nervous."

"In tangles."

He offers me his arm. "This is your throne, Kalinda. Tarachand is your empire to defend."

Gods willing, I will represent our homeland well.

I slide my arm through Ashwin's, and we start off for the procession.

<hr />

Ashwin and I part ways at the palace gardens. The storm clouds from yesterday have gone, but the sweltering air still scents of wetness. Rohan goes with Ashwin, and Opal escorts me to the line of waiting elephants and extravagant wooden litters.

Elephant warriors ride bareback atop their steeds in showy dress uniforms of plum tunics and loose green trousers. A machete hangs at each warrior's hip, and a khanda is strapped to their backs, gold hilts glinting in the sun. More soldiers prepare to march alongside us. The dragon cobra emblem of Janardan adorns the soldiers' tunics and the emerald banners they carry.

Opal pushes a step stool beside the elephant I will ride. A servant stands near the mighty beast's head, stopping it from moving. I rode an elephant to my rank tournament, but it had a howdah carriage. This elephant is bareback, no saddle to secure myself into.

"Can I ride with the prince?" I ask, motioning at Ashwin climbing into one of the litters.

"It is tradition for the duelers to ride bareback," says Opal. "Don't fret. The elephant has been trained to stay in line."

A couple yards in front of me, Citra straddles another elephant. A green-and-gold training sari displays her toned body and gentle curves, and her shiny dark hair is braided into tiny sections and clipped up in swooping strands. A thin gold-chained crown rings her head, a teardrop beryl gem dangling from it over her forehead. The kohl around her eyes sweeps out to dagger points, lengthening her eyelashes and deepening the severity of her stare.

She smirks, a patronizing curl of her rouged lips. "Afraid of a short ride?"

Nothing is *short* about the elephant, but I cannot dishonor our hosts' tradition. Opal steadies the stool as I step to the top. Bracing against the elephant's side, I hop up onto it and fling my leg over its back; its girth is wider than my stride. I immediately slide forward to its narrower neck and stop myself by grabbing behind the elephant's ears.

The elephant sidesteps in agitation. The servant pacifies the animal, and Citra snickers. My face burns. I look a fool, but at least I am still astride the great beast.

"Rohan and I will ride ahead to the amphitheater," says Opal. "Only native-born Janardanian soldiers are allowed in the procession. We'll be waiting for you there."

She pats my leg to put me at ease, but a storm of anxiety wreaks havoc on my nerves.

A gong sounds, and the procession starts down the stairs that Citra made alongside the cliff. One after another, the elephant warriors and foot soldiers disappear over the edge. Servants lift Sultan Kuval's wooden litter. He sits beneath a shade canopy atop silk pillows. Delicately carved orchids decorate the posts of the four open sides. He sways as his servants heft the litter to the top of the stairway and downward, falling out of sight. Ashwin is carried next in another ornate litter, and then more foot soldiers and elephant warriors follow.

Citra is the next royalty to descend from the palace, and then my elephant lumbers closer to the sheer drop. I grip its head tighter as it starts down the stairs. I slide forward, my legs clamping around the elephant's hard neck, and train my gaze on the zigzagging stairway. I duck often to avoid an overhang or lean away from the spray of the waterfall.

Once we reach the ground, Janardanians line the roadway, cheering for their princess. Citra smiles broadly and waves in return. I am so taken aback by the sincerity of her affection for them that I do not see the mango soaring at me until it strikes my arm. The rotten fruit splits open, and sticky juice sprays down my side.

Numerous people lining the road boo at me and throw more fruit. I hunch down over the elephant, and my back is pelted. A papaya hits the side of my head, and chunks of it mash into my ear. I wait for the foot soldiers to step in and stop my assailants, but they stay behind and in front of my elephant, plodding onward without a care.

Ahead, I can barely see Ashwin's litter winding through the packed roads. He is too far in front to view what is happening. I cover my cheeks, hot with humiliation, and leave my head down. Along with their booing, the rabble shouts names. "Filthy bhuta." "Slag." And the most insulting, "Kur's pet."

Angry tears sting my eyes. Sultan Kuval knows his people hate Burners. He should have anticipated this uproar. Perhaps he did, and he is trying to browbeat me into conceding.

I choke down a burning lump of fury and sit up tall. I lift my chin high and draw a dagger. The next piece of fruit that flies at my face, I block with my blade and forearm. The spectators near me shrink away, as they do not know that I am without my powers. But not all are afraid. The anonymity of the mob and inaction from the soldiers encourage

231

their loathing. I do not stop all the rotten fruit from hitting me, and I cannot halt their heckling, but a fierce stare and the gleam of my dagger slow a portion of their wrath.

Our procession turns away from the city, weaving into the outskirts of the Morass, down a road lined with massive banyan trees. The tree-tops arch above, the branches threading together like clasped fingers. Children dangle from the boughs overhead. One child leans down and yanks hard on my braid and then swoops out of reach before I can swat him. The relentless hounding almost releases my tears, but I concentrate on each shaky inhale, matching it to the sway of the elephant.

Almost there. A little longer.

Twin teak trees mark the entrance to the outdoor amphitheater. Far ahead, Sultan Kuval's servants set down his and Ashwin's litters. The rest of the procession halts in succession. I slide down off the elephant, and Opal comes to my side. She takes in my sticky clothes and hair.

"Kindred, are you all right?"

"I've faced far worse than rotten fruit. Once I'm wearing my armor, no one will see the stains." I throw a smile at Opal that I doubt is convincing and then leave her to meet the others.

Ashwin spots my blemished sari as I approach the entrance to the amphitheater, and his face sets in anger. I plead silently with him not to cause more of a spectacle. Citra is already smirking at me like she has a blade to my throat, and Sultan Kuval looks me up and down with pompous satisfaction. I clamp my molars together at their tiresome ridicule and garner every scrap of dignity I have left. *Let them think I'm unshaken. Let them worry if I have my powers.*

I join Ashwin's side, and he views the full damage. "What happened?" he demands.

"The spectators on the roadway expressed their opinion of me."

He faces Sultan Kuval and Princess Citra, and his voice slices at them like an arrow. "Why were your people permitted to accost my kindred?"

Citra jolts at his use of "my kindred." *Oh, yes. Ashwin knows where best to retaliate.*

"The voice of the people may declare their favored warrior," answers Sultan Kuval.

Ashwin risks staining his tunic jacket by pulling me against him, resting his hand on the small of my back. "Kalinda doesn't need the voice of the people. She has me."

Citra chirps an uncertain laugh. Ashwin glares at her, stone-cold. She sniffs in dismissal of his resentment and revolves away. Sultan Kuval twists the end of his mustache, his gaze troubled. Doubt is a powerful motivator, but it will only take me so far.

The sultan leads us down the path to the sunken amphitheater. The wide oval stadium and arena are dug into the ground, the steps leading downward. The rows of seating for spectators are made of hard-packed land that rings the massive pit in the jungle floor.

Green pennants with the dragon cobra symbol rap in the breeze above the upper row of the stadium where we stand. All of the spectators are Janardanians. Sultan Kuval must not have permitted my people to attend due to the outbreak, not that they would cheer for me. As a chambermaid, Natesa was not allowed to come. Indah and Pons are seated near the sultan's imperial box. My solitary supporter from home is Ashwin.

I slip my hand into his clammy one and anchor myself to his unwavering faith in me. He is my blood, my ally, my rajah.

Drummers line up alongside us and strike a furious beat. The audience rises and faces the top of the stairs. While the drummers thump a marching rhythm, Sultan Kuval and Citra start down the stairway.

Ashwin tugs my hand, urging us to go next. As we descend into the amphitheater, I pray that the gods will have mercy and restore my powers before I reach the bottom. I avoid the defiant stares of the Janardanians and reach for my inner flame. My soul-fire is quiet, like a muffled voice. A hand has smothered it to silence, but it is there.

At the bottom of the stairs, the crowd towers high as the sky. Citra kisses her father's cheek, and then Sultan Kuval leaves her and enters the imperial box that overlooks the arena.

"I'll be right here," Ashwin whispers to me.

I have wrung his hand so hard my fingertips are numb. He gives me an encouraging squeeze and then enters the imperial box. The sultan's wives and courtesans occupy another reserved area above Kuval and Ashwin. Tevy is with the women, come to support her sister. *If only Natesa could be here.*

Bladesmiths heft heavy armor onto Citra and me. One drops a helmet that is too big onto my head, and the other straps a breastplate on me too tightly. They offer me a khanda. I refuse, opting for my lighter daggers. The armor is heavy, sinking me further into this pit of doom.

Standing before his throne, the sultan lifts his arm, and the drumming stops. "Welcome to the finale of the trial tournament! Our first challenger is Princess Citra—"

Spectators stomp their feet to demonstrate their support. Citra leaps over the barrier and drops down several feet into the arena. She lands without difficulty and then raises her arms to the stomping and starts to pump them. Her arms start slowly and then push faster. The audience matches her rhythm with their stomps, and soon the entirety of the amphitheater tremors under their feverous thumping. Finally, her people launch to their feet, their thunderous acclamation shuddering through me.

Citra grins and sweeps her arms down into a regal bow.

The cheers of the crowd peter off so I can hear my crashing pulse.

Sultan Kuval lifts his voice to finish the introductions. "Our second competitor is the kindred of the Tarachand Empire."

Boos begin before the sultan can say my name. Ashwin scowls up into the crowd and then faces forward, deciding the group is too big to silence with a fierce look.

"Hailing from the Turquoise Palace in distant Vanhi, welcome Kalinda Zacharias!"

Yells of discord bang at my back. I search inside for my temper, for my Burner powers to spark in defense, but they are still a far-off star, cold and unreachable.

A bladesmith motions for me to join Citra in the arena. Seeing no stairs, I hoist my leg over the rail and leap down. The added weight of my armor throws me off balance, and my knees buckle as I land. I fall forward onto all fours. Uproarious laughter cascades across the piers. Their cruel amusement, like nettles, rakes over my skin.

Citra's shadow falls over me. "You know how to make an impression."

I push to my feet before her. Citra's frame carries the heavy armor like it is an exoskeleton. She struts to the sparring ring etched into the ground. The arena floor is an endless slab of unforgiving stone that reeks of old blood. I pad across the flat surface into the ring and face her.

The drummers begin an ominous, slow beat. Citra draws her khanda, and the rhythm rolls faster. The start of the tournament is coming, dragging me forward like a landslide. I pull my daggers and settle into my fighting stance. The drumming surges to an earsplitting thunder.

I am directly beneath the storm. I cannot run from the terror flooding me.

I am going to die without my powers.

My next thought overwhelms me with sadness.

I'll never see Deven again.

The beat stops.

In the sudden silence, Citra throws out her free arm. The stone floor lifts to her command, and a raised culvert of rock heaves at me. Dust and pebbles spray my face. I dive out of the rocky deluge, and my helmet falls off, rolling away.

Citra materializes through the cloud of dust, running around me on stones that elevate beneath her feet, each taller than the last. When she is above my head, she leaps at me with her sword poised to strike. I lift my daggers, and they clash against her khanda. With our blades connected, Citra heaves the land beneath me, knocking me off balance. I rearrange my weight and avert another khanda blow to the head.

"Where are your powers, Burner?"

I wedge a knee between us, thrusting her back. "Don't pretend you don't know."

Citra raises her khanda, confusion crossing her face. "Know what?"

"The tonic I took yesterday hasn't worn off," I explain, perplexed by her response. "Your father poisoned me."

"No, he didn't."

"Yes, he *did*."

"He didn't tell me," she replies, stepping back.

"Did you let your blood today?"

"Yesterday evening. My father said it was to cleanse me for battle."

My mind spins with reasons why the sultan would not tell her, and from Citra's hurt expression, we come to the same conclusion—he does not trust her to win on her own merits.

"I don't need help defeating you," Citra growls.

She sweeps her khanda and cuts my right side. Pain explodes across my abdomen. I bend over, grasping my wound. She kicks me in the knee, and I fall in an agonized crouch, bleeding through my fingers.

Citra kicks me again, in the back. I groan from the bruising strike. "I can win without my powers," she snarls.

The loss of blood weakens me, but it also tears down the wall between me and my blocked powers. The star of my soul-fire is closer, like a comet blazing in my direction. The poisons are bleeding out.

I push to my feet, suffering the agony of every excruciating movement, and lower my wet hand from the cut. I allow the blood to flow and free me from my poisoned prison. Daggers ready, I strike at Citra.

She evades and smashes the hilt of her sword into my lower back. I stumble forward and raise my dagger in time to parry her sword and plunge my second dagger into her shoulder.

She cries in pain, and then again as I wrench out the blade. The audience pours out a round of boos and curses at me. Blood splatters around Citra and me, the iron scent nauseating. I cannot tell which crimson specks are mine or hers, but my powers are returning.

I push soul-fire into my hands. Citra lifts the ground beneath me, plunging me into the air. I am level with the center of the amphitheater, high above the arena.

Citra rises up on another pedestal, her shoulder bleeding. "Now this is a fair fight."

I throw a heatwave at her, and the spectators gasp. Citra dodges, leaving her teetering close to the end of the pedestal. She throws a cloud of dirt up to blind me. I shield my face from the raining pebbles and lower my arms to the clearing dust.

Citra leaps onto my platform and knocks me down, landing on top of me. I roll her onto her back and push her head over the edge. The audience chants Citra's name. She elbows me in my injured side. I moan on a fresh wave of pain and roll off her. She hacks down with her khanda, and I grab the blade. Before the metal can cut me, I push forth my powers. The blade glows red-hot, and the heat surges up to the hilt, scalding Citra. She drops the warped khanda, cradling her palm.

As I stand, the Trembler princess lifts more pedestals around us and leaps to the next. I throw a blast of fire after her, and the audience gasps again, enthralled by my rare abilities. The tail of my flame connects with Citra midjump, and she falls short of the pedestal, scrambling to pull herself up.

I jump to the pedestal between us. She forms a foothold, saving herself from falling, and grins at me. The ground beneath me crumbles.

I drop, going down with the rocks and boulders. The sky turns hazy. I hit the ground, and rocks pummel me. I throw up a blast of fire, burning some to dust. A boulder lands, pinning my leg. Something snaps in my knee, and dizziness reels through me.

Citra struts over to me through the falling dust, her face smeared with dirt. I try to tug out my leg, but it will not budge. Citra punches me in the nose. I flop back, the world swinging away to the crowd's joyous cheers.

She throws off her helmet, kneels beside me, and grabs my face. With her hands on my cheeks, grinding presses through me; chisels hack at my bones. I arch against the pain, agony silencing my cries.

Citra lowers her face over mine. "I've been told grating is excruciating. Some say it feels like termites are gnawing away your insides. Your legs, arms, spine, even your skull, are slowly filed to dust."

She lifts the floor beneath us while I am pinned. We surge into the sky above the dust cloud. "Everyone is going to watch me claim your throne," she says.

I reach out to scorch her, but my body spasms, little jerks of torture. Citra's powers grind deep, mining the last of my strength. My sight grays to a sky of granite. My rib cage pokes into my lungs, and my joints crack together like smacking rocks. Soon, I will be no more than dust.

Then I remember—Citra's skin-to-skin connection goes both ways.

I funnel all of my powers, everything I can rally inside me, and I shove it into her hands on my face. Smoke puffs around us. The scent of singed hair and burned cloth fills my nostrils. She screams and stumbles back to the edge, teetering on the lip of the pedestal.

I place my hands on the boulder pinning my leg and burn myself free. Citra grabs on to my other leg as an anchor, and her weight drags us over the edge.

We drop fast, clinging to each other. Citra throws out her hands to lift the arena floor to catch us, but she reacts too late. We land, her on the bottom. The impact drives up through her and into me, jarring my weakened bones. I slump off of her. Blood streams out behind her head, and her eyes glaze over with a film of nothingness.

The audience goes silent. My pulse stutters, and my world washes to shadows. I cradle my wounded side and lie back. Behind my eyelids, my soul-fire wanes to a wisp of light. Blackness embraces me with a chill that defies all winter. My insides freeze under the impenetrable cold, and I am beckoned into the night.

29

KALINDA

A cool, soothing sensation wakes me. Ashwin hovers near my bedside and dabs my face with a damp washcloth. Indah stands on my other side and heals my khanda wound with expert concentration. Pons assists her, holding a jug of healing waters. Ashwin slides his hand into mine. Dried blood and dirt stain his jacket.

"Where am I?" I rasp.

"We brought you to my chamber," he says. "I suggested we go straight to Indah's boat, but we wouldn't have made it through the city. Indah insisted we return here so she could start healing you immediately."

"Kalinda wouldn't have made it any farther with her bleeding," Indah replies. "She's fortunate she's awake."

I turn my head and see Opal in a chair, washing her scraped knees. Rohan stands guard out on the balcony. His cheek and chin are bruised. "What happened?" I ask.

"We had trouble getting you out of the arena," Ashwin replies. "The spectators rioted. Opal and Rohan reached you first and shielded you from the mob. I carried you out, and they cleared our path back here."

"Thank you," I say, aware that gratitude cannot fully repay them.

"Rohan thought it was exciting," Opal says, shrugging. "We don't usually get to knock people over with our powers."

Rohan grins. "Our winds flattened the mob like chaffs of wheat."

"Thank you," I repeat, extending my appreciation to include Indah, Pons, and Ashwin.

Ashwin lifts my hand to his warm chin. "You scared me into my next life. When I reached you in the arena, you were ice cold."

"Is Citra . . . ?" I start.

"Gone. We're no longer welcome in Iresh. As soon as you can travel, we'll leave for Lestari with Indah and her party."

"And our people?"

"I have a boat on standby for us," Indah says. "More are coming for your people. They'll arrive the day after tomorrow and begin the evacuation."

"We might have to leave before then," Rohan says, striding in from the balcony. "Vizier Gyan is coming, and he's bringing guards."

I try to sit up, but Indah forces me back down. "Don't," she says gently. "You broke your leg, and your side wound is severe."

"Indah," Ashwin says, "pack your things and ready your boat. I don't know what the vizier wants, but after the riot, we must be prepared for anything. Opal and Rohan, find Brother Shaan at the civilian encampment and then help Indah prepare to leave."

Vizier Gyan's bhuta guards throw open the door and march inside. The vizier surveys my protectors and barks, "All of you, leave us."

Indah, Pons, and our guards go, filing past Vizier Gyan stationed at the door. His nose and eyes are red from crying.

"My niece is dead," he states with bitterness.

"The trial-tournament proceedings are over," Ashwin replies evenly. "I understand the sultan is no longer willing to offer us aid, so I'll take my people and go."

"You'll go nowhere," counters the vizier. A guard drags Natesa through the open door and shoves her to her knees.

"I'm sorry," she weeps, begging my forgiveness. "He threatened to kill Yatin. Don't give him what he wants, he—" Vizier Gyan hits Natesa square in the face, and she crumples to the floor.

"Leave her alone," I exclaim. "She's a servant, nothing more."

"She proved valuable to me." Vizier Gyan holds up a book, and my heart retracts in on itself.

The Zhaleh.

"Your servant insisted she doesn't know where the vessel is hidden." Vizier Gyan crosses to my bed, the Zhaleh firm in his grasp. Ashwin tries to block him, but the vizier shoves him out of the way and bends over me, his glare frightening. "Where is the vessel?"

"I don't have it."

He raises his fist to strike me, and Ashwin calls out.

"Here." He lifts the necklace from under his shirt, the vessel dangling. "Let us go, and I'll give it to you."

"You're in no position to bargain, boy," the vizier sneers. "We have your people, your army, and, soon, your palace." Ashwin balks. Ridicule fills the vizier's long, cruel face. "Our troops are nearly to Vanhi. I'll soon join them to deliver the vessel and the Zhaleh to Hastin. Now hand it to me."

Ashwin rips the chain free from his neck and holds it out beside him. "Come any closer and I'll crush it."

Vizier Gyan signals to his soldiers. They manhandle the vessel from Ashwin and pass it to the vizier.

No, no, no.

The vizier gazes at both powers in his hands. I fear he will take them and go, but he hesitates. Can he hear the call of the Voider? He opens the Zhaleh and flips to the incantation. He runs his fingers over the page, enthralled. Desire builds in his greedy gaze. He desires the power of the Voider. He seeks the promised favor for himself.

But the incantation is written in ancient runes. His lips start to move, and a warning blares inside me. "You can read runes?" I ask.

He smirks, an arrogant twist of his lips. "I've studied the language of the gods. Haven't you?"

Ashwin yanks himself from the guards' grasp, his expression distraught.

Vizier Gyan lifts his palm from the book, his stare firm with resolve. "I don't think I will pass this on to Hastin after all."

He has succumbed to the call of the Voider.

I tense to attack, but I have no powers to stop him. My abilities were expended in the arena, and my sheathed daggers are hanging off my bedpost. I can almost reach them with the foot of my leg that is not broken, but I cannot sit up to grab them.

Vizier Gyan lays the book at the end of the bed and flips open the vial. Ashwin springs at him, but the guards drag him back. The vizier drinks the blood, and then, with his lips stained crimson, he reads the incantation. "Fire to smoke and smoke to—"

"One scream and the palace guards will be here," I cry, drowning out his voice. He pauses, but darkness flows out of the open book like black fog. "What will Sultan Kuval say when he finds out you're betraying him?"

Vizier Gyan sets the vial beside the book and grabs my throat. "Don't be noble, Burner. I have drunk the blood and spoken the first words of the incantation. I cannot be stopped."

Choking for breath, I kick the bedpost with my good leg and foot. My toes knock down my daggers, drawing the attention of the guards. Ashwin rounds on the nearest one, slamming him in the chest with his shoulder and seizing the sword. Lifting the blade against the second soldier, Ashwin backs up against the bed. His free hand darts out and rips the page with the incantation on it from the Zhaleh, and then, with the same hand, he fists the discarded vial.

Vizier Gyan lets up on his grip slightly. I gasp, gulping in air, and his crazed gaze snaps to Ashwin. "You waste your strength, boy."

Ashwin tosses the khanda on the floor. Thunderstruck, I watch him take the incantation in both hands to rip the parchment in half.

The guards move to charge the unarmed prince, but Vizier Gyan waves them off. "Give it to me or your kindred will die."

Ashwin scans the loose parchment. It smokes, though I see no flames. "I want justice for bhutas too," he says. "But this is not the way."

"Where was justice when Tarek was slaughtering my people?" the vizier yells, his bloodshot eyes frenzied. "Where was mercy when my sister was killed? My legacy is of the gods. Your legacy is of treachery and butchery."

"I *love* my empire," Ashwin proclaims.

"Your empire has fallen." The vizier's grasp remains on my gullet. I dare not move to oppose him. He is overcome with the call of the Voider, desperate to finish the incantation. Leaving it unfinished will drive him mad. He growls, "Give me back what belongs to my people, or I will grind the kindred's bones to powder."

He means his threat, and Ashwin cannot stop him. Ruining the incantation is a temporary diversion. The darkness is coming; the fog rolling off the parchment is inescapable. Vizier Gyan will unleash the Voider, and we will lose more than the empire—we will lose the world.

Ashwin's face falls. He has foreseen the same devastating future.

"Gods, forgive me." He tears the incantation in two and drops the pieces.

Vizier Gyan lunges for the fluttering sections. While he is down, Ashwin licks the bloody rim of the vessel and says, "Fire to smoke, and smoke to dark. Let the light fall and the night rise. Shadows be one. Darkness open the Void and awaken the evernight."

Coils of shadow shoot out from the torn incantation in the vizier's hands and splay across the chamber like crooked, grasping fingers.

I gawk at Ashwin. He finished the incantation. He must have memorized it.

A malevolent chuckle echoes around us, and more darkness slinks in from the fringes of the chamber. Ashwin steps over to me, paling with fright. Vizier Gyan's guards try to flee, but they are lost in the voracious shadows. They scream as spiny threads of the dark whip out, strangling their cries to helpless gurgles.

Vizier Gyan scrambles back to the door, but the shadows seize him with grasping claws. The ground trembles, and cracks snake up the wall from his feeble attempts to retaliate. I lose sight of the vizier and his dying soldiers in the blinding dimness, and then the trembling stops.

Shadows eclipse the light, smothering my senses in bone-chilling obscurity. Despair crawls far inside me and expands into my bones. We are lost to the evernight.

<hr />

I exhale a startled breath at the sudden night, and the darkness stirs. Something shifts nearby. A hand grasps mine, and a shaky voice speaks my name. Ashwin. I clamp down on his fingers, struggling to sit up.

The balcony door flies open, ushering in harsh daylight. I squint and see the figure of a finely dressed man standing in the doorway. Sunlight falls over one half of his familiar face.

"Father," Ashwin gasps.

"My son."

My veins run to ice. *It's him. It's his voice.*

Ashwin drifts to Tarek in a daze, meeting him at the end of the bed. Their resemblance is astounding, but no more will I mistake Ashwin for his father. His younger face lacks malice, whereas Tarek's is cold and unfeeling. Even with those dissimilarities, Tarek is not as I recall. He has a different air about him that pulls my hairs on end.

Tarek embraces Ashwin, clutching him by the shoulders.

"How . . . how have you returned, Father?"

"You asked the gods to defeat your enemies and reclaim our empire." Tarek opens his arms wide, indicating the fallen soldiers and vizier. "The gods heard your prayer."

My sense of wrongness festers. The gods would not send someone deceased back into their prior mortal state. The spirit would return to a new form, not the same. *This isn't Tarek,* my instincts scream.

The door flings open.

"What's happening in my palace?" Sultan Kuval bellows. He scans the dead soldiers, his departed brother-in-law, and, finally, he spots Tarek. "It . . . It cannot be."

Tarek—or whatever *it* is—stalks over to him. "You've betrayed us, dear Sultan, and schemed to take our land. The gods revealed all while I was in the Beyond."

Sultan Kuval recovers from his shock enough for him to shout, "Guards!"

Palace guards charge in armed with machetes. Tarek throws out a hand, and blue fire explodes from his fingers, slamming the soldiers into the wall and knocking them out. A second onrush of guards enters. Tarek tosses them aside with another blast of the same blue flames.

His ruthless display of power and his otherworldly azure fire startles the sultan. He freezes alone inside the threshold. Tarek closes in on him with slow, purposeful steps.

"I helped your son," says Kuval. "I gave your people refuge. I—"

Tarek's hand darts out like a snake's tongue, grabbing the sultan's thick chin. Sultan Kuval shrinks away from him. "Look at me when you lie," Tarek says, dead calm.

Sultan Kuval lifts his gaze and pales. "No, please. No!"

Tarek pushes his powers into him. Cold flames dry away Kuval's skin, and he crumples to the floor in a heap. The air scents of freeze-burned flesh. Tarek faces his son. "Spread the word that the sultan is dead."

My gaze pleads with Ashwin. *Don't leave me.*

He casts a worried glance my way. "Perhaps Kalinda—"

"My kindred stays." Tarek's order is definitive. Gooseflesh prickles up my arms. He has not looked at me once, but he is aware that I am here. "Did you forget my command, son?"

"No, Father." Ashwin bows and hurries out.

I am alone with Tarek, and as in my nightmares, I am powerless.

Tarek's unfeeling gaze meets mine. As he strolls to me, I compare my memory of him to this man. He is an impeccable replica, uncanny in his rare beauty, a compromise of masculinity and pampered imperious deportment. Except for his eyes. His irises blaze blue with an inner fire that dries out my mouth. He sits next to me on the mattress and twirls a strand of my hair around his fingertip. Even his hands are as I remember, always touching and taking.

"Did you miss me, love?" His voice is a dangerous purr.

"You aren't Tarek."

A smirk reveals his amusement. "I am a stronger, purer form of you, dear Kalinda. By now, you must have heard the tale of Ki and her lover, the demon Kur."

"That's a myth."

"All myths are grounded in truth." He winds my hair even more, tugging sharply at my scalp. "Ki and Kur *were* lovers, and together they fathered a child. Their son inherited his father's powers. The same venom burned in his blood as did Kur's. They named him Enlil. Ki pretended Enlil was Anu's son so the sky-god would not smite down the infant. Anu took the child in and raised him, not knowing his son, the fire-god, was the offspring of a demon."

"That isn't true," I say, harnessing boldness in my faith. "Anu bestowed man with fire powers in honor of Enlil, not Kur."

"The other bhutas are descendants of the wretched sky-god. But you . . ." Tarek hisses near my ear. "You and I share the same venomous demon blood."

I shake my head, rustling the pillow. My powers are god-given. Brac would have told me if Burners were descendants of Kur, or does he know? This is a Janardanian myth. Perhaps Brac has not heard of this, or, like me, he scoffed at it.

"It isn't true," I repeat.

"You know it is. You saw your soul's reflection in the flame. Fire shows you dragons, serpents of the dark."

My soul's reflection in fire *is* a dragon, but that is not me. Despite all my wrongdoings, I was born a bhuta. I am *good*. This man is inherently evil.

"You're the Voider," I say. He smiles with Tarek's lips, but he is not Tarek. This is not the man who claimed me from the temple, not the man who brought life to Ashwin. He is not a man at all. "How do you know me?"

"Tarek was sent to the Void after his death. We became well acquainted."

Souls that abide by the five godly virtues go to the Beyond, where they await judgment and are rebirthed into their next mortal state. Disobedient souls are sent to the Void. I should have supposed Tarek's tyranny would not qualify him for rebirth.

"But why did you return as Tarek?"

"I must repay my debt to Prince Ashwin for releasing me. His heart's wish is to regain his palace. Thus I assumed the form of the person who could aid in fulfilling my favor to him."

He strokes my cheek and moves in to kiss my neck. I recoil, my hand glowing threateningly.

The demon rajah picks up the Zhaleh from the end of the bed and offers it to my glowing hand. "If you want to burn something, burn this." I do not take it, so the Voider lights his fingers and holds the book over the blue flames. I watch as the Zhaleh, my only means of returning the Voider to darkness, burns.

Panic kicks deep in my chest. I cannot let this demon stay in our world. After he fulfills Ashwin's heart's wish, he will destroy everything. I grab his forearm and feel inside him for his soul-fire. His skin is cool, and within I sense a feral, destructive heat.

"I would not do that," he singsongs.

I use my powers to scorch the demon rajah, but instead, *his* cold-hot powers rush into *my* veins. I cry out and yank free. Tears of agony fill me.

He smirks. "I warned you."

"I'll tell everyone what you are," I say, panting through the pain.

"No one will believe you. Even my own son thinks I am the rajah . . . and you are my kindred." The demon rajah bends down, his lips above mine. His musty breath sours my stomach. "It's been a long time since I've had a body to touch and feel with. Bhutas revolt me with their godliness and divine light. But you and I are kin."

"We are not," I croak.

"You killed your husband and aided in the fall of Vanhi, the very act Prince Ashwin employed me to reverse." The demon rajah rubs his thumb over my bottom lip. "You know I speak the truth. You belong with me in the dark."

"Father," Ashwin says, returning. He sees Tarek close to me, and his expression goes flat. "The guards want proof of the sultan's death."

The demon rajah aims a prolonged stare at Ashwin. *Please let Ashwin be stalling. Please let him realize this man is not his sire. Please let him discern that this replica of Tarek has no humanity whatsoever.*

"We will give them proof." The demon rajah waves at a dead guard's sword. "Hand me that khanda. We'll show these people what happens to traitors."

Ashwin does not move. "I won't rule with fear."

The demon rajah rises with deliberate calm, dispassionate as he picks up the khanda. "Fear is the only way." Clenching the sword with both hands, he arcs down the blade. I grimace at the sultan's severed head. Natesa still lies motionless on the floor, unconscious.

The demon rajah straps on the sword and returns to my side. "Wait here, love. Soon we will march on Vanhi, and I will return us to our rightful thrones."

He presses dry lips to my cheek, lingering as Tarek once did. While the demon rajah faces me, Ashwin reaches for one of my daggers. *Gods' mercy. He* does *realize his father is an imposter.* I curtail my revulsion and withstand the demon's chilling touch long enough for Ashwin to pocket a blade. Then I jerk away.

The Voider picks up the sultan's decapitated head. "We will go down to the prison camps and show our people their rajah has returned."

Cooperating with the demon will put Ashwin in danger, but he understands the ramifications of his heart's wish more than I do. He does not spare me a glance as they walk out.

Alone in my chamber, I lie on my back and stare up at the ceiling in frustration. I must get up. I have to wake Natesa and warn our people, warn Deven. My broken leg is bandaged, and my side still weeps blood. Ignoring the pain, I scoot to the side of the bed and try to stand. My injured leg gives out, and I wind up on my back again.

Footsteps echo closer. I brace, anticipating palace guards or perhaps the demon rajah's return, but Brother Shaan rushes in with Pons and a limping Indah. They falter to a stop and scan the bodies.

"Kalinda," Brother Shaan stammers. "I saw . . ."

"The Voider."

Brother Shaan lifts his chin, praying skyward. "Gods protect us."

Natesa groans and sits up, holding the side of her head. "What's going on?"

Pons kneels down to help her, and I explain what they missed. "Ashwin released the Voider to stop Vizier Gyan from doing the same. The Voider came disguised as Tarek to help fulfill Ashwin's wish to take back the empire. I tried to stop the demon rajah, but he is immune to my powers." Brother Shaan prays more fervently. "Ashwin and the demon rajah are headed to the camps. We have to warn Deven." I try to sit up again, but a sharp pain pushes into my side, and I double over. Beads of sweat from the exertion of trying to stand wet my forehead.

Indah helps me lie back. "You're bleeding through your bandages, and you shouldn't stand on your leg. Pons will carry you to the boat."

"Where are Opal and Rohan?" If I cannot go to Deven, I can send someone else.

"They brought Brother Shaan here and then went to the boat," replies Indah. "We have no time to go to the camps. Iresh will fall into disarray without the sultan ruling or the vizier leading their army. The city is beyond saving."

"He has Ashwin," I protest. The Voider recognized Ashwin, Sultan Kuval, and me. Will the demon remember Deven betrayed Rajah Tarek?

"Kalinda, we cannot stop the Voider," says Brother Shaan. "He does not need to refuel his powers and rest like bhutas. Demons are immortal, like the gods. We must run while we can."

"But our people—"

"Will follow their rajah," he finishes. "Even with your tournament win, the people will not stand with you, a bhuta, against their ruler. The Voider is a master deceiver. Our people will believe the demon rajah *is* Tarek."

Shrill screams of panic and terrified shouts spill in from the garden. The Voider comes into sight out the open balcony door. He has set the sultan's head on a pike and lifts it for all to see.

"This is what the gods think of traitors," the demon rajah proclaims. "Anu raised me from the dead to punish my enemies. First Vizier Gyan and Sultan Kuval. Next the warlord Hastin!"

Janardanian bhuta guards rush at the Voider. He throws blue fire, and the guards are blasted backward in a radiant explosion. Those overtaken by the blue fire melt away. I gawk in amazement as the Voider cuts them all down. His blue fire eats through bhuta winds and rocks, banishing all hope of reprisals.

The demon rajah continues across the courtyard. At the cliff, he stakes the pike in the ground so the people of Iresh can see what is left of their ruler. Then Tarek and Ashwin disappear over the cliff's edge, traveling the stairs down to the city.

"We have to go now," Indah says, trying to help me to my feet.

Hot tears flood my eyes. "I cannot go like this."

Indah sweeps my hair from my clammy face. "I can take away your pain for a time by tricking your body into thinking you're better."

"You can do that?" Natesa asks.

"The pain blocker is temporary," answers Indah. "Kalinda will be pain-free for about half an hour."

Explosions crash nearby, and blue flames lick the sky as the demon rajah carries on his way to the encampments.

"That's all I need," I say.

Indah runs her hands up my leg and over my abdomen. She chants under her breath, and the pain falls off of me like a leaden weight, lightening my whole body. Adrenaline pulses through my limbs. I stand on my broken leg, my stance offset and my balance not quite right. My body will punish me later, but for now, I can walk.

Indah hoists her trident, and Pons fills his blowgun with darts.

Natesa borrows a khanda from a fallen guard. A bruise darkens her cheekbone where Vizier Gyan struck her. "I'm going to find Yatin."

"My healer is still in camp," Indah says. "He'll help you bring Yatin to the boat."

"Bring him and Deven back," I add, trusting Natesa to find them both. "We'll send Opal and Rohan to help you if there's time."

Natesa hugs me, a quick embrace. "Send them no matter what," she says and then darts off.

I sheath my one dagger. Indah's pain blocker is holding, but this invincibility will not last. I need to make the most of it. "Let's get to the river."

30

DEVEN

Vibrations rumble through the ground around me. I try to move, but the pit holds me like a clenched fist. The guards outside shout orders to launch a defense attack. More quakes shake through the land, the whole world trembling.

The cell door is blown off, devoured by incredible sapphire flames. A figure manifests in the smoky haze. I cough and blink to clear my vision. *Tarek?* The man looks like Rajah Tarek, except his hands weave blue fire.

The rajah casts more cobalt flames at the guards, and they fly back against the walls. He marches past the open cell door, Prince Ashwin behind him. Neither sees me buried up to my chin in the cell, but someone sneaks in.

Natesa kneels beside me and begins to dig me out.

"What in the gods' names is going on?" I demand.

Natesa presses a finger to her lips to shush me. "We don't have long. You have to show me the way to the sick tent."

More bhuta guards are flung back by the rajah's power. When no more Janardanians charge him, the rajah raises his arms. "My army! Come out from hiding!"

The men gradually leave their tents. Natesa unburies me faster, releasing my shoulder. I pull my arm out and help her dig out my other side.

"My good people," Rajah Tarek calls. "Sultan Kuval sought to betray us. Prince Ashwin learned of his deceit and called upon the gods before our enemies infiltrated our city and claimed our homes. Anu has seen your suffering. He sent me back in my previous form and bestowed upon me the power to avenge you."

"He lies," Natesa whispers. "Prince Ashwin unleashed the Voider, and he came as the rajah."

"Impossible," I say. The man before us is a demon? He looks exactly like Rajah Tarek. But Natesa's assessment must be true. That *thing's* power is not of this world.

"We will march on Vanhi, and I will lead you," the demon rajah continues. "But we will not leave the land of our enemies until our wrongs have been righted. Janardan has taken advantage of our weakness. Now is the time to rise up in strength of numbers. We will bring down Iresh, and then we will march upon Vanhi stronger than before!"

Our men listen in stunned rapture. The Voider's strategy is clever but horrible. He will topple Iresh and then cannibalize the city to supply his army with food, weapons, and more soldiers. Once preparations are finished, the demon rajah will target Hastin.

Natesa digs my other arm free. She tugs while I push, and together we liberate me from the pit. I brace against the doorway, my legs stiff from disuse. Manas stands at the front of the crowd, captivated by the return of our ruler.

"Surrender," the Voider yells to our captors, "and the gods will spare you."

A Galer throws a wind at the demon rajah. He dissipates the gust with a blast of blue fire. The burning ball throws the guard down. Those around him drop their weapons and raise their hands in the air. In a matter of minutes, the demon rajah has defeated guards that have held us captive for days. An ominous feeling inside me spreads.

"Natesa," I say quietly, "where is Kali?" I heard the cheers from the amphitheater as the vizier said but have not heard the outcome of the tournament.

"She won the duel, but she's injured. She's on the way to the riverfront. A boat is waiting to take us to Lestari. I'll bring Yatin. Can you get Prince Ashwin? Opal and Rohan will arrive soon to help. They may already be here."

I waiver, debating whether or not the prince is worth the risk. Prince Ashwin released a demon. He deserves to suffer the fullness of his consequences.

"Captain!" Natesa snaps. "I don't know if you're jealous of Kalinda and Prince Ashwin or if you have another reason to abandon your ruler, but you're an imperial soldier."

"I know what I am." And I am certain that this is my godly purpose. I *am* a soldier. I may not have been born with powers that enable me to knock down walls or heal people, but I still have the gods on my side.

"Then do your duty." Natesa points at the Voider. "*That* is not our rajah. Ashwin is."

Before I can reply, a blast of blue fire brightens the sky. We flinch away from the explosion, and then I peer around the corner. The men have broken into the guardhouse.

"The sick tents are on the other side of the quad," I say. "You should go. The men will break into the small armory in the vizier's study and soon be armed."

"Get the prince. We'll meet at the waterfront. And, Captain? Kalinda will burn me alive if she finds out I left you, so don't die." With a half-joking grin, Natesa slips out of the hut.

Men run out of the guardhouse armed and wearing Tarachand soldier jackets they must have found inside. The demon rajah and Prince

Ashwin wait at the gate for the soldiers to fall into formation. On the other side of the exit, bhuta guards gather to defend their homeland. I remain out of sight until the Voider's back is turned, and then I dart across the yard and slip inside the guardhouse.

The vizier's study has been ransacked. The last weapon left is the decorative khanda hanging on the wall above the desk. I take down the sword and spot one last uniform on the floor. I hold up the bloodred jacket with the black scorpion emblem on the front. This is not how I envisioned I would earn back my uniform, but I tug it on. The familiar fit is like a second skin.

I peer out the door. The men are ready to march out. The Voider leads the newly armed ranks through the open gate and blasts the bhuta guards with blue fire. They fall back, and our soldiers cut down the remaining Janardanian guards at the barricade around the civilian camp.

The Voider destroys the gate to the second compound and addresses the shaken refugees. "I have returned to free my people. Come join our crusade against our enemies!" The demon rajah blows open the main armory door with his powers. The people descend on the weapons like ants on ripe fruit.

A handful of men have stayed behind in camp to round up the Janardanian soldiers who surrendered. They hold them captive across from the guardhouse.

Gods above. Opal and Rohan are crouched at the back of the group of prisoners.

I cross camp with short, official strides and wave Opal and Rohan forward. "You two come with me." One of my men raises his arm to halt me, but I beckon them again. "These Galers were personal guards to Prince Ashwin. He wishes to discipline them himself."

The guard lets Rohan and Opal pass. I pretend I am leading them to the prince. Once we are out of the gate, I urge the Galers into a run. We scurry around the corner of the north wall and duck into the jungle. We sink low in the bushes, my heart thudding against my ribs.

Opal listens for pursuers. "I don't think anyone saw us."

"We need to get to the riverboat." I will think of how to sneak past the army once everyone is accounted for. "Where are my brother and mother?"

"We thought you knew," Rohan answers. "The sultan closed the border two days ago. Brac and Mathura haven't crossed into Janardan."

They aren't here. I am struck by an unsatisfactory blend of relief and worry. "Can you take your wing flyers and find them?"

Rohan sets his chin. "We want to stay and fight."

"You look like you've had enough of that," I remark of his injured face. "Please. I need your help."

Rohan starts to protest, but Opal speaks right over him. "I'll find your family. Rohan will stay with you. My wing flyer is on the other side of the civilian camp—"

She cuts off, and then both she and Rohan dunk into the ground cover.

"Captain?" Manas calls from beyond the tree line. I unbend and face him. The underbrush conceals Rohan and Opal near my feet. "Where did the prisoners go?"

"What prisoners?" I reply.

"The palace guards. I saw you exit the gate and come here with them." Manas lowers his hand to his khanda and starts cautiously into the trees.

"Oh, those prisoners. They ran off that way." I point at a bamboo thicket that would be nearly impossible to traverse through.

Manas stops a handful of steps out, near Rohan. "How did they escape?"

"They were Galers. They overpowered me."

Manas pulls his sword. "They were Kalinda's guards. You let them go."

"How do you know Opal and Rohan were guarding Kali?"

"I . . . I heard about it," Manas stammers.

He could only have heard about them from someone who was in and out of our compound. None of the prisoners were, so the messenger had to have been a guard or . . . The truth rattles me. "You're Vizier Gyan's informer."

Guilt radiates from Manas, but he shuts it down with hardened pride. "Hastin let me live to serve as his informant. He sent me to tell the vizier what I knew about you and Kalinda." I lock my jaw against a string of curses. Manas jabs his sword at the air between us. "Don't look at me that way. *You're* the traitor. You fell in love with a filthy bhuta."

"This isn't about bhutas. Vizier Gyan found the Zhaleh. That *thing* that came back to free us isn't Rajah Tarek; it's a demon."

"All you do is lie!" Manas slashes at me. I block his khanda with my ornamental sword, but my dull blade bows. He strikes again, hacking my sword off in the middle.

I throw the useless stub away and step back from Rohan, closer to Opal. They both remain down. Neither of them can summon their winds without revealing our presence to the army beyond the trees.

"I am not lying," I say to Manas. "You need to trust me."

"No." Hatred dispels all traces of the boy who was once my friend. "You were my captain. You didn't just betray the rajah; you betrayed me too."

Manas raises his khanda to stab at me. Opal lunges from the undergrowth and grabs his leg. He tries to kick her off, but Rohan rises from the ferns and punches Manas in the back. Manas whirls on Rohan and aims his blade at his chest.

As I move to intervene, Manas jerks and then goes still. Rohan scrambles away, and Manas drops his sword. He clutches at his throat, choking. Opal pulled up his pant leg and pressed her hand against his skin.

Manas's eyes bulge, his lips bobbing for air. I remember the agony of having the sky squeezed from my lungs.

"Opal, stop," I say. She continues to hold on. Manas falls beside her, bucking on the ground. I fortify my voice. "I said enough."

She lets go and shrinks away from what she has done. Manas claws at the ground, panting. I pick up his sword. He rolls onto his back, too weak to run.

"I'm letting these Galers go," I say.

Manas scrunches his face and spits at Opal. "Dirty demon."

Tears shine in her eyes. She regrets winnowing him, but Manas would kill her without remorse.

I hit him in the head with the hilt of his sword, and he droops into the dirt, passed out.

Rohan crawls to his sister and holds her.

"I couldn't let him hurt you," Opal says.

The Voider yells in the distance. "Onward to Iresh!"

The army is moving out. I have to join them, or I could lose track of the prince.

"Does anyone else know we're here?" I ask the Galers. Rohan listens to the wind and shakes his head. "Go, Opal. Find my family."

"I'll go too," Rohan says, helping his sister up. "We'll find them twice as fast with both our winds."

Opal brushes away a piece of hair flopping in his face. "All right."

"Be safe," I say. "We'll meet in Lestari."

They run west through the trees. Although I want to go with them, my duty to the empire requires that I stay. I cannot leave until I have brought the prince to safety.

Great Anu, let Opal and Rohan find my family. Send them fair winds and the cloak of speed.

Manas has not moved. In a little while, he will wake up with an awful headache. I am not the least bit sorry.

I step out of the cover of the trees and jog toward the demon rajah's army.

The late-day sun shines down on the soldiers' gleaming machetes and khandas lifted to the sky. The demon rajah, visible by his glowing blue fire, leads the armed soldiers and civilians toward the city. Prince Ashwin marches near the front with him. I blend in with the amassed troops and fall in line with the ranks.

At the city gates, a line of elephant warriors, all bhutas, obstructs our way. A regiment of foot soldiers holds the line behind them.

"You cannot pass," calls out a commander. He rides upon a large elephant with great tusks. He holds out his hand, and the ground trembles. A fissure opens up in the land, and a crack spreads, creating a gap between our army and his.

The demon rajah throws a stream of blue across the divide, striking the commander in the chest. He falls off his elephant, and the ground stops parting. The unnatural flame scares all the elephants, and they stampede away with their riders. The demon rajah jumps over the crevice to engage the rival regiment.

Our soldiers charge forward to defend their ruler, but he needs no aid. In one swipe, the demon rajah's blue fire flattens the first line of men. Prince Ashwin leaps over the divide and joins his imposter father. I jump over the gap and rush after him. The opposing regiment breaks its line. Our troops barrel past them through the gate and into the city. I try to maintain sight of Prince Ashwin, but I lose him in the foray.

The demon rajah pushes into the roadways lined with huts, his blue fire burning homes and trees and markets. Crimson soldier uniforms fill the roads like streams of blood. Screaming women and children run everywhere. I spin around and spot the prince slipping between two huts. I run after him and seize him from behind.

Prince Ashwin points a dagger at my face, struggling against my hold, and then recognizes me from his peripheral view. I release him, and he lowers his blade. I identify the dagger's turquoise handle as one of Kali's.

"Did you rob that from the kindred before you abandoned her?" I growl.

The prince recoils from my rancor. "I only left her to draw away the Voider."

"Don't pretend you're a hero. You unleashed this thing."

A blast of blue flames illuminates the sunset sky.

"I had no other choice," Prince Ashwin says, glowering.

"Tell that to the people whose city is being destroyed." I check around the corner for the demon rajah. "A riverboat is waiting to take us out of here."

"What about Kalinda?" the prince asks, eyeing the palace high up on the hill.

"She's meeting us at the river. Try to keep up."

I take off down the road. Prince Ashwin matches my speed, and we run downhill for the waterfront. Slivers of the dark-green river can be seen through the huts. *Nearly there.*

Blue flames explode at us from behind. The demon rajah casts another blast of fire at the hut in front of us, and the walls collapse. I haul Prince Ashwin out of the path of the raining debris, and we roll away. The prince turns onto his back and groans. He was struck in the forearm, his flesh burned white.

"I wondered if I would see you, Captain Naik." Rajah Tarek's voice sends a torrent of memories down upon me. I spent years serving this man. I saved his life over my brother's during an attack. A small part of me still seeks his approval, but this is not Tarek. "I am unsurprised my son is with you. He has always been a disappointment."

Prince Ashwin sits up, biting down on his pain. "Stop lying. I know you're not my father. *Tarek* was the disappointment. He failed the empire."

"Tarek's work was left unfinished, but I have come to put everything right."

The demon rajah collects a blue fireball in his hands. We cannot outrun him, so I hunch over the prince and prepare for agony.

Real fire flares above us, red as a sunset, and pushes away the Voider's icy blue.

Kali plants herself between us and the demon rajah. Her hands are aglow, her face set in a defiant glare. Her soul-fire brightens her veins like rivulets of gold and reflects off her dark hair. Life and light glimmer around her, radiating supernal power, a beacon casting away shadows. Almost immediately, my eyes ache like I am staring into the sun. Kali resembles a goddess destroyer, terrifying and glorious.

"Get Ashwin to the boat," she says.

The river is not far, but upon a closer look, Kali's side is bleeding, and one of her legs is misshapen. My fears warn me that if I leave now, I may never see her again.

The Voider collects more blue flames for attack, his powers endless.

Kali bends into a fighting stance. "Deven, go! Protect the rajah."

The rajah. My ruler. Our future.

I heave Prince Ashwin to his feet and push him into a run. He cradles his burned arm, the scent of charred flesh rank, but he meets my speed. We dash around the corner for the riverfront, and I lose sight of Kali.

31

KALINDA

My fire streams through the Voider's blue flames, dispersing them to plumes of smoke. Deven and Ashwin depart, on their way to the boat. I was there moments ago but ran back when I saw how close the demon rajah was to us. Indah is still at the vessel, waiting with the others, including Natesa and a fatigued Yatin.

The Voider starts toward me, his hands glowing with aberrant powers. "You are bold, Kalinda."

I lock my trembling knees, rooting myself to the ground. I hoped, *prayed*, I would be given the opportunity to stop the flood of wrongs I undammed by killing Tarek. Ending his life was the gods' will—fate. So this must be fate too.

"I've been waiting for this," the demon rajah says.

"So have I." The Voider has been plaguing me through my nightmares of Tarek. My burning hands and the eerie eyes I saw were signs of my real tormentor, this demon. Whether my soul is tied to Tarek's or not for eternity, I am done with him in this life.

No more Tarek. No more guilt. No more mercy.

I throw a blast of fire. The Voider wisps it away as he would a pesky fly.

"You cannot earn redemption, Burner. None of this would have happened if you had been a dutiful wife. Tarek is very angry with you. He yearns for you to suffer for your betrayal."

"You don't strike me as the type to fight a mortal man's battles."

"This is my battle too, a vendetta as old as the ultimate betrayer, the sky-god Anu." The demon rajah thrusts another blue flame at me. I blast it away with a stream of fire, and our tangled flames strike a row of huts. My flames attack the houses, feeding off the bedlam. "Anu ripped this world from Abzu and Tiamat and then left it to weaklings. Bhutas are an abomination, created to ease Anu's conscience for abandoning the mortals he enslaved. No longer will demons be confined to the shadows."

Smoke from the raging fire stings my eyes. Inside the flames, serpentine dragons slither. I extend my fingers to them. *Protect me.*

On my command, the serpents encircle the Voider, lunging and snapping at him. The demon rajah fends them off with his powers. One by one, the fiery dragons shriek and puff to smoke.

"You cannot hurt me with fire. Tiamat created the First-Ever Dragon. The demon Kur is my master. I am born of fire *and* venom."

The demon rajah knocks me back with a blue burst. I hit the wall hard, rapping my head. With temples pounding, I reach for my power and throw heatwave after heatwave to slow his approach. He bats away the searing strands of light and gains on me. I brace against the wall. My injured leg aches sharply, and my side has begun to bleed once more. Indah's pain blocker is wearing off.

He steps up to me and brushes the hair from my face. "So pathetic. So weak."

He slams me against the wall with more frosty fire. While I am pinned by numbing cold, he presses his lips to mine and blows blue fire into my mouth. Icy flames flow inside me, chilling me so deeply my soul-fire begins to suffocate. He steps away, yet the wintry inferno still burns through me, freezing my veins.

I crash at his feet, immobilized by excruciating pain.

"My fire would have burned a mortal to ash by now. But you . . . I could leave you in this blistering misery forever." He bends over me as I shiver in agony. "Wait here, love. I will end your dear captain and prince and then return to usher you into the evernight."

The demon rajah starts for the waterfront. Shards of ice pierce my lungs. I search inside for my soul-fire. Only embers remain. The frosty blaze will fester until it smothers my powers completely.

A chunk of burning rubble falls near me, blowing ash into my face. I wait for Jaya to appear, searching for the same shining spirit that visited me when I was drowning, but she does not come. I must not need her, for she has never failed me.

Nature-fire feeds off the debris, the serpents staying near. I stretch out my fingers. *Come for me.* Nothing happens, so I direct the last of my strength to lifting my hand and pulling at them harder. *You will obey.*

They shed off of the firestorm and slink over, dancing around me. Their warmth radiates into my limbs and thaws the worst of the Voider's chill.

I climb to my knees, shuddering in spasms. "Do it now," I call at his back, my teeth chattering violently. "Or do you think I'll get the better of you?"

He pauses with a disdainful smirk. "You err, Burner. I am not your husband."

"My husband wasn't afraid of a woman."

He bares his front teeth like a snake preparing to strike. "I am the shadows. You are to fear *me.*"

I push to my feet, favoring my injured leg, and call to nature-fire. *Rise up and show him who should be afraid.*

The slithering flames amass beside me, entwining together with single-minded purpose. They weave into a smoldering mass that hisses and snaps like wildfire. I detect no immediate shape, but then the chaotic blaze rises taller than the highest hut and takes form. A face materializes with a long, distinguished snout and whiskers. The body stretches out into a sleek, curving wave, extending down the road, and sprouts short hind legs. Ridges rise and fall across its long, winding back. Spindly flames elongate into a regal neck and slide down into a slender, proud breast and strong front legs. A pair of red eyes burn hotly on its striking face.

A fire dragon.

I reach for its side, transfixed by the entity's fearsome beauty. The fire does not burn me, nor does my hand pass through, but it meets a tangible body as real as if a cloud became solid ground. I rest my palm against the dragon's serpentine form that burns a vengeful ember red. Blessed heat flows into my chilled veins. I do not understand how I created this dragon born of nature-fire, but I do not question its vitality or my ability to command it.

"Your serpent cannot stop me," says the Voider.

The fire dragon bares its fangs.

Dropping my chin, I glare across the road at him. "I was created to light up the sky. I do not fear you."

He pushes crackling blue fire into his fingertips. "You will."

Get him, I call to the fire dragon, and it snaps at the Voider. He reels away, but as he turns back, he shoots at the dragon. A hole opens in its flank. The Voider throws more fire, and the gap widens. If he can outmatch nature-fire, he can beat me to the boat.

I leap onto the fire dragon's back. *Fly away.*

The wingless beast carries me up. As we soar above the city, the Voider discharges blue flames after us. We dodge them, banking toward the river. Muddy green waters spread out beneath me. Indah's boat waits below.

Arrowlike flames zip at us. I maneuver the fire dragon away, but the Voider's cold fire pierces its breast. The crater spreads as the dragon is ripped apart by a hail fire of frosty blasts. The fire dragon falls apart around me, bursting to smoke, and I am knocked into the burning sky.

32

Deven

·

Kali is falling.

I run for the edge of the boat and dive into the river headfirst. I rise to the top; the golden surface reflects the remnants of her fire dragon fading in the sky. She hits the water a short distance away. Panic seizes me as I swim to her body floating in the waves and drag her back to the boat.

A young Lestarian woman, an Aquifier, coaxes a wave that lifts us up to the deck. I heave Kali out of the river with me. She hangs limply in my arms, her skin icy cold.

"I'm Indah," says the Aquifier. "I can help."

The image of Kali tumbling through the sky shocks me into compliance.

Indah rests her hand on Kali's forehead and murmurs. "Blood is water, and water is mine." Kali coughs up fluid but does not rouse.

Blue flames burst at our stern. The demon rajah nears the riverbank. Indah's guard yells to the pole pushers with their bamboo rods on both sides of the wide, flat boat to draw us from shore. But man power will not move us out of the line of fire quickly.

"Pons!" Indah yells.

Her guard, Pons, shoots at the Voider with his blowgun. His poisonous dart strikes the demon square in the chest, but does not slow him.

Indah runs to the bow and summons a wave beneath us. I clutch Kali against me as the Aquifier propels us downriver on the swell. Once we are at a safe distance from the city, Indah relaxes her hold on the river, and the boat lowers to a level surface. The pole pushers begin their work, propelling us onward with the river's current.

Brother Shaan appears in the doorway to the wheelhouse. "Bring Kalinda here."

I carry her inside, dripping water across the floor, and lay her on an empty cot along the wall. She is still unresponsive, little breaths her lone movements. A healer treats Prince Ashwin on the next cot over. Indah sweeps in and commands two more Lestarian healers to set to work on Kali.

Watching her slack face, I can scarcely fathom that moments ago she flew on a serpent built of flames. When did she learn to command nature-fire—and harness it into a dragon? She has surpassed even Brac's talents. I do not know of a more powerful Burner than her.

She is the woman the gods sent to save the empire.

And now, she is so *still*.

I stand back and pray while the healers attend to her. *Anu, let her wake. Let me see her skin glow with veins of gold, her soul-fire unscathed within her. Bring her back to me intact and whole.* Despite my insistence, her complexion remains ashy and dull. Before long, the healers' distressed frowns undo me. I fist my hands in my hair. *She cannot die.*

"Will she be all right?" Prince Ashwin cradles his bandaged arm at Kali's bedside. He brushes a wet strand of hair from her cheek.

I throw him back. "Don't you touch her."

Prince Ashwin stumbles sideways and retreats out the wheelhouse door. I storm after him, trapping him against the rail. He bends backward, his top half hanging over the water.

"You doomed us all!" I shout in his face.

"Vizier Gyan began the incantation," he explains in a rush. "I had to release the Voider before he did."

"Kali could die because of you!"

His face hardens to an angry mask. He pushes me forward, standing upright. "I didn't see you there to defend her."

I fist his collar and strike him in the face. The prince falls to the deck, cupping his mouth. I hoist him up to flatten him again, and Brother Shaan hurries out of the wheelhouse.

"Deven, this won't help," he says.

Prince Ashwin wipes his bloody lip, his gaze stricken. "I'm sorry."

I shove him away, sending him staggering. "You're a murderer. I know what you did to Brother Dhiren."

"You go too far, Captain," warns the prince.

"You killed your mentor."

"I *loved* my mentor. Rajah Tarek discovered Brother Dhiren was a bhuta and ordered he be stoned to death. I couldn't bear to see him suffer. Brother Dhiren was old and frail. I offered to end him quickly. The whipping . . . He didn't survive ten lashes." The prince tugs down his tunic, tears of indignation simmering in his eyes. "I had to make a choice, just as I did today. *That* is the burden of the throne. *That* is the duty of the rajah."

I point upriver at the blue fire devouring the city. "Those people are paying for your 'choice' with their lives. You can rationalize this all you want, but the fall of Iresh is on *your* head."

I bang inside the wheelhouse. Lanterns have been lit to compensate for the twilight hour. Out the forward window, Natesa and Yatin sit near the bow. A blanket covers Yatin's shoulders, and Natesa is urging him to drink from a cup. Yatin has lost some of his girth, but I am relieved to see him upright. His little lotus will take good care of him.

Indah steps back from Kali's bedside and studies me, determining whether or not I will accost her too. "That's all we can do for now," she says.

"When will she wake up?"

"Difficult to say." Indah's golden eyes brim with sympathy. "You should get some air."

I rest on the corner of Kali's cot. "I'm fine here." Prince Ashwin is still out on deck. The mood I am in, I will toss him overboard and leave him to the crocodiles.

Indah signals to the healers. They collect their water jugs and step out of the wheelhouse, leaving Kali and me alone.

I lift her hand and inhale her scent, jasmine and midnight rain. *Please don't leave me.* With Brac and Mother stuck in Tarachand, Kali is my family. Our group has been pulled apart since leaving Vanhi, and no matter how much I desire all of us to be together, I do not have wide enough arms to keep everyone close and safe.

Night blankets the jungle, the nocturnal noises drifting over the river. Rain begins to fall. The sway of the boat pushes me toward queasiness. I ground myself to Kali, cupping her hand in mine. She wears a cuff around her wrist identical to the one I saw on Prince Ashwin. Has she promised herself to him? I cannot bring myself to ask the prince. At a loss for what to do, I return to my prayers and plead with Anu to save my love.

33

KALINDA

I wake to steady rocking and dull, ceaseless pain, the most vulnerable parts of me turned inside out, exposed and bare. Lanterns swing gently above, casting pale light on my memory. Last I recall I was falling . . .

Warmth hugs one side of my body. Deven sleeps beside me, sharing my pillow. I snuggle into his dormant strength, and his eyes flash open.

"How long have I been asleep?" I ask, my voice hoarse from disuse.

"Three days."

Quiet relaxes between us, raindrops drumming against the wheelhouse roof.

Deven props his head under his hand and observes me closely. A full beard blankets his jaw. "How do you feel?"

"Like a washcloth wrung and hung to dry." I tip my forehead against his, inhaling his sandalwood scent. *Home.* "Are you all right?"

Emotions stream across his face: relief, joy, and yearning that stirs an ache inside me. "I missed you."

His low voice eases through me like a warm drink. He cups my chin, and his tender lips seek mine. My nerve endings spark with happiness. Deven shifts closer and packs all of his longing into deepening our kiss. I drown in him, my dull pain replaced with singing pleasure.

Forgetting my injuries, I reach up to finger his full beard, and my injured side pinches. I gasp, and he pulls away, apologizing.

"I'm fine." I kiss him again for proof. As I lean away, I notice Ashwin gazing in the window at us. Anguish tarnishes the prince's handsome face, and my own expression falls.

Deven turns to look behind him, and the prince rushes off. I consider calling Ashwin back, but anything I say will only hurt him more. I do not care for him the same way I do for Deven, but I *do* care.

Deven turns back to me and touches Ashwin's cuff around my wrist, his gaze cool and reserved. "Did you promise yourself to him?"

"I'm not promised to anyone. Ashwin and I are friends."

"He wants you to be more."

Deven's jealousy exasperates me. "You hardly know him."

"I know he cannot be trusted. He unleashed the Voider."

I understand how Ashwin's actions could be seen as a betrayal, but Deven is wrong to blame him. "He had no choice. The vizier had started the incantation and wouldn't stop until it was finished. Ashwin couldn't have foreseen who the Voider would return as." An image of Tarek throwing blue fire fills my mind, and dread threatens to throttle me. But I do not blame Ashwin for the physical form the Voider took. "I trust Ashwin. He respects me, and he isn't afraid of my powers."

Deven tempers his voice. "I'm not afraid of you either. When I saw you flying on that fire dragon, you nearly stopped my heart."

"With fear?"

"Admiration. You were spectacular." He caresses my chin. "I'm proud of you."

His praise itches in an uncomfortable place. "I'm only one-quarter bhuta," I confess. "The Janardanians have a myth that Ki and Kur were lovers and had a child together. I didn't believe it at first, but it's true. Enlil is Kur's son."

"If you're right, all that means is that you're equally bhuta and demon."

Deven's answer is terribly inconclusive. "So am I good or bad?" I ask.

"We're all a little of both." He holds my hand to his chest. "Anu claimed Enlil as his son. Regardless of who fathered the fire-god, Anu believed Enlil was good and gave his powers to mortals. You're born from goodness, Kali. It's in your soul."

I remember the pain when I tried to scorch the Voider. Nothing good dwelled within it, only cold, ruthless fire. My soul-fire is not the same, and that is enough to satisfy me for now. Deven's comfort is precisely what I needed, but I also needed him during the trial tournament. My aching for him erupts all at once, and hot tears crowd my vision.

"I'm sorry, Kali." He lifts my hands and kisses the backs where my rank marks have faded. "I didn't want you to leave. I was too focused on our duties to the empire."

"I'm more than my throne."

"Of course you are." He rests his forehead against mine. "I love you. I thought about it a lot since we've been apart, and what a fool I was for not telling you."

"Even though my hands don't carry my rank, I'm still the kindred. I cannot desert Ashwin to save the empire alone." Too many people died for peace, Citra being the freshest wound on my heart. Blood is on my hands, and the only way to wash it away is to earn the peace others have died for. "This is who I am. I belong to my throne."

"And I'm still your guard."

My fingers thread through the silken hair at his nape, my other hand roaming his soft beard. "I fell in love with my guard."

Deven presses his forehead against mine. I graze my lips over his, and he bundles me nearer. Our kiss drowns out most of the fears hanging over us. The sunrise will bring with it preparations for war. A battle must be fought against the Voider, and we must win. But for one treasured moment, I nestle into Deven's side and let all else be.

ACKNOWLEDGMENTS

Many thanks to the following:

Marlene Stringer, thank you for your patience with my numerous e-mails and your heartfelt enthusiasm for this book. I took a screenshot of the lovely tweet you posted right after you finished reading this manuscript and will keep it forever. Thank you for continuing to be amazed.

Thank you to the best editor I could have asked for, Jason Kirk, for jumping on board with this next installment of my characters and world. Your guidance and unfailing support are a dream come true. I'm thankful for Clarence Hayes, who helps me dig out the heart of my story and polish it to a shine. Also, thank you to everyone else at Skyscape and Amazon Publishing, especially Brittany and Kim. I am grateful to work with your amazing team.

Kate Coursey (rhymes with "horsey"), thank you for loving something I thought was unlovable and handling my stress texts with admirable grace. Kathryn Purdie, thank you for your love, understanding, and much-needed line edits. Tricia Levenseller, thank you for advising me to stick to the story I originally envisioned.

Thank you to my fabulous crew of talented supporters: Angie Cothran, Erin Summerill, Veeda Bybee, Lauri Schoenfeld, Kate Watson, Michelle Wilson, Breeana Shields, Rebekah Crane, Shaila Patel, Charlie N. Holmberg, and Becky Wallace. Your texts, IMs, and phone calls bring me joy. Thank you.

Michal Cameron and Catherine Dowse, thank you for your excitement and awe. Jessie Farr, my self-proclaimed handmaiden and on-the-side editor, thank you. I'm grateful for my primary group: Cassidi Mecham, Kate Morehead, Gloria Wright, and Brenda Hartvigsen.

Thank you to my mom and dad, for being my top cheerleaders. I adore you both. For Eve and Chris, you are my favorites (ha ha).

John and our four kiddos, Joseph, Julian, Danielle, and Ryan, you inspire me to do better. Thanks for putting up with the long hours, quick meals, and spastic mood swings. I could not do this without you.

My lovely readers, I am your biggest fan.

Lastly but most importantly, my father in heaven, thanks for making all of this possible.

ABOUT THE AUTHOR

Photo © 2015 Erin Summerill

Emily R. King is a writer of fantasy and the author of *The Hundredth Queen*. Born in Canada and raised in the United States, she has perfected the use of *eh* and *y'all* and uses both interchangeably. Shark advocate, consumer of gummy bears, and islander at heart, Emily's greatest interests are her four children. She's a member of the Society of Children's Book Writers and Illustrators and an active participant in her local writers' community. She lives in Northern Utah with her family and their cantankerous cat. Visit her at www.emilyrking.com.